A Novel
By David Alexander

WWW.DAVIDALEXANDERBOOKS.COM

Triumvirate

Publications
New York • London • Sydney

CHAIN REACTION

This is a work of fiction. Names, characters, places and incidents are either the product of the author's imagination or are used fictitiously, and any resemblance to actual persons, living or dead, business establishments, events or locales, is entirely coincidental.

A Triumvirate Publications International thriller novel. Published by arrangement with the author.

For more about David Alexander:
www.davidalexanderbooks.com.

Copyright © David Alexander. All rights reserved.
ISBN-10: 0-9995493-1-6
ISBN-13: 978-0-9995493-1-5

Triumvirate Publications International
2001 Madison Avenue
New York NY 10035

DAVID ALEXANDER

Excerpts from Co-Co-Caleevio
A Mafia Novel
By David Alexander

Dominick "Dee" de Venise's textile warehouse has been in the family for generations, but he'll have to torch it for the insurance money. De Venise has no other choice. The Mezzatesta family is into him for boo-koo bucks and if he doesn't pay off, he's history.

The only other option de Venise has is to stage a big-money heist planned by his crooked lawyer friend Arnie, but he's already turned down that particular deal. Arnie's plan was too risky, and besides, de Venise knew Arnie long enough and well enough not to trust him. De Venise doesn't trust anyone to torch the business either. Wanting it done right, he plans to do it himself, then set up an ironclad alibi.

Everything goes like clockwork until the insurance company refuses to pay off on de Venise's policy, leaving him with no business to run and no money to buy off his wise guy creditors.

With no more cards to play at this point, de Venise agrees to do the heist for Arnie. If nothing else, it will get him out of the country, and if de Venise is really lucky and really smart, there's even an outside chance of him scoring the bucks he needs to get him straight with the mob and put him back in action. Just like when he was a kid, the name of the game is Co-Co-Caleevio – single, double, triple. Catch the ball to win.

The only difference now is that if de Venise winds up out, this time he could also wind up dead.

CHAIN REACTION

Crime Does Pay
Co-Co-Caleevio pulls the trigger with a bang!

Co-Co-Caleevio is a crime novel that begins and ends on the mean streets of Gravesend, the toughest neighborhood of New York City's toughest borough and the heart of notorious West Brooklyn. It's a place where organized crime still rules and where wise guys have to think fast, hit hard or get whacked. In between, the novel crosses international boundaries and time zones with the speed of sound as West Brooklyn's most accomplished safe and loft burglar takes on a European job in order to pay back the markers held on him by boss of bosses Tony the Pug. This is a caper novel to end all caper novels, a non-stop pager-turner from start to finish, and one of Author David Alexander's boldest books ever.

■

"Where's the statuette? I've made a rather thorough ransack job of both cabins, but can't find anything. I'm assuming its inside the corpse you and the lady are transporting."

"It's not there. I have it in one of the drawers. I'll show --"

"Don't move. Tell the truth or I'll cause considerable pain."

"All right, I should have known better. Yes, the *Bambina* is inside the corpse in the casket we're taking back to New York."

"What happens then?"

"The funeral parlor gets it, opens up the stiff and takes it out."

"I see. How do I believe you?"

"If I tell you will you let us live?"

"That depends on whether you're honest with me or not. But if you don't give me what I need, I promise I will cause you and your whore pain. Her first, as you watch."

"No, okay. Yeah, I got the proof," de Venise said. "No problem."

"Where is it?"

"My phone. It's in my pocket. Cut the cable tie, and I'll get it."

"Tell me where it is."

"Okay. You win. The phone's in my back pants pocket. The right one."

"This better not explode in my face."

"It won't. I can do it for you."

"Shut up. I'm warning you."

He flipped it on and thumbed to the photo folder. He scanned the MRI they'd done of the Greek's remains to show the morticians at Bassamontagna where the statue was. The passenger in the white suit nodded.

"You didn't lie. That's good. I'll make it easy for you. After you die, I'll rape the bitch and make it look like you killed each other on drugs. One shot. You won't feel it."

"Wait, lemme smoke some grass. I got some joints rolled in a Baci tin."

"You get nothing."

"I can pay for it."

"How?"

"The cross around my neck. It's solid gold. I been wearing it all my life. It's worth a lot. You can have it."

The assassin reached for the crucifix. He fingered it, seeing it was pure gold, the real thing. With a tug he yanked it off the chain.

--excerpted from unrevised Co-Co-Caleevio chapter.

5

CHAIN REACTION

■

Today Brooklyn, tomorrow the world ... David Alexander has the names of two conquering heroes and Co-Co-Caleevio is world-class ... a thriller with style, guts and endless quantities of Brooklyn *chutzpah* applied as thickly as mozzerella cheese on a Brooklyn pizza. Alexander is an author who is going places. Hopefully one of them is not jail, as some of the criminal capers described in the novel read almost like he was present at the scene of the crime taking notes.

■

When he came in, hands free, the assassin was flopping on the bed, trying to get up. Blood pumped from his neck. He was still alive.

"You dumb prick."

The torso was still partially intact.

"You can see me right? You can understand, right?"

The killer's eyes registered that he did.

"You listen up. I was crying for Mario, who gave this to me. Now I'm sending you to wipe his fuckin' ass in heaven."

De Venise took off his sports coat then took off his shirt and pants. He stood naked with the gun in his right hand.

"I can wash your fuckin' blood off, and the powder grains will usually come off too. I'll give it three washes. They usually get the shit off your clothes anyway."

De Venise wrapped the butt of the assassin's silenced gun around his hand. He didn't have much longer. The eyes of the Infessura were rolling up in his head from shock. De Venise hoped he could still understand him.

"I hope you choke, you cocksucker," de Venise said, as he shoved the silenced muzzle into the killer's mouth as hard as he could, and jerked the trigger once with the killer's stubby forefinger. There wasn't much noise as the head

6

jerked and the pillow was suddenly stained with glop from the brains that shot out the back end of his skull.

--excerpted from unrevised Co-Co-Caleevio chapter.

■

Could he also face a murder rap -- as a cop or JFK guard or customs officer was killed in the course of the robbery? It wasn't Dee's fault -- he never carried a gun -- but as an accessory to murder commited during a robbery he could get the hot shot.

There's this cop after him. For years already. He's like a stone in his fucking shoe, this cop. The cop hates him because he's half-Sicilian. He's some kind of fuckin' nut job.

The DA is is in league with the cops. The DA is on a vendetta against corruption with a holy zeal not seen since the Gotti trials. He's going after everybody.

Dee is smarter and more tech savvy than he appears at first glance.

The Boost is an old crony from even before the Aer Lingus heist days.

So there's a progression from the 1st safe and loft job in Red Hook (and from those that preceded it in back story) to the III-V job, and then it connects up with the *tombarolo's* "grave robbing" of ancient tombs. (Cracking safes is like cracking tombs in a way.)

Arnie may use his knowledge of Dee's involvement with the Aer Lingus heist as a lever to force his compliance with the III-V job -- and the rest that follows after the heist is eighty-sixed.

--excerpted from unrevised Co-Co-Caleevio author's notes.

■

Authors don't come any better than David Alexander, and his tough-as-nails global thriller Co-Co-Caleevio represents his taking the fine art of mayhem to an exciting new level of accomplishment. The depth of insight into the world of the Mafia, black intelligence ops, tomb raiding *tombaroli*, historical arcana, exotic military technologies and the inner mainsprings of political intrigue -- to name but a few of this book's points of focus -- seems at times close to envisaging actual   events.

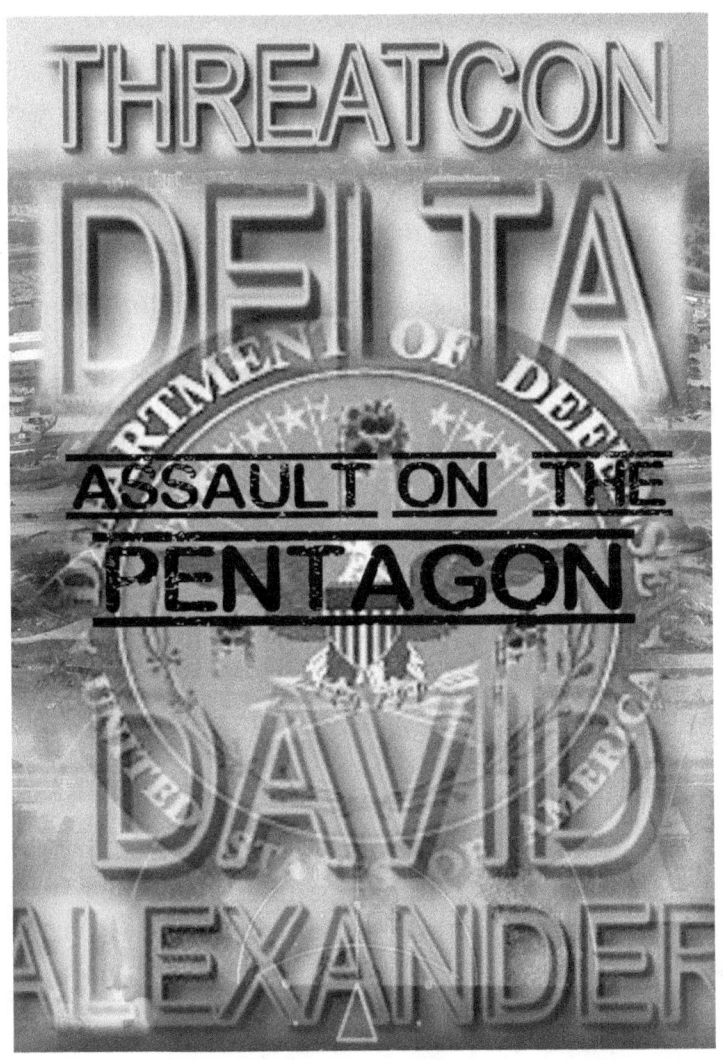

Chain Reaction

A Global Thriller
By David Alexander

In this superb achievement by a master storyteller, a New York City police detective caught in a web of international terrorism and global intrigue becomes the central focus of an expertly told story that's so exciting it may actually make you sweat.

Chain Reaction features scenes rich in gripping narrative, striking action and punchy dialog in a plot armed with superweapons and power-mad bad guys who rival or exceed any encountered in real life. This amazing thriller offers a feast of surprising twists and turns that suddenly appear with mind-boggling rapidity that make it a milestone in the annals of thriller fiction.

Carried along by a strong, clear and powerfully cinematic prose line that benefits from extremely accurate portrayals of all the elements of the cop's, spy's and soldiers' trades, Chain Reaction is top-notch writing and a great reading experience. The opening and closing chapters go off like a shock and awe campaign, and nothing in between gives readers enough time to even catch their breath. The cumulative effect of Chain Reaction is overwhelming in the sheer impact of the powerful prose and the slick, commercial, though uniquely original plot and style.

DAVID ALEXANDER

David Alexander is one of those rare authors who can write fiction that has the power to relentlessly carry the reader onward, and who can blend a wit and humor as sharp and cutting as a samurai sword and combine it with in-depth analysis and the deft touch of a master technician. David Alexander's superb thriller Chain Reaction is more than a great read, it's an awesome experience that is sure to keep readers on the edge of their seats, addictive adventure writing at its boldest and brightest -- the stuff from which great thrillers are made.

High Praise for The King of West Brooklyn

"The Mezzatestas, David Alexander's fictitious crime family in The King of West Brooklyn, are the new Corleones." -- USA Today

"If mob-related hits haven't already put Gravesend, the crime capital of West Brooklyn, on the map, The King of West Brooklyn is destined to do so." -- Daily News

"Today Brooklyn, tomorrow the world ... David Alexander has the names of two conquering heroes and The King of West Brooklyn is world-class ... a thriller with style, guts and endless quantities of Brooklyn chutzpah applied as thickly as mozzarella cheese on a Brooklyn pizza. Alexander is an author who is going places. Hopefully one of them is not jail, as some of the criminal capers described in the novel read almost like he was taking notes at the scene of the crime." -- L.A. Times

"If James Bond wore athletic shirts, spoke with a Brooklyn accent and drove a candy apple-red 1973 Plymouth Barracuda, he'd be Dominick de Venise, the edgy protagonist of David Alexander's smashing crime thriller The King of West Brooklyn." -- Kirkus Reviews

"Bestseller! Bestseller! Bestseller! The word should be shouted at least three times as a kind of Brooklyn cheer, because David Alexander's crime thriller The King of West Brooklyn has "Bestseller!" written all over it." -- NY Daily News

"... All muscle, no flab..." Daily News

"What Tom Clancy did for submarines, Alexander has done with the contemporary realities of global terrorism, high-tech weapons and the robotization of the battlefield." -- Jack Phelps / Independent Reviews

"This boat ride through the Tunnel of Fear nails you to your seat. Don't get on unless you have the guts to finish the ride!" -- Stun Gun Sam / Independent Reviews

High Praise for David Alexander's POTUS

"Perhaps the best thriller of its type to have come along all year!" -- New York Times

"Always the consummate prose stylist, David Alexander also speaks tech talk like no other. What's more, the tech specs are undoubtedly real, including those that pertain to ostensibly stolen or covertly obtained Russian and Chinese weapons that have been reverse-engineered by [US military technology development agency] DARPA. Alexander's security clearance is probably higher than the president's, and his knowledge of military systems better than any three members of the joint chiefs of staff." -- NY Newsday

"Among the possible three finest thriller authors today, Alexander takes first place." -- USA Today

"Here, as elsewhere, Alexander convincingly blends action, intrigue, adventure and startling glimpses behind the walls of the CIA, Oval Office and Pentagon that seem far too real to have been completely invented ...throughout he shows off the masterful skills that have placed him high amid the ranks of the world's thriller authors." --London Times

"Three R's for David Alexander's POTUS -- riveting, relevant, remarkable." -- The New Yorker

"A happening of a thriller. Alexander grand-slams the competition with this latest action-adventure masterpiece!" -- Village Voice

High Praise for Threatcon Delta: Assault on the Pentagon

"If you read no other technothrilller this year, read this awesome action yarn by David Alexander ... it's guaranteed to make you lose sleep."--Arlington Times

Critical Applause for Brothers of the Gun

"Brothers of the Gun is faster than a speeding bullet ... slicker than the slickest contender out there. Go and get this book today!" -- St. Paul Intelligencer

Critical Acclaim for Snake Handlers

"Alexander once again turns newspaper headlines into riveting high-tech military action fiction with that special combination of cinematic thrills and chills and fly-on-the-wall accounts of back room crisis management in the making ... surely one of the best technothrillers to come along in a great while." -- Salem Record

Critics Hail Under Attack

"Alexander is so far ahead of the pack that they must be howling like wolves running at his back, hungry for even just a taste of his immense writing talent. There's no doubt that in the action wolf pack

Alexander is top dog, and the canine whose scent the others follow." -- F. C. Dubrow, Book Reviewer

Critical acclaim for Kill Chain

"Passenger jets disappear out of thin air ... terrorist armies drape black flags across failed states ... chaos in the streets of American cities ... and the threat of terrible doom gathers steam as this thriller draws to a powerful climax ... Alexander ... has thought of everything and then some...." -- Voice Book Reviews

"This is not just another novel; this is history in the making ... a game changing ... thriller." – Booklister

Also by David Alexander:

I Kinda Spy
Snake Handlers
Habu Patch
Under Attack
The King of West Brooklyn
Co-Co-Caleevio
Trainjack
War Pigs
Sword of the Mahdi
Death Pulse
Brooklynese
Bloodbath
Puzzle Palace (nonfiction)
Military-Industrial Complex (nonfiction)

When the swords ran among one another like red-spotted serpents, then did our fathers become fond of life; the sun of every peace seemed to them languid and lukewarm, the long peace, however, made them ashamed. How they sighed, our fathers, when they saw on the wall brightly furbished, dried-up swords! Like those they thirsted for war. For a sword thirsteth to drink blood, and sparkleth with desire.

--*Friedrich Nietzsche, Thus Spake Zarathustra.*

Author's Note:

The Thirty-ninth Precinct is a fictitious New York City police command. Some place names and descriptions of weaponry and military procedures have been modified where necessary to suit the needs of   the   story.

DAVID ALEXANDER

PROLOGUE

SHOCK WAVES

CHAIN REACTION

One

*T*he three-man commando unit had been operational for seventy-two hours conducting pre-strike reconnaissance on the complex of low-rise cement block warehouse structures in the sand desert south of Rabta, Libya.

The team and its specialized equipment had been inserted by CH-53K helo drop at 0400 hours zulu on a moonless night approximately five kilometers from the mission zone.

The team had traveled the rest of the way by desert patrol vehicle armed with a front-mounted 7.62 millimeter MAG gun and a .50 caliber Barrett machinegun mounted on a pintle stand at the rear of the militarized dune buggy.

On reaching their destination and selecting a recon site, the team had broken out entrenching tools, dug in and settled down beneath camouflage netting for a protracted vigil.

Through high-powered night vision binoculars the team had surveilled the installation, noting patterns of personnel and vehicle movement, and then transmitted their assessments to the mission command center.

This was located on the Arleigh Burke-class destroyer USS Hopper, flagship of a Combined Task Force in the US 5th Fleet's area of operations. Anchored off the coast of Kuwait at the extreme northern reaches of the Persian Gulf, the CTF's mission was twofold. It patrolled the Gulf states' coastal regions and served as a maritime staging base for long-range missions inland, including to operational sectors located well beyond the Gulf littorals.

At 0340 hours on the second day of their insertion, the forward observation team had gathered sufficient intelligence on which to base a mission assessment profile. Unshipping and initializing the satcom unit, the team leader punched in the main encrypted transmission channel to the combat information center on the Hopper and proceeded to call in an air strike whose outcome would be the complete obliteration of the target.

■

At a secret base in the Negev desert some five hundred statute miles northwest of the Hopper's position in the Gulf, the sortie of Israeli F-16F Desert Falcons rose straight up into the night like immense screaming raptors forged from death visions of hallucinating metal. The fuselages of these fighter plane heavy haulers bore a camouflage pattern designed to make them difficult to recognize by ground- or air-based observers.

The long-range fuel tanks or "fastpacks," and electronic countermeasures pods to jam enemy radars and air-to-ground munitions clustered beneath their wings plainly indicated that the Falcons were engaged in a long-range mission against a high-level threat. Two large bombs stood out amid the other ordnance.

These were fuel-air explosives; conventional air-to-ground-munitions that nonetheless packed a subnuclear punch. Paveway seeker heads had been mounted on the FAEs. These would enable the bunker-busting munitions to home in on the beam painted by a ground-based laser target designator with nearly pinpoint accuracy.

DAVID ALEXANDER

While the Israeli jets flown by Israeli pilots were carrying out the bombing of the biological weapons complex at Rabta, the operation had in fact been planned and was in fact being run by the United States Central Intelligence Agency. Because of the always delicate political situation in the Middle East, and despite the best of reasons, the United States could not afford to be seen as flexing its military might against even an international outlaw state such as Libya.

The Israelis were another matter entirely. Despite overtures toward regional peace, they would remain pariahs among the Arab states forever, or at least until the waters of the Red Sea parted again. Because they had nothing to lose on that front, the Israelis had long been useful as a clandestine surrogate of American military might and strategic policy in the region.

It would not be the first time that Israeli jets had been sent in to bomb a target while American troops on the ground designated the strike zone.

In Lebanon, air strikes against Hezbollah targets as paybacks for the Beirut car bombing in 1983 of US Marine

25

barracks was one notable example, but there were numerous other and more recent instances, including a previous raid on the Rabta complex a few years before tonight's mission, resulting in severe blast damage due to causes which are still officially classified by the US State Department under the catch-all heading of "unexplained." For the Israelis this raid on a military target inside Libya would simply be another case of same business, same official denials, new democratic government, different day.

■

Major Nazir Falashia of the Libyan Defense Forces, whose position as commander of the army barracks at Jalabad, a city twenty kilometers north of Rabta, made him responsible for the safety of the weapons development facility, was awakened from a pleasant dream in which he was enjoying cunnilingus with the dancer at a local tavern.

His subordinate reported to Falashia that a Libyan AWACs aircraft orbiting in a loiter pattern had picked up a fleeting radar track that might have indicated the approach of enemy planes traversing restricted national airspace in on a low, nap-of-the-earth flight trajectory, which strongly they were engaged in an offensive military action against Libya.

Having been awakened the previous night by a similar report which had turned out to be a false alarm, Falashia dismissed the present report as yet another example of the ineptitude of his country's military personnel and their fascination with expensive electronic toys. He promptly went back to sleep, hoping to again meet the dancer and resume what they had been doing.

Had he known that the previous night's brief border penetration by Israeli F-16s had been intended to lull him into just such a state of false security, he would certainly not have acted as he did. But this thought never crossed Falashia's sleep-drugged mind, and he began dreaming again of the dancer, whose parted lips beckoned him forward to taste delights he would know only in his dreams.

■

CHAIN REACTION

The Israeli F-16 bomb trucks swept low over the desert using nap-of-the-earth flying techniques.

Hurtling along no more than a dozen feet above ground, the veteran combat planes flew under the curtain of Libya's Russian-supplied Flat Jack radar, their terrain-following radars keeping the fighters on a precision course to their mission objective. At a distance of less than a mile from the target they executed a flaring maneuver, rapidly gaining altitude before leveling out to place the aircraft into position to pickle off their bomb loads.

When the sortie had reached the designated altitude of three hundred feet above the desert floor, infrared detectors in underwing pods registered the invisible laser beam painting the target. The beam, emanating from a tripod-mounted device deployed by the commando unit on the ground, was directed at one of the structures of the doomed installation complex, a building housing stockpiles of CBWs, chemical-biological weapons.

The target now framed in a glowing kill box on their head-up displays, the weapon systems operators in the back seats of the two F-16s pickled off the FAEs whose Paveway seekers followed the beam down to the point of explosive impact as the pilots executed steeply banked turns and turned the planes around at supersonic speeds.

■

Only a few moments after the Libyan army commander's neglected warning had been dispatched and ignored, a series of explosions suddenly boomed and thundered through the ruptured stillness of the night. The fuel-air explosives detonated with the destructive power of subkiloton nuclear weapons. Gasoline vapor clouds, ignited by the same high-speed Kryton switches that triggered nuclear explosives, generated shock waves of superheated compressed air that smashed concrete retaining walls to flinders. A thermal pulse ignited anything that could burn. In a matter of seconds, the base was engulfed in flames and the CBW stocks inside the facility destroyed by intense heat.

From their clandestine observation post out on the desert, the three-man special warfare detachment watched the base consumed by a howling firestorm like something out of Biblical myth.

The team confirmed that the mission had achieved closure via another encrypted satcom transmission that was bounced off a Magnum electronic intelligence satellite in orbit one hundred thousand feet overhead and received at a National Security Agency listening post in a secure section of the glass-walled NSA headquarters building at Fort Meade, Maryland in near-real-time. The commandos were so close to the target site that their faces were lit by the flickering orange glare of the crackling flames that licked up into the night skies above Rabta.

With the Libyan weapons facility destroyed and the Israeli F-16s now vectoring eastward toward their hidden underground runway in the Negev, it was time for the target designation team to extract. Filling in the "spider" hole that in the wake of Desert Storm has come to mean much the same as the "fox" hole of World War II, and sanitizing the observation post, the team obliterated all traces of its presence.

Mounting the DPV they had ridden from the drop zone, the unit quickly reached the predesignated rally point where a backtracking CH-53K Super Stallion, guided to its LZ by infrared strobes activated by the team and which were only visible to airborne observers, began a cross-border return trip toward north Persian Gulf and the waiting USS Hopper.

Two days later the team would be back at Fort Bragg, North Carolina, being debriefed in the Delta Force compound known as "The Stockade," men who had officially been vacationing in Florida, Puerto Rico and the scenic Virgin Islands when the preemptive strike on Rabta had taken place.

Two

*T*he tall blond man touched the thin white line of old scar tissue that ran between the lobe of his left ear and the corner of his surly mouth. His pitiless gray eyes missed nothing as he watched the training cadre from the Irish Republican Army renegade splinter group drill on the firing range at the secret camp in Tajura, Libya.

The consignment of advanced caseless weapons had arrived only yesterday via their licensed Saudi end-users from the manufacturer in Ashburn, Virginia. The lightweight plastic frames of the Heckler & Koch G-11s belied the awesome firepower that the specially configured tactical weapons could deliver.

The renegade Provos, now calling themselves the Real IRA or RIRA, had demonstrated themselves to be the most gifted shooters among the varied nationalities present at the camp, excelling the Palestinians, the Basques, the Kosovar Albanian separatists, and even the American skinheads from the White Aryan Warrior paramilitary organization. Because of this superiority,

they had been permitted to train on the
new advanced weapons. As such they had
become the envy of all the other self-
styled freedom fighters at Tajura.

The blond man was interrupted by the
sudden thuk-a-thuk sound of helicopter
rotor blades that had risen to a deafening
crescendo above the bolt clatter of
automatic weapons fire from the target
range. Looking up, he saw the Russian-
built Mil Mi-26 Halo transport helicopter
whose brown and black camouflage-
patterned hull was emblazoned with the
single green circle that was the insignia
of the Libyan Air Force.

The appearance of the chopper at the
training camp had been completely
unannounced. He knew that it could only
signify a matter of great importance,
though he took care not to permit even a
flicker of interest to register on his face.

Within minutes the chopper had
touched down, the fierce cyclonic wind
churned up by its spinning blades
creating a swirling funnel cloud of fine
ochre dust.

The Halo's side hatchway slid open,
disgorging two soldiers outfitted in
camouflage fatigues, polished black jump

boots and the red berets of the Libyan special forces. They carried Belgian versions of the Israeli-made Uzi submachineguns.

The troops stood erectly at either side of the open hatchway and smartly saluted the high-ranking Libyan officer who next emerged from the belly of the rotorcraft and strode directly toward the blond man across the packed earth compound. The officer was garbed in the same camouflage dress and red "blanket" as his bodyguards, but with shoulder flashes indicating that he bore the rank of full colonel.

"His Excellency, the Guiding Father, has requested your immediate presence," said the officer as he approached the man with a bodybuilder's physique and long, straight blond hair that he would have considered an effeminate affectation on most other men. "Can you leave immediately?"

"As soon as I make arrangements," he replied, knowing better than to question the reason behind the summons. That, he supposed, would be made plain enough to him in short order.

Turning to his second-in-command, a stocky Basque with hard eyes of gleaming cobalt and the face of a ferret, the blond man instructed him to carry on the weapons training with the new high-technology rifles.

Moments later he accompanied the Libyan colonel toward the chopper which lifted from the desert floor, rose to its cruising altitude of two hundred feet and soon completely vanished from sight as it banked steeply to the south.

■

The chopper set down at a secluded military base deep in the vast sand desert of central Libya after a flight of approximately twenty minutes duration. There was a large Berber tent of striped flaxen cloth in the near distance, festooned with fluttering pennants colored the unbroken green of Libyan socialism.

The fact that the tent was kept under heavy guard left no doubts as to the identity of the individual who was to be found inside it.

Nafeeq al-Sharqi, the military dictator of the Democratic Arab Libyan Peoples' Republic, sat on a colorful array of cushions of various shapes and sizes. As was his custom, al-Sharqi was garbed completely in the Bedouin manner of loose-fitting white robe, leather sandals, and a plain red and white checked *kufiya* of spun cotton covering his head. His single concession to Western dress was the dark aviator-style sunglasses that shrouded his eyes.

The Shark of Libya did not invite the blond man to sit and the visitor continued to stand at a respectful distance from the Guiding Father of the Great Democratic Revolution, as al-Sharqi styled himself, near the entrance to the tent.

"Gregory Vanesco."

Al-Sharqi spoke in Arabic after selecting a page of typescript from the open red-striped dossier lying in front of him on a cushion. Although a political innovator, he was puzzled by e-paper and never used it.

"Thirty-eight years old. Born in the Romanian town of Sigetu Maramureš in the foothills of the Carpathian Mountains and believed to be part Gypsy. Fluent in Russian, Czech, Hungarian, English, French and Arabic." He studied the blond man for a moment and asked, "I think of Romanians as a Latin people, yet your hair is the color of straw."

"My mother was an American woman."

"Yes, of course," al-Sharqi said, returning his attention to the dossier. "Your family managed to emigrate to the United States when you were quite young and settled in the town of Seattle, Washington."

"Seattle is a big city, Excellency," Vanesco interjected.

"Yes, of course," al-Sharqi acknowledged, but there was tension in the tent; it was not a good idea to contradict *al-Qaid*, the Leader, even on a trivial matter.

"You enlisted in the US Army Special Forces and were accepted by 1st Special Forces Operational Detachment-Delta, otherwise known as Delta Force, where you were engaged in Operation Backslash exercises which took place after the Russian reoccupation of Minsk in eastern Belarus. Tell me more about these, please."

"I was attached as a scout to a nuclear demolition unit employing SADMs," Vanesco began, pronouncing the acronym as "Saydum" per US military usage. "These backpack nuclear devices were to be seeded throughout the periphery of

Riga Pact countries in order to cause severe damage to the Neo Soviet Union in the advent of war, which then seemed likely.

"Because the town of my birth was close to the Russian border on the east, and the Hungarian and Czech borders on the west, and because of my familiarity with the terrain, language and customs of the area, and because I physically resembled the Slavic peoples of the region, I was considered a prime candidate for inclusion in the unit."

Vanesco paused in the event the Guiding Father had further questions.

"Go on," al-Sharqi said with annoyance, gesturing with his be-ringed hand.

"We conducted numerous practice runs under highly realistic conditions, as it was known that Soviet Spetsnaz units were doing in the continental US, Mexico and Canada," Vanesco went on. "We were required to be completely self-sufficient and trained to use any methods available to carry out our brief."

Al-Sharqi nodded and selected another page from the dossier.

"With the easing of East-West tensions you were stood down from your unit. Discharged from the US military you sought employment as a hired mercenary and security consultant," he read. "During the course of these years your political sympathies began to change and you aligned yourself with the causes of the oppressed masses of the Third and Fourth Worlds."

"The information is accurate," Vanesco affirmed as al-Sharqi paused.

The Libyan dictator closed the file folder and handed it to an aide, then asked, "You know about the unprovoked air strike on the sterilization plant for babies' milk at Rabta that took place last night?"

Vanesco nodded.

"Yes," he said, not adding that he was also well aware that not sterilized milk but CBWs, chemical-biological weapons, were being manufactured there. The plant had been the subject of intense diplomatic efforts on the part of the United Nations and equally intense stonewalling and denials by the Libyan government.

CHAIN REACTION

According to his reliable sources, a joint US-IDF operation using advanced low-flying Israeli F-16F fighter-bombers guided by American commandos on the ground operating laser target designators had vaporized the weapons complex with enhanced blast yield fuel-air explosives.

That the stalemate would end up broken in the manner that it had been the previous night, Vanesco considered inevitable under the circumstances. That the Americans had again used the Israeli Defense Forces as its clandestine military surrogate came as no great surprise. While the US could not unilaterally afford to stage unsanctioned preemptive attacks on targets in the region due to the sensitive political situation in the Middle East, Israel was another matter entirely. Despite overtures toward regional peace, it would remain a pariah among Arab states for decades to come, and thus had little to lose.

"The world believes that it was the Israelis who bombed the plant," al-Sharqi went on. "But this is not so. It was the Americans who, as usual, were controlling the fawning puppets of their Zionist client-state."

DAVID ALEXANDER

The blond man remained silent. The Guiding Father, having grown more long-winded with time, would get around to what he really wished to talk about if he kept his patience.

"It is time we taught the Americans and Zionists a lesson," the Libyan stated at last. "I have heard that you are a man capable of administering this lesson to them."

Behind the tinted lenses, al-Sharqi's shrewd eyes played across the stern face of the long-haired man as though he doubted this last remark.

Vanesco had detected the faint rustle of cloth behind him while speaking with the Libyan dictator. Although he knew what was about to happen, he did not permit his gaze to leave al-Sharqi's half-hidden eyes.

Sidestepping at the last possible moment, he pivoted in place, reached out and unerringly seized the gun hand of the muscular man in camouflage fatigues who had been aiming the Chinese Type-59 semiautomatic pistol at his back.

In an almost effortless movement, Vanesco inserted his index finger behind the nine-millimeter weapon's trigger, and with the gun now prevented from firing, turned it fully around to stick its muzzle into the commando's suddenly fear-contorted face. With his thin lips set in a grim smile, Vanesco forced the trooper down to the carpeted floor of the tent and held the muzzle of the gun against his head.

Vanesco looked toward al-Sharqi who answered his silent question with the slightest possible nod.

Unblocking the trigger Vanesco fired a single round directly into the now helpless assailant's right eye, blowing a large, bloody entry hole in his face and bespattering the Ottoman rug covering the packed sand floor of the tent with bits of tissue and bone and dark droplets of arterial blood.

Blowback snapped the slide of the pistol into the open position where it remained firmly locked in place, indicating that the weapon was empty. Vanesco had suspected as much from the weight of the gun the instant in which he had gained a complete grip on it.

He had extrapolated that only a single bullet was chambered, and that the bullet was reserved either for himself or the hapless soldier.

Vanesco felt no remorse.

He had not the slightest doubt that had the situation been reversed, the other man would have had orders to kill him and would have carried out his instructions without a moment's hesitation.

Vanesco straightened up from a crouch above the disfigured corpse that leaked blood onto the fabric of the carpet and faced al-Sharqi, staring straight ahead with impassive features.

"Report back to camp," the dictator proclaimed, a new tone of respect apparent in his voice. "You will be given further instructions."

BOOK ONE:
THE MEDUSA FACTOR

Three

Lieutenant Jack Keller of the New York City police department rounded the corner of Forty-sixth Street and turned onto a section of Vanderbilt known locally as Crack Alley thanks to the drug bazaar that had sprung up in the Midtown enclave around Grand Central station.

Vanderbilt, an urban canyon that ran from Sixth down to Second, was permanently cloaked in shadows in the vicinity of Midtown because of the skyscrapers that flanked it, and attracted scum like a dirty rain puddle.

For this and other reasons, including its central location, it had become an oasis for New York's more enterprising drug dealers. They catered to a prestige clientele made up of lawyers, bank executives, insurance agents and other Manhattan plutocrats to whom discretion was as much a way of life as it had been for Cornelius Vanderbilt himself.

Busting the Vanderbilt Avenue drug concession would cause embarrassment to a number of prominent New Yorkers, including some city officials, and so the

CHAIN REACTION

NYPD had never come down hard on it, and it remained an invisible and -- in the eyes of some -- necessary, evil.

Keller caught the razor-edged glance that the tall dreadlocked Rastaman in tie-died denim suit and oversized reverse-billed ball cap was giving him as he approached the corner of Vanderbilt and Forty-fourth. He smiled in return as a familiar notion crossed his mind.

Keller thought about the old black-and-white movie in which Edward G. Robinson made sure that the criminals he tolerated in his precinct turf doffed their hats in a token of respect and submission to his authority as a cop.

Today, Keller merely smiled at the parasitic lowlife as he habitually did. But Keller feared that someday he would not be able to resist the compulsion to make one of the drug dealers of the Vanderbilt Crack Alley doff their ball caps to him or perform some similar genuflection.

Envisioning how the department and the media would respond to such actions made the grin on Keller's long, boney face more diabolical, and as he crossed the street, he turned on impulse to see the Rastafarian still eyeing him with barely suppressed hostility.

Keller stretched out his arm and held his index finger pointing straight out and his thumb sticking straight up.

He crooked his index finger several times as though pumping the trigger of a gun, a dangerous gesture for anyone not known to be a cop in New York to be making.

The rude boy from Kingston did not move a muscle. This was Keller's turf, and he knew better than to fuck with a cop with Keller's reputation for being a class-A scumbag, even if he knew that the heat never came down on his corner and probably never would.

■

Continuing down Vanderbilt, Keller reached what many area denizens called the "ass-end of Grand Central," and walked through one of the swinging bronze-clad doors of heavy steel frame construction.

A bearded bean-counter type in a dark business suit carrying a hard shell attaché case of monogrammed brown kidskin walked directly toward him, hurrying out of the station and deliberately not moving aside to permit Keller enough room to pass.

Keller took a wicked delight in shouldering the brisk-walking executive aside with precisely enough body English to make him stumble but not knock him to the ground or bounce him off the wall. He had sized him up as the kind who would continue on his way without as much as a sidelong glance. As well as the kind who deserved all the trouble he got from the great levelers that were the streets of Manhattan.

Deeper within the Beaux Arts rail terminal beneath a cathedral ceiling bearing the time-stained constellations of the zodiac, the post-lunch hour crowds were thick, but not as heavy as they would be at the rush hour, still some time away. A chamber ensemble was practicing on one of the balconies high above the terminal's main concourse and strains of music echoed across the enormous room as they fitfully started and stopped after playing a few bars.

Keller ascended to the Grand Central Cafe and glanced around in search of Augie Watson, the man he was to meet. Augie, a habitual latecomer, had not shown up yet, but Jack hadn't expected him to.

Keller ordered a bourbon on the rocks and sipped the rich amber fluid as he leisurely watched the activities taking place around him.

The musicians had started up again in earnest and launched into a brassy version of "Mame."

A uniformed transit cop went into the entrance to the Grand Central police command center at a lope, his cheeks puffed out as he crammed the last of a meatball hero sandwich into his mouth.

A bored railway porter in a dark blue uniform stared at a homeless man with the face of Jesus who was asleep on a bench in the ticketed waiting area beneath a crystal chandelier made up of a large, brilliant cluster of tiny white lights.

Two men leaned over the balconies and looked down into the terminal concourse, so alike in appearance that they might have been brothers. Keller studied them for a moment and then caught sight of the waiter.

"Hit me again," he said.

■

CHAIN REACTION

Inspector Augustine Watson had been detained downtown at One Police Plaza where he worked for the NYPD's Police Intelligence Unit. Since the recent terrorist near-miss on the halls of Congress in Washington and the close-call here at the Statue of Liberty the mood at headquarters was as tense as it had ever gotten since 911.

The public might have forgotten by now that international terror had finally set up a franchise in the City of New York, but not the police department, nor the New York branch of the FBI. Watson was aware that Keller was waiting for him at the cafe. He regretted being late but there had been no alternative.

Now he got out of a yellow taxi driven by a turbaned Sikh who had whistled Dixieland jazz and hurried through the terminal's Lexington Avenue entrance doors.

Preoccupied though he was, Watson was still a cop. The sudden mental click between a wanted photo from Denard at French Interpol he had seen days before in an email alert, and the blond man he had just spotted standing by a news kiosk near the stairway to the IRT made Watson do a double-take.

"Got some change, bro'?"

The hulking man in foul-smelling rags was suddenly in his face, blocking his view as he held his large, calloused hand out open-palmed. Watson shoved past the beggar but in the instant his view had been cut off the guy he'd scoped had vanished.

"Mother-fucker!" he heard the beggar shout behind him at the top of his lungs, pronouncing the final syllable with special vehemence. "Put a nigger in a suit an' he think he fuckin' ass be white!"

Watson ignored the shouted taunts; he understood that the man's poverty fueled his hatred and felt guilty about not having given him some money. But his only thought was to once more get the tall blond man in sight, and now that he was unable to pick him up again, Watson could not be certain if he had ID'd him or not.

Crossing into the terminal's high-ceilinged "Great Hall," Watson spotted Keller waving to him from the upper level of the cafe and turned his attention to other matters.

CHAIN REACTION

Watson waved back and headed toward him, anxious to order a drink. There was no sign of the blond man in the terminal concourse, and Watson felt he had probably been mistaken after all. Fatigue played tricks with your mind, and Watson had been functioning on caffeine and adrenaline for weeks.

"Christ, I'm sorry I'm late, Jack, but I got sandbagged at Nadelman's office," he apologized, meaning veteran NYPD Commissioner Erick Nadelman.

Augustine Watson was a black man of middle height whose hair had begun to go gray at the temples. But his eyes were alert behind the wire frame glasses he wore.

"So how are your friends on Vanderbilt?" he asked with a chuckle, knowing all about Keller's fantasy.

"Passed one of the home boys standing his corner," Keller said taking a sip of the potent rye whiskey. "I went like this." He repeated the intimidating hand gesture to Augie that he had made on the street corner.

Watson shook his head in disbelief. "I'd think twice about those famous hand gestures of yours, Jack," Augie suggested. "One of these days a brother might pull his jammie and light you up."

"If I wind up looking down the barrel of a gun I'll only have myself to blame," Keller said. "Besides, it wouldn't be the first time."

"You trying to remind me of Anh Seh, by any chance, Jack?" asked Augie.

"I told you then I'd never let you live it down."

The year had been 1990, the place had been a Cambodian border town in the northwestern Anlong Veng stronghold, the last redoubt of the almost beaten Khmers called Anh Seh, on the night when the Khmer Rouge had staged a sudden all-out attack from crossborder staging areas in Thailand and Vietnam.

Jack had then been assigned to Gator Force, a covert CIA rapid-deployment paramilitary team, fighting a secret war that officially was not taking place. Army Captain Augustine Watson ran the team's intelligence support unit, headquartered in an old mansion dating back to the time of French colonialism in Indochina.

During the melee Jack received word via radio that the Khmers were storming the palace. Jack's team of special forces personnel, ex-French Foreign Legionnaires and fierce Nung tribesmen took down most of the attackers. But there were still a few Khmers left inside who had not yet been dealt with and had dug in their heels for a confrontation. One of them was holding Augie hostage at gunpoint.

The Khmer Rouge ordered Jack to lay down his Uzi submachinegun, one of the special weapons Gator Force personnel were permitted to draw from ordnance stocks, and when Jack did, the "Red" Khmer laughed and said he was going to shoot him anyway. In the instant he leveled the Chinese automatic pistol, Jack had already pulled the Walther .38 he'd secreted behind his back and shot the guerilla insurgent through the head, saving Watson's life. The round had passed so close to his skull that Watson would remember the whistle it made as it cut through the air for the rest of his life.

After Cambodia, Jack and Augie had both done stints with the CIA. Though presently assigned to different branches of the New York City Police Department -- Keller to the Homicide squad at the

Thirty-ninth Precinct in Midtown Manhattan and Watson to the Police Intelligence Unit based at One Police Plaza in Lower Manhattan's Wall Street district -- they still kept periodically in touch, renewing a close friendship that had lasted for almost twenty-five years.

"So let's talk about why you wanted to meet today," Keller suggested. "Or do I already know the answer?"

"You might, Jack," Watson returned, "but hear me out this time. One of my key personnel has just retired. With the worsening terrorist threat conditions in the city, your expertise is desperately needed. This is not just me talking, Jack. We ran names through the server. Yours came up at the top of the short list."

"I told you before, Augie," Jack answered, "I'm out of the spook business for good. If I wanted more of that cloak-and-dagger crap I would have stayed with the Company where at least I was playing with pros."

"I'll level with you, Keller," Augie pressed, his features going hard. "I brought your name up with Nadelman today. He agrees you're the man we need to fill the post. You may not have a choice."

"Augie, you sonofa -- "

Keller noticed Watson's attention focused on something down below in the crowded terminal concourse and fell silent. Keller followed the direction of his gaze in an attempt to understand his sudden change of demeanor.

"What is it, Augie?"

"That guy over there," he said, not looking at Jack, "the tall blond dude with a scar on his face, I spotted him when I came in. Thought I was seeing things."

"So what?" Keller asked, noticing the long hair and almost pretty features. "Didn't want to give you a blowjob, is that it?"

"No, he's .... " Watson' mouth was set in a tight, humorless line. He continued to stare at the blond man then stiffened. "Sweet Jesus!" He was now completely certain. "That guy's wanted by Interpol ... He's a fucking major league terrorist ... Jack, listen to me. No shit. We have to -- "

Watson had fallen silent as the blond reached down to the duffle bag at his feet. It was unzipped and there was no mistaking the wedge-shaped buttstock of the G-11 rifle that he was now in the process of extracting. Watson muttered an oath and unholstered his service automatic, one of the new Glock ten millimeter pistols recently authorized by the department for service use.

"No Augie! Wait!" Keller shouted, but events had overtaken them. Watson had already bolted down the stairs of the balcony area on which the cafe was located to the floor of the terminal concourse below, shouting for the guy with the assault weapon to freeze.

Keller took off after Watson, drawing his own service pistol, a compact Sturm-Ruger P93 semiautomatic. He held the gun pointing upward, its safety thumbed to the etched dot and its hammer cocked.

Jack's full attention was riveted on the blond man as he unshipped the wedge-shaped black plastic high technology rifle and fired a burst into Watson's belly at pointblank range, hurling him to the terminal floor amid a spray of blood.

Seeing the second armed man running toward him, the shooter pivoted and tracked the gun. In the split instant before he fired their eyes locked, and

CHAIN REACTION

Keller saw the pure malice reflected in their ice-cold depths.

The weapon cycled and bullets chewed up the information booth on the lobby floor behind which Jack took cover, killing the Metro North ticket clerk inside the booth as he frantically reached for the phone. When Keller popped up again, blood poured down the side of his face. A shard of glass had gouged his temple.

Using his sleeve to wipe the blood running into his eyes, he caught a brief glimpse of the gunman, who vanished into one of the numerous side corridors connecting with the main concourse to street and basement levels -- and to two suburban railroad and several subway lines that ran beneath the station.

Keller paused for only a second where Watson lay in a spreading wine-colored pool. The fact that there was gunfire coming from all directions had only dimly begun to register. His main focus was that Augie was gone.

Still in shock, Jack was aware that other individuals stationed on the balcony level that encircled the Great Hall had extracted automatic weapons from similarly shaped carryalls and were now indiscriminately firing them into the crowded terminal. There was a sudden flash and an explosion from the Grand Central police command center as a rifle grenade detonated.

A cold fury gripped Keller as he booked along the corridor into which his quarry had run, edged to a corner of the wall and quickly moved into the open, leveling the Ruger in a two-handed combat grip.

"Halt! Police!" he yelled, as the shooter jumped a turnstile and hustled down the steps toward the IRT subway platform below.

Unable to fire for fear of hitting a citizen, Jack took off after the cop killer, intent on his capture. Only part of his mind took note of the automatic bolt clatter and screams of terror coming from behind him. The blond's accomplices were firing continuously on the crowd in the terminal.

Keller got hold of a baby-faced transit cop as he ran along the platform.

"Call this in! A terrorist situation is in progress in the terminal concourse. A police officer is down," he shouted, taking notice of the rookie's terrified expression. The dilated pupils of her eyes registered the telltale symptoms of shock.

Keller noted the fledgling cop's badge number.

"You fuck up and you'll personally answer to me," he underscored, then ran off after the felon without a backward glance.

Midway along the platform he saw the shooter turn and braced to take sudden fire. As Keller dodged behind a large pill-shaped metal trash container, he saw the flicker of muzzle flash against the white tiles of the tunnel wall and heard the sequential thuds of close-impacting rounds.

When he popped back up again seconds later, the heavy casing of the cylindrical trash receptacle was perforated with bullet holes. Keller saw the blond running down the tracks into the darkness of the IRT tunnel.

DAVID ALEXANDER

Four

*K*eller heard the klaxoning of a siren that indicated a subway train was minutes away from arriving at the station. Since there were two tracks on the platform, a local and an express, he could not be sure which of them the train would come in on. But he had no time to play wait-and-see. With over 850 miles of underground track and 468 stations, the New York City subway system was the largest in the world next to the London Tube.

Beneath Grand Central Station itself, the tunnel system was a vast, multilevel labyrinth with a total combined size of 48 acres. It contained not only the active electrified railway tracks for the IRT subway and the Long Island Railroad, Harlem-Hudson, Metro North and PATH commuter lines, but also depots for parked trains, storage chambers for maintenance equipment and feeder tunnels connecting to the city's underground electrical and sewer system.

Numerous ventilation shaftways and safety exits led directly up to steel gratings on the sidewalks above. It would be an easy matter for the felon whom Keller was chasing to lose himself in the dark, meandering tunnel complex and, having done so, use one of the many routes to street level to escape pursuit.

Sizing up the situation, Keller jumped down onto the debris-littered track bed. He ran into the tunnel, feeling the concrete foundation in which the steel rails were embedded vibrate beneath him as a steadily increasing roar filled his ears.

The IRT train pulling into the station was close by. Keller shrugged off a sudden flashback to a childhood nightmare of being chased by a demonic black locomotive as he plunged deeper into the encircling darkness.

Keeping close to the tunnel wall, he inched his way carefully along as his night vision began to predominate.

Up ahead he heard a sudden noise and saw one of the bare incandescent light bulbs set at intervals along the tunnel walls flicker out. Keller's lips drew back in an expression that was part smile and part grimace. His quarry was directly ahead of him, smashing the tunnel utility light bulbs as he went along.

DAVID ALEXANDER

As the roar of the incoming subway train increased to a deafening crescendo, Keller saw a powdery white light begin to play along the curved concrete walls, leaving no doubt that he was on the same trackway as the arriving local.

Forcing himself to concentrate on his quarry, he moved along the wall on a half-crouch until he had rounded a curving stretch before the tunnel straightened out again.

He caught his breath as he saw his man loping through the tunnel about fifty yards in front of him, silhouetted against the tunnel wall by the faint glimmer of light from a ventilation shaft high overhead.

Keller raised the Ruger semiautomatic, risking a quick glance behind him. The IRT local was just beginning to move again. He had only a second or two in which to take his shot and make it count, and he took a deep breath to steady himself. Sighting on his man's back, he pulled the trigger and fired twice.

The figure seemed to stumble, but turned quickly and sprayed automatic fire in his direction. The burst forced Keller to flatten inside one of the niches cut in the cement wall and used by MTA maintenance workers as shelters when subway trains passed by.

Before he could reemerge, the southbound IRT train roared past his position, throwing up hot yellow sparks as it sped down the electrified track. Keller saw the faces of passengers through the lighted windows, oblivious to what was taking place around them.

He was ready to jump from the niche and flatten himself on the track bed as the last car passed him, taking advantage of the light thrown off from the subway car's interior to scan the tunnel. As the two red taillights receded into the blackness around a tunnel bend, Keller swept the tunnel ahead of him.

There had not been sufficient time for the shooter to do anything more except take cover in a maintenance niche as Keller had just done. He would have to come out sooner or later. But after several minutes of waiting in the darkness, Keller had the feeling that his man had somehow managed to flee the scene.

Getting to his feet, he proceeded cautiously along the tunnel wall toward the approximate point from which the gunman had last fired. When Keller reached it, he saw traces of fresh blood covering the track bed and smeared along the adjacent section of wall.

A few feet ahead of him, beneath a screw socket that contained the shattered fragments of a smashed incandescent light bulb, Keller saw the signposted entrance to a ventilation shaftway. More droplets of blood had been recently shed onto the concrete steps that ran straight up to the street above.

Cautiously ascending, Keller reached the mouth of the shaft in a matter of seconds.

The grating above cut the daylight into small blue squares that fell across his upturned face in a checkerboard pattern. Keller heard the honking of car horns, police sirens and the footfalls of passersby overhead.

Nearby, on the refuse-littered concrete apron ten feet below the sidewalk, he found the advanced design automatic rifle that had been left behind by the killer before he had lifted a hinged grating cover and exited onto a side street several blocks away from the scene of the attack.

■

From the balcony encircling the Grand Central terminal concourse, the terrorist death squad continued to fire their automatic weapons. They paused only long enough to jam fresh ammunition clips into the rifles as they kept up a steady tempo of unremitting slaughter.

Jagged shards of splintered glass burst from the shattered windows of ticket booths and shops lining the perimeter of the main concourse and from the three huge windows of the terminal's Forty-second Street-side atrium. They fell to the floor in a deadly rain, littering the corpses that had piled up everywhere and mingling with their congealing blood.

■

Directly outside Grand Central Station on Lexington Avenue, two men in a rented Jimmy panicked as screaming commuters poured from the terminal and the aggregate wail of police, EMS and fire department sirens converged on the scene of calamity.

DAVID ALEXANDER

Forced to move by a traffic cop, the driver of the truck collided with an ambulance double-parked immediately in front of it. The ambulance driver got out, caught a glimpse of a weapon concealed under the front seat of the Jimmy, and began to holler for a cop.

The driver and the man sitting in the passenger seat of the Jimmy simultaneously jumped out of the vehicle, and the driver of the truck shot the EMS driver in the face at nearly pointblank range.

The second man ran for the ambulance and jumped inside, shifting the idling vehicle into drive.

The ambulance lurched away, its tires squealing, plowed into the fenders of the two vehicles pinning it between them, and bolted into the street.

Two harness cops from the Thirty-ninth Precinct that had just pulled up in a blue-and-white had seen what happened, and were ready with combat shotguns hastily pulled from their cruiser.

The windshield of the ambulance shattered as they opened fire and blood from the head and upper torso of the mortally wounded driver sprayed the cab.

CHAIN REACTION

The second man jumped out of the side door and began wildly firing the short-barreled automatic weapon in his hands. He managed to get as far as the next corner when his rifle jammed and he was nearly killed by a mob of pedestrians. The police rescued him, cuffed him, and took him into custody.

■

Keller scanned the streets to either side of him, focusing his concentration in order to detect any sign of the killer's presence amid the troubled sea of pedestrians. There had been no more blood spoor to follow after emerging from the ventilation shaft onto the sidewalk.

In any other metropolis on earth, a man emerging from the bowels of the city with a massive police and emergency services presence only a few blocks away would have aroused suspicion. But not in New York where a see-no-evil attitude was the norm.

Keller had just emerged carrying a pistol and pedestrians had studiously looked aside. As long as the gun was not pointed in their direction, nobody seemed to give a damn.

Keller holstered the pistol, realizing that he no longer needed it. The blond cop killer had gotten clean away. The man who had gunned down Augie Watson before his eyes had slipped from his grasp.

■

A line of blue-and-whites blocked off Lexington Avenue between Forty-second and Forty-fifth Streets and the immediate crime scene was roped off with yellow hazard tape.

The whirling gum ball lights cast kaleidoscopic patterns on the walls of the tall surrounding buildings. Minicam crews from the local news stations were already at the scene, interviewing bystanders, whom a detail of harness cops kept back from the cordon of blue sawhorses bearing the stenciled words: Police Line Do Not Cross.

Inside the Grand Central Terminal main concourse, a joint NYPD-FBI forensic team was already at work sorting through the carnage. Spattered with blood and littered with fragments of broken glass, the bodies of both the strike's many victims and several of its perpetrators lay scattered about the spacious railway terminal in grotesque death postures.

Police photographers snapped pictures from a variety of perspectives while the forensic team outlined the positions of the corpses using white adhesive tape. On the sidelines, a detail from the coroner's office stood waiting for the forensic crew to finish its work, and the chief pathologist to give it the go-ahead to cart the DOAs to one of the temporary morgue barges on the West Side piers pending shipment to the city morgue on Clarkson Avenue across the river in Brooklyn.

DAVID ALEXANDER

Five

*T*he Thirty-ninth Precinct was a four story red brick turn-of-the-century building in the district west of Times Square and north of the Port Authority docks called Clinton and Midtown West only by real estate brokers but known as Hell's Kitchen by real New Yorkers. A line of patrol cars emblazoned with the words "NYC Police" was angle-parked in front of the station house. A hand-lettered sign on its institutional green steel door warned that all visitors were subject to unannounced weapons searches.

It was the morning after the terrorist hit on Grand Central Station.

Junkies and hookers screamed at bored cops in the precinct house's large, crowded muster room that served double-duty as a place to question alleged crime victims and suspected offenders. Having entered the building, Keller walked through this area into a large open bullpen in which other members of New York's Finest sat performing various tasks at desks which seemed haphazardly placed around the room.

CHAIN REACTION

Some pecked out reports on newly upgraded computer workstations that were already beginning to look shopworn from maltreatment and grimy fingers. Other denizens of the Thirty-ninth's bullpen listened and occasionally nodded assent as stories identical to scores of others they had encountered during the course of too-long careers poured from the lips of participants in the city's unending drama of endemic criminal violence.

Keller's office occupied a recently constructed room with sheetrock drywalls fronting the bullpen. The coroner's preliminary report lay on the scratched and chipped gunmetal gray surface of Keller's steel desk as he sat on the oak swivel chair worn smooth by decades of polishing by the seats of cops' pants.

The chair had come with the office. So had the dingy row of olive-drab metal filing cabinets and the dirty, steel-mesh covered window with a dreary view of an Amoco service station on Tenth Avenue and the riverfront one block west, with the gray shapelessness of the New Jersey shore line hulking in the overcast distance.

DAVID ALEXANDER

Keller flipped through the ten-page, double-spaced printout filled with the coroner's medical jargon, and tried with his usual lack of success to translate it into plain English.

After five minutes, Keller flopped the report back down on the desk and got up to grab some coffee.

The row of coin-operated machines dispensing hot coffee, brand-name chewing gum, sugary cakes and other junk food with no known value in human nutrition was located in the corridor at the other end of the bullpen.

Upon reaching it, Keller fished in his pockets and realized he didn't have enough change even before he'd finished counting the assortment of quarters, nickels and dimes that lay in the hollow of his outstretched open hand.

As he stood there he felt a tap on the shoulder and turned to see O'Downey, an Irish sergeant and veteran cop of the old school whom he recognized from the Safe and Loft Division.

"Lou, I was just in the captain's office," O'Downey said to him. "He told me to tell you he wants to see you if I saw you, so since I seen you, I'm telling you." And O'Downey was gone.

■

Captain Frank Abernathy was a 35-year veteran of the force. He had survived everything from the Yeng and Stallings anti-corruption commissions to a major coronary suffered when the heat was turned up during the municipal scandals of the Jimenez mayoral administration. His basic character flaw of speaking the truth when he recognized it had kept him from rising any higher than the command of one of the most problem-plagued precincts in the borough of Manhattan.

A portly man with pallid skin, a small, well-formed mouth and the broken nose of an ex-street fighter, Abernathy nursed his gastric ulcers like a mother hen, and was due to retire with full pension benefits within six months. No matter what the time of day it happened to be, the captain's fleshy cheeks seemed to sport a blue haze of stubble. Twice divorced, he was looking forward to spending his golden years in Fort Lauderdale. The last thing he needed was the bedlam that had suddenly erupted on his watch and the pressure put on him by Borough Command in the bloody aftermath of the Grand Central terror attack.

Abernathy unscrewed the cap from a two-ounce bottle of liquid Gelusil and took a long, measured swallow while poking his index finger into a battery-operated electronic device that calculated blood pressure based on the human pulse rate.

Keller watched him perform this familiar ritual from his seat on a hard chair of molded Formica in front of the captain's desk. He lit up the Bull Durham he had just hand-rolled, blowing a dense stream of fragrant pipe tobacco smoke in his chief's direction.

"Don't fucking blow that in my face, Jack," Abernathy swore.

He flicked his eyes to Keller, then back at the small liquid crystal display on the beeping device which monitored his vital signs. After a few more seconds the machine emitted a long, continuous beeptone to indicate that it had finally taken a reading.

CHAIN REACTION

"Goddamn it!" Abernathy cursed. "This contraption's all fucked up. It says my ticker's stopped."

"Throw it away, Frank," Keller suggested. "Life's too short to worry about your health."

"Maybe you got a point there."

Abernathy contemptuously flung the blood pressure meter into the top drawer of his desk and lit up one of the acrid-smelling Dutch cigars he habitually smoked.

Abernathy had known and worked with Lieutenant Augustine Watson for many years. In the aftermath of the bloody terrorist strike on Grand Central Station, Augie's death had taken on the dimensions of an especially cruel personal blow.

Amid the body counts, strategy sessions, press conferences, blame casting and soul searching in the wake of the shootings, the police department had found itself bearing the added trauma of burying a hero cop struck down in the line of duty.

Keller flashed back on the funeral services for his longtime friend and fellow police officer.

He remembered listening to the minister make a speech over Augie, not daring to let his eyes wander to where his widow, Celia, was sobbing in the first row.

Keller had known Augie Watson for at least twenty-seven years and was his best friend, but he had declined making a funerary speech. He had suffered guilt and more than once had picked up the phone in order to tell Celia that he would do it.

But now that he had been to the funeral Keller was glad he hadn't given in. Had he stood up there he would have broken down and wept like a baby. Keller had instead paid his respects to Celia and promised to attend the wake at their house in Jamaica, Queens.

Keller was jolted back to the present by Abernathy, who he realized had been speaking to him for some time.

"I thought I'd lost you there for a second," he remarked.

"Sorry, Frank. I suppose all of this has really ground me down."

"I was saying that there were no prints on the gun your man dropped. Either he wiped them off or he wore gloves. And that was a pretty advanced weapon. I've never seen one like it before."

"Few have," Jack explained. "Not even in the 'hood. It's a caseless rifle. It fires bullets fused inside solid propellant blocks. There are no shell casings and very little recoil. Beyond that, the G-11 has yet to go into standard non-military production. Meaning this gun was a specialty item."

"Well," mused Abernathy, "maybe there's a lead in there someplace. You check it out?"

"Yeah, I did," said Keller. "The weapon was manufactured at H&K's US division facilities in Virginia and sold under a Pentagon-approved export license to the royal weapons procurement office in Dhahran, Saudi Arabia. My sources were the Defense Department and ATF. I'm still checking with Interpol, though don't bet your chips on any leads from this angle."

"What else?"

"Goddamn blood type didn't tell us much," put in Keller. "It was Landsteiner Group-O, the most common in the world."

"Keep the faith, Jack. We have those two suspects in custody and international APBs on the big kahuna that escaped. I have a hunch that pretty soon we'll have - - "

Suddenly the PBX on Abernathy's desk rang. He lifted the handset and Jack saw his face go through a transformation while he listened intently.

He said, "I'll tell him. He's right here," hung up, and stared at Jack distractedly for a second or two.

"What is it?"

"Jack, I think we might have found the cocksucker who iced Augie," Abernathy announced.

"Where?" Jack replied, instantly galvanized, a muscle on his lean jaw throbbing and tight with anticipation.

"A blond man matching his description down to the facial scarring was positively ID'd on the Manhattan piers ten minutes ago by a Customs agent to whom he presented seaman's papers. The Customs agent said he was acting suspiciously.

"He's on a freighter now but we have to make the collar before he reaches the three-mile limit and is in international waters where he's out of our jurisdiction."

Abernathy added that a crack police SWAT unit had already boarded a Harbor Patrol cutter and was in pursuit. The SWAT crew had been trained in counterterror techniques at the FBI's special law enforcement range at Quantico, Virginia, and was considered among the best in the country.

The captain went on to tell Keller that a fast police port and waterways launch was waiting at the Forty-second Street pier and would remain moored at the Port Authority maritime facility no longer than fifteen minutes.

Jack tugged on his ear but said nothing.

"What's the matter, Jack?" asked Abernathy. He was already heaving his sizable bulk up from behind his desk. "You should be smiling. We've got the rat bastard as good as cornered."

"I'll smile when we have the shooter in custody," Keller said, standing to follow Abernathy to the door. "And not a second sooner."

■

The two cops reached the pier minutes after the Harbor Patrol cutter carrying the SWAT unit had sailed from its base at the Peck Slip piers on the East River.

Once they had come aboard, the launch sped into the harbor amid a wash of frothing salt spray. The boat caught up with the Harbor Patrol cutter within a matter of minutes.

Keller could see it in the swell just up ahead. The pilot radioed the helmsman of the cutter that they were bringing two passengers onboard. The cutter slowed its speed and hove to as the launch approached to starboard of the fantail at its stern. The deck crew let down boarding stairs and Keller and Abernathy scrambled aboard.

"Glad you're here," the captain of the cutter said as the new arrivals came onto the bridge. Radar showed the track of the contact which was now approaching the Verrazano-Narrows near the mouth of the Hudson.

"That's her," the captain announced. "We'll be abreast of the boat in about twenty minutes."

■

CHAIN REACTION

The suspect freighter lay dead ahead, cutting at flank speed through high, rolling seas two miles beyond the tip of Coney Island at the edge of Lower New York Bay, apparently hurrying to reach the security of international Atlantic waters.

The police cutter had just passed under the under-level of the massive Verrazano-Narrows Bridge and was closing with its target at a speed of thirty maritime knots. At the prow of the boat, the commander of the SWAT unit picked up a loudhailer and his amplified voice boomed across the choppy gray water.

"This is the New York City Police Department," he announced. "You are ordered to cut your engines and stand to. Failure to do this will result in our taking immediate action to stop you."

The freighter did not stand to as it had been instructed, but continued on without noticeably slowing its speed.

The SWAT commander picked up a compact Motorola radio and issued commands to the cutter's gunnery crew to put a warning salvo across her bows. The .50 caliber deck guns began to boom and the white neon dashes of tracer ammunition arced across the freighter's foredeck.

The deadly threat made its intended point. Within seconds the freighter's speed was reduced and she heeled to starboard. The SWAT team cast off boarding gaffs, securing her to the port deck of the cutter. Crossing over, with combat shotguns and submachines in their hands, they fanned across the freighter's decks, making anyone they encountered lie face-down under armed guard.

Once the upper decks of the boat were secure, the SWAT team fanned out below decks, carefully combing the cabins, cargo hold and engine room for an individual matching the suspect's description.

Jack waited with anticipation on the freighter's upper deck. Cold salt spray showered him from six-foot swells and the chill northeasterly wind whipped his black hair around as he stared at the skyline of the financial center at the tip of Lower Manhattan in the near distance.

Jack turned around as he heard his name called.

CHAIN REACTION

The commander of the SWAT unit faced him and shook his head.

"Bad news," he said. "Your man isn't onboard."

"You're sure of that?"

"Positive. My personnel have combed every inch of this tub and questioned the crew. If your man had been onboard you'd be reading him his rights instead of talking to me."

"Okay. Thanks," Keller answered, not entirely surprised to have come up empty.

It had felt too easy.

As he had suspected, the freighter had been used as a diversion all along to throw pursuers off the shooter's true escape route. The killer had used a variation on an old tactic, seeding avenues of escape that were certain to be under close scrutiny with look-alikes sure to arouse suspicion.

"We have the man who was originally identified as the terrorist in custody," the SWAT commander went on. "You want to question him?"

Keller nodded. He would go through the motions, but he had no doubt that the ringer would be a low-level operative, hired through cutouts and paid to leave the ship and then re-board her at the end of the forty-eight hour shore leave period granted under international maritime law and knowing nothing about the operation as a whole.

Six

*B*ehind the in-flight magazine, the passenger in the first class compartment was in a state of heightened alertness. The small .38 caliber pistol that he had smuggled with absurd ease through two airport security checkpoints, including a state-of-the-art body scanner was nestled in a crotch holster, ready in case he had to play the hole card and take the plane as a last resort.

Vanesco had pre-boarded the commercial jet with the other first class passengers at JFK International after changing his appearance. It now matched the photo on the forged passport that had been provided him for use in extracting from the strike zone in the wake of the attack.

The shooters had been provided with fallback options of their own, but Vanesco had never been part of their cadre and had escape routes and fallbacks of his own in place.

The direct transatlantic flight would take him to Paris where he could go to ground in a safe house in the vicinity of the Rue Clichy. It was an area of tourists, artists, cabarets and houses of prostitution bordering the infamous Pigalle quarter. There transients were the rule rather than the exception. His presence would not attract undue notice.

In Paris, Vanesco could, in relative safety, await further instructions before committing to return to the Middle East, despite the operational plan which had called for his departure following the retaliatory terror hit.

The raid had only been semi-successful, thanks in large part to the unforeseen interference by the American policeman who had spotted him only minutes prior to the commencement of the action -- and who he had subsequently killed.

His paymasters would not be pleased and might be motivated to act on their displeasure by exacting an appropriately savage retribution, *pour discourager les autres.*

Vanesco had been warned by *al-Qaid*'s military planners that his direct participation in the strike would be counterproductive. But he had overruled them all and unilaterally announced that it was his mission. He would act as he pleased.

CHAIN REACTION

Had the mission been an unqualified success, he would have been praised as a hero. Now he would be branded an American cowboy, a loose cannon, perhaps even a Zionist tool and other unpleasant things.

However, Vanesco had plans to mollify his paymasters by offering *al-Qaid* a far more delectable morsel than the one the self-styled Guiding Father and politically reborn patron saint of guerilla fighters had ordered him to carry out.

Based on information from his days as a grunt in the shadow war, he had knowledge of a dire secret. It would make possible a strike that would be remembered throughout history as the most ambitious undertaking of its kind.

Vanesco would offer his paymasters the plan from his protected hiding place in Paris. He would gamble that he could sell *al-Qaid* on his plan, because he knew that despite any misgivings he might entertain, he would in the end be unable to resist it.

Seven

"Y ou better get a grip, Jack," Abernathy warned. "The FBI people don't like the way you handled the interrogation yesterday. They're calling you a wise-ass and a loose cannon and a couple of other things besides. I won't even tell you what the D.A. said."

It had been Jack's turn to run with the ball after Falmouth, the Bureau's chief interrogator who's name and style had both earned him an eponymous nickname, had struck out.

Jack had been watching Foul Mouth perform from the shadowed sidelines beyond the cone of intense white light in which one of the captured suspects sat on a metal-frame chair, a snarl of contempt on his middle-class European features.

Keller's assessment of the FBI's interrogation procedures was not favorable. They -- and their retinue of representatives from the office of the D.A., who were themselves scrutinized by a court stenographer and two court-appointed public defenders -- were playing textbook head games, using psychological peashooters when they needed bare-knuckle howitzers to accomplish the job.

Jack lit the cigaret he had freshly rolled and stepped directly in front of the prisoner, ignoring the urge to exhale a stream of smoke directly into his smug face. A bandage covered the bridge of the suspect's nose; it had been injured during his capture.

"You participated in the vicious killing of at least fifteen people," Jack began.

"*Suspected*, Lieutenant," the public defender chimed in. "You left that out. My client has yet to be convicted of any crime."

Jack nodded, but kept his eyes on the prisoner.

"Alright," he said. "You are *suspected* of blowing away a priest, a pregnant woman, a fifteen-year-old school kid, a blind beggar and eleven other innocent bystanders."

"Lieutenant, I warn you! You're pushing the envelope."

Jack ignored the public defender and went on.

"You are *suspected* of irreparably fucking up the lives of people who never did you any harm," Jack continued. "And you are *suspected*, you shitfaced little prick, of being an accomplice to the cold-blooded murder of my friend Augustine Watson, a guy who I loved like a brother."

"I have nothing to say," was the reply Jack got in guttural, accented English.

"Fine," Jack said, smiled tautly, and smashed his fist hard into the bandaged bridge of the prisoner's nose, breaking it again in a second place before the combined efforts of five FBI men succeeded in dragging him away.

"Fuck the Feebs," he now said as he flashed back finally to his being unceremoniously ordered to leave the interrogation room. The suspect had gone berserk, howling like a wounded animal while blood gushed down his shirt from his shattered face.

Abernathy slammed his fist down on the table making paperwork jump. He rose to his feet, his pale, doughy face crimsoning in anger.

"'Fuck the Feebs?' What the fuck are you saying, Jack? You're a cop, not some street corner punk out to settle a vendetta. You lose your professional perspective and you're on your way to the bughouse or a prison cell. Do you understand what I'm saying?"

CHAIN REACTION

Jack held Abernathy's stare, returning the captain's gaze with a hard, blank expression Abernathy had seen before on psycho cases, leaving no doubt in his mind that Jack was a man who right now was teetering on the edge.

After a long beat the mad eyes cleared and Jack slowly nodded.

"Okay, so I was out of line," he said, conceding the truth of the captain's observation. "But I couldn't just stand there and let that murderous fuckin' -- "

"Look, I know you and Watson had some shared history," Abernathy affirmed, sliding his massive rear into his seat and uncapping a fresh bottle of the antacid liquid he habitually swilled.

"But the matter is out of your hands now, Jack. You've gotta lighten up. You've gotta accept it."

"Sure, I'll accept it," he said and got up to leave the office, adding, "like hell I will," under his voice.

Abernathy morosely watched his office door close after Keller had left the office.

He thought about the warm Fort Lauderdale weather and the hardbodied coeds with nice firm tits that came down there every year to party during spring break. He promised himself that if Keller deep-sixed his dream retirement, he'd have him checking parking meters in the South Bronx so fast it would give him jet lag.

∎

The nightmare gripped Keller in its dark, fetid embrace. He cried out in terror and came awake with a sudden start. Greasy fear sweat stood out in beads on his face and his heart pounded in his chest like blows from a sledgehammer.

"Jack, snap out of it!"

He turned to see Christine's face hovering in the darkness of the bedroom. Her fingers were pressed into his arms and she was shaking him with all her might.

"Okay, okay," he snapped and shook her off. "I'm alright."

"You sure?" she asked. "I mean, you were talking some crazy shit for awhile."

"Like what?" his fingers mechanically groped for the rolling machine, Top papers and packet of pipe tobacco which he habitually kept nearby on the bed stand.

"I don't know ... weird things. You said the word 'snake.' It seemed as if something was chasing you. And then you were talking in what I thought was German."

"Could be, *mein Schatz*," Jack proposed, lighting the cigaret and inhaling deeply. "I speak German. Some French and Russian too."

"You never told me," she returned, looking dubious.

"I never told you a lot of things," Jack replied as he lay back down and admired Christine's lean body. "Then again, I'm sure there's an equal number of things you've never told me. Like for instance, where you were on a certain night last week when I waited up for you."

"That's my business," Christine stonewalled.

Keller laughed. He reached out to touch her shoulder and his fingers brushed against her plump, naked breast. Christine was something of a departure for him. Since his wife had left him two years before, Keller had confined his sexual activities to two or three semi-regular partners who he knew were "safe."

DAVID ALEXANDER

He had quickly found out that he was not alone in this practice. Promiscuity in the age of AIDS had become a waltz instead of a watusi. Two of his girlfriends were married, one to another cop. The third was a gynecologist who practiced partial celibacy and who had stopped performing lucrative operations for fear of being infected by contaminated blood from her patients.

Among his more staid liaisons, Christine was an unknown quantity. She was younger then Jack's other women, and though not necessarily hornier, she embodied the reckless sensuality of youth rather than the more mechanically precise, though less earnest, lovemaking of his more seasoned lady friends. He had met her at a yacht party thrown by the commissioner and they had immediately hit it off.

Christine's job as a sales rep for a surgical supply company kept her on the road frequently, and she breezed in and out of Jack's life, never staying long enough for entanglements to form.

Sometimes he regretted the impermanence of their relationship, but most of the time he was grateful for it being the way that it was. Jack would have been a fool to permit himself to believe that it would ever work between them. When it ended, it ended, and there would be no regrets on the part of either.

Jack slid his hand down Christine's cool, flat stomach until he found a place of warmth. She inhaled suddenly and her body shuddered. He lifted himself slightly.

"You're gonna need my help, Jack," she said with a sincerity that did not mock him, and gently pushed him on his back.

Jack watched Christine's lips kiss his belly and stroked her shoulder-length ash-blonde hair. He blew smoke at the ceiling where headlights of passing cars cast moving shadows, like wraiths encountered in some half-remembered dream.

Stubbing out his cigaret, he changed position to finish what Christine had started.

∎

It was still dark when Jack awoke to the electronic Roc cry of the bedside alarm clock. Christine muttered in her sleep and turned over to show him the pink roundness of her bare ass cheeks. Jack got out of bed naked and made coffee.

By sunrise he had left the apartment he owned in Manhattan's Chelsea district with a note reminding Christine to make sure to turn off all the lights when she left and wishing her luck with her upcoming business trip to L.A.

He ate breakfast at a greasy spoon eatery on lower Broadway made from a converted diner car -- probably the last of its kind in an age of plastic franchise fast food places -- and checked his watch. It was time for his appointment.

■

A gentrification-resistant wedge of bombed-out Lower East Side neighborhood between 13th Street and the East River south of Avenue C was what the residents of Alphabet City called "The Kasbah."

The cops who policed it just called it trouble. The turf was the location of open-air heroin bazaars, hooker strolls and the hangout of crack dealers, dime store pimps, pinball macks, stone killers, drug-crazed voodooists, and others on the lunatic fringe.

CHAIN REACTION

It was also the place where a computer hacker and self-styled cybercriminal calling himself "Tim Buck Three" lived.

A legendary figure on the cyberpunk circuit, Tim Buck Three owed Keller bigtime for a favor he had done him during his spook days in Indonesia, when his activities had brought him afoul of elements of the US intelligence community. Because of that favor, Jack had periodically come to him for information that only Tim's unique skills made it possible to acquire. In return he adopted a policy of salutary neglect regarding what in fact were major-league felonies.

Tim Buck Three's specialty was in big money extortion schemes from multinational corporations. Keller knew he had already raked in hundreds of thousands by this means. That was not all that Tim was into, though. Apart from cyber crime, industrial and even political espionage was another gray area in which Tim Buck Three was a true innovator.

During the Gulf War, for example, he had contracted with the Iraqi secret services, the Mukhabarat, to hack into the Cray supercomputers that at that time controlled spy satellites run by the National Security Agency. During the second go-round in the Gulf, Tim Buck Three had hacked for corporate interests seeking a competitive edge in the highly profitable domain of private sector defense contracting the Pentagon was using for a host of operations in theater. In part payment for these services, the hacker had been secretly given live real-time feeds from Predators and other UAVs as well as military imaging satellites which he then sold to the highest bidder.

Keller had no love for the spooks and had overlooked that particular bit of Tim Buck Three's wheeling and dealing too. The CIA had, after all, been routinely supplying Saddam Hussein with high-grade satellite photography on Iran during the eight-year-long Iran-Iraq war. Jack was a firm believer in the old adage that what comes round, eventually goes round.

If nothing else, Jack's past leniency meant that Tim Buck Three owed him some serious quid pro quo. Now he was about to call in his markers.

■

CHAIN REACTION

"Let's see what we can do for you," Tim said as Jack entered the loft space. It was crammed with more sophisticated electronic equipment than the situation room at NORAD headquarters inside Cheyenne Mountain.

Jack watched graphic displays phase in and out on several large digital video screens as the hacker penetrated the NSA/CIA computers at Fort Meade, Maryland. A series of database windows suddenly came up as a three-note warning tone sounded. Each of the windows bore a digital photo on the upper right-hand corner of the display, with text data filling the remaining part of the screen.

"No, not that one." Keller said. He scanned the faces being shown him, flicking his eyes to the accompanying biographical entries. "Not him either."

Continuing to scroll, Tim showed Jack a few more screens.

"That's the one," Jack suddenly exclaimed as he recognized the killer.

In the left hand corner of the screen was a photo containing the image of the blond man he had seen at Grand Central, the same man who had cold-bloodedly gunned down Augie Watson.

"Gregory Vanesco," Jack said, his eyes riveted to the screen, reading off the terrorist's name.

■

Tim Buck Three waited a few minutes until he was certain that Jack had left his studio. He then seated himself in front of one of the large flat panel screens on a long steel table and began to input commands using the keyboard and a trackball pointing device.

The dedicated server, coded by this particular black screen bearing a large Mickey Mouse stick-on, and connected to a black component case below the table, was his firewalled direct link to CIA headquarters at Langley, Virginia. Mickey Mouse was Tim's inside joke. It was an icon which stood for what he thought of the Agency's computer security people.

As he entered his access code, this time a legitimate one, a report template was painted across the brightly lit rectangular plastic square in front of him. The security heading across its top indicated that the list of those authorized to view it -- its "bigot list" -- was restricted to a handful of individuals occupying the very apex of the broad-based pyramid of covert intelligence.

■

Driving north along the FDR Drive after leaving the hacker's studio, Jack noticed a low-slung black Camaro that seemed to have been following him since the Avenue A turnoff onto the highway.

Keller wrenched the wheel savagely and goosed the accelerator as he swung the vintage Pontiac Grand Prix into the left lane, his rear fender inches from the cab of a mammoth trailer truck loaded with Japanese cars. As the truck driver leaned on his horn and flipped Keller the bird from six different angles, Jack speeded up and shot ahead of the much slower truck.

Studying the rearview, Keller saw the black Camaro pull abreast of the truck and snap into lane directly behind him. There were two men inside the car, both occupying the front seats.

Images of the carnage in the Grand Central terminal concourse flashed through Keller's brain. It would not be an unlikely presumption that the shooters could have targeted him to die.

Reaching under his jacket, Keller pulled the Ruger semiauto which he carried loaded, cocked and locked and flipped the safety catch into firing position. Jack's heart thundered in his chest as adrenaline coursed through his bloodstream. He saw the Camaro tailgate him, then swerve smartly into the parallel lane.

He prepared to open fire on the driver as the muscle car sped up and almost pulled abreast of his own vehicle.

The driver's side window rolled down.

Instead of the terrorist hit team he feared, Jack saw a kid with long, unkempt hair flipping him the finger as the Camaro shot ahead at better than one hundred MPH and took the turnoff onto Fourteenth Street.

Eight

*K*eller left the Commissioner's office in the company of Captain Abernathy. The hastily convened meeting had been tense, the strain of the past few days on its participants evident from the outset in the form of badly frayed tempers and an accusatory air that hung ominously over the proceedings.

The Deputy Mayor had sat in for the Mayor, who was unable to attend because she was stranded, due to a severe storm, in one of the conference rooms on the third floor departure level at Stockholm-Arlanda Airport in Sweden, where she had canceled a "Sister City" goodwill trip because of the troubles back home.

The city's chief official was patched into the session by a video telephone conference linkage, and her disembodied face and oddly distorted electronic voice lent a bizarre ambiance to the already distressed atmosphere of the meeting.

Word had leaked out through the usual channels that matters of unprecedented importance were to be on the agenda, and the newsmedia were as thick as locusts in a plague year. A reporter from a local TV station rushed at Abernathy and Keller as they emerged from the meeting room into a long corridor that led to a flight of stairs to the ground level of the building.

Annie Wong was a feisty -- some used the word "pushy" -- anchorwoman for one of the city's top-rated local evening news programs whose warm smile was a perpetual fantasy ingratiating her to millions of TV news junkies. The charcoal gray suit she wore bespoke another fact. Annie Wong was all business.

Eying Abernathy, she jammed the business end of her hand-held voice recorder into his face and flashed one of her famous hundred-kilowatt grins.

"Captain, is there any truth to the rumor that Delta Force has been called in by Mayor Jimenez."

"If they have I don't know anything about it," he remarked gruffly, intent on getting past her. "Go ask the Mayor."

She was tenacious if nothing else. Unperturbed and still smiling she directed her next question at Keller.

"The cop killed in the attack, Detective Lieutenant Augustine Watson, was a friend of yours, wasn't he?" she asked, expertly keeping the small recorder near Jack's mouth despite his having turned to jog briskly down a flight of stairs toward the lobby.

"No fucking comment," Jack barked.

"Lieutenant, is it true the Mayor has authorized a secret retaliatory strike against the terrorists?"

"Eat shit, Annie," Jack said, adding with a smile, "that's strictly off the record, of course."

"You're being difficult, Lieutenant," Wong replied in saccharine tones, wishing she could use that particular sound bite on the eleven o'clock local news but knowing her producer would see her in hell first. "The public has a right to know. People are terrified."

"That's the business of terrorists," Abernathy cut in, "and bastards like you media shit flies aid and abet them in the performance of their acts of violence."

By now they had reached the foot of the stairs and strode toward the entranceway's revolving doors across the building's marble-floored lobby.

"There'll be a news conference later today," Keller said. "You'll get everything then."

"But Lieutenant -- "

Jack and Abernathy brisk-walked through a cordon of harness bulls toward a waiting police limo, finally leaving an exasperated and no longer smiling Annie behind.

"Morons," she cursed and looked toward her cameraman. "Kill the lights Sal, and let's get the hell out of here."

On the way toward the vehicle somebody took advantage of the anonymous crowd to punch Jack in the face.

Jack, hearing the words "Fuckin' pig motherfucker!" and catching a flash of glittering gold on the brown knuckles and the hues of a multicolored ski jacket, shouted an epithet as he reflexively fingered his nose to see if it was bleeding. Though he stopped for a moment to rubberneck, he was unable to spot a likely candidate for the perpetrator amid the surging crowd.

Inside the car he massaged his hurt nose.

"Cowardly fuck," he grumbled. "Jesus, it's like feeding time at the shark tank out there."

CHAIN REACTION

"That Annie was pretty damn close to the truth," Abernathy commented as he reached into his coat pocket and took out his electronic blood pressure gadget.

"You learn a lot when you keep your nose to the grindstone," Jack replied, as City Hall receded in the distance.

"Yeah," agreed Abernathy, "and your mouth to the right dicks."

In fact the purpose of the meeting at City Hall had been to craft a plan to retaliate in some way for the spasm of terrorist violence that had struck the city.

The decision had been cleared through the Mayor herself after Jack had produced secret computer files obtained through his hacker contact, Tim Buck Three, that proved conclusively that both the Company and the feds were lying through their teeth about their intelligence on the persons responsible for conducting the strike and their reasons for doing so.

The cover-up, if that was the precise word for it, went beyond the normal covetousness of intelligence agencies obsessed with keeping a lid on what they considered proprietary data in light of the nature of the crime committed.

DAVID ALEXANDER

Familiar with the practices of the spooks from his stints with Gator Force and the Agency, Jack argued that there was something that reeked distinctly of clandestine maneuverings blowing in from the Washington Beltway.

He had spoken plainly of his fears that information on the blond man was considered operationally "sacred" and would never be duly provided to the city's police department, and that while underlings and tyros would be fed to the fire, the prime architects of the bloody massacre would forever remain anonymous if the spooks' will held sway.

The mayor, having won a victory in the last election with her tough anti-crime posture, could not afford to do nothing when a vicious act of such magnitude had occurred in the city. Violent crime was violent crime, despite its motives or international repercussions, and if New Yorkers were getting gunned down in the streets, then Mayor Lucy Jimenez saw it as part of her mandate to do something about it, no matter how those in Washington might proceed.

CHAIN REACTION

The City of New York -- the former Columbia college professor had declared from Stockholm during the meeting using one of her famed historical analogies -- was no ordinary city. It shared closer ties to the city-states of old, such as Troy or the Venetian Republic, than it did to most contemporary American cities.

As such, New York had always had its own special brand of foreign policy. That was why she was in Stockholm at that very moment, and it was why New York would, after its own fashion, strike back at those who had spread violence and chaos among its populace.

It had been the mayor's idea, with the reluctant backing of the police commissioner, to send Keller to Europe where the information he had gathered indicated the terrorist leader might be discovered. Once there, as she put it, Keller would be "The voice and conscience of every New Yorker, a person who like many others has suffered a deep personal loss, and who may bear witness to atrocities for which this heinous individual must be made accountable."

If nothing else, sending Keller overseas to track down the terrorist would be a major public relations coup for the mayor. Keller's overseas connections, his intelligence background, and above all his direct involvement in the assault made him a natural choice.

The media would have a hero to show the citizens of New York that they were being avenged, one who every New Yorker could identify with, and some of the heat that would otherwise come down on Gracie Mansion might be directed elsewhere.

And -- though it had never been overtly stated but was plain to Keller from the first -- by sending a single individual the city administration could further limit its accountability. If the terrorist honcho were apprehended, fine. If he were not, then ways could be found to make Keller, hero cop and embarrassment to the department, into a sacrificial lamb.

"Well, this is one scoop Annie won't get. The news conference this afternoon will lay it all on the table," Abernathy said, shaking his head at the high pressure readings taken by his diagnostic toy before tucking it back in his pocket. "You'll be officially on sabbatical due to the emotional strain of the past couple of days."

"Won't be far from the truth," Jack interjected.

He was tired. The meeting had stressed him out and he had stayed up late studying the twenty-page single-spaced printout of the downloaded data file that his high-tech stool pigeon had pulled down from the cloud.

He had not only burned the image of Gregory Vanesco into his mind, but, through the extensive biographical data included in the dossier, had crawled into the killer's psyche. From now on, Jack would be Vanesco's mental double. What Vanesco thought, Jack would think. What Vanesco felt, Jack would feel. And when Vanesco made a move, Jack would know it almost before it happened.

He thought back to the specifics mentioned at the meeting that had sanctioned his traveling to Europe. Though glad for the opportunity, Keller felt he was being needlessly hamstrung by the arrangements. There were more thou-shalt-nots than the Ten

Commandments to which he would be expected to pay heed, a result of accommodating a plethora of political factions who ran the City Hall establishment.

Officially, Keller's role was limited pretty much to liaising with Interpol in Paris. He was to file reports through Abernathy with the Mayor's office. The Mayor could in turn make tough-talking pronouncements regarding efforts to stem the terrorist tide and avenge the deaths of innocent New Yorkers that were being instituted on her orders.

Keller was not to carry a weapon. Furthermore, he was to, in the Deputy Mayor's words, "uphold the dignity, ethnic diversity and gender neutrality of our city at all times."

Jack had been about to shove a verbal fist into the deputy mayor's bearded face for having uttered such abject bullshit, when he caught Abernathy's warning glare. He had kept his mouth shut and suffered the court jester of City Hall in livid silence.

Jack had other ideas about his role and other plans about how to play it, though for the moment he kept these to himself.

If the trip turned out to be a wash, then so be it. But if he saw the slightest chance to run down the case and apprehend the blond man who had brutally murdered his friend, Jack swore he would play the string out, no matter where it led, what it cost and who was hung politically out to dry.

■

Keller stubbed out the cigaret and poured himself a drink from the half-empty bottle of Old Grand Dad. He had bought it after a solitary dinner following a visit to the Watson residence where Augie's family sat and grieved.

He had sworn off the bottle and except for the occasional social drink had been on the wagon for three months. But after having gone to Augie's house to attend the wake for his dead friend and a straight-up cop, Keller had fallen victim to a steadily mounting depression.

Half-hoping that something or other would have prevented Christine from leaving on her trip that morning, he had unlocked the door with guarded expectation. The apartment was empty, though. That meant television for company, the bottle to warm his heart and the war cries of stone junkies and partying bridge-and-tunnel kids from across the Hudson Tubes who nightly chased each other through the streets of yuppie Chelsea for comic relief.

Keller was scheduled to leave on the redeye the following morning, but he realized he would never manage to get a decent night's sleep the way things were going. He had updated his will and arranged for neighbors to look after his apartment in his absence.

His single piece of luggage containing a change of clothes and assorted toiletries was already packed and waiting near the door, ready to go when he was.

There was an attaché case which, among miscellaneous papers, contained the file on Vanesco. Jack thought about opening it and studying the dossier one more time, but was too wired and tired; there would be plenty of time to read it on the eight-to-ten-hour transatlantic flight to Paris.

He checked the cable TV listings but none of the movies seemed remotely appealing. He'd already seen the old

CHAIN REACTION

Schwarzenegger flick in which the Austrian-born actor was pitted against a deadly creature from outer space.

Keller flung down the cable listings and flipped through his video collection. "Across the Pacific," a black-and-white classic starring Humphrey Bogart, Mary Astor and Sydney Greenstreet caught his attention. It had been a long time since he had watched it and he retained only a vague recollection of its plot.

Keller slid the disk into the DVD player and poured himself a tumbler of bourbon over ice as the images of a bygone Hollywood era flickered across his retinas, and a tale of romance, intrigue and mayhem unfolded in an easy progression almost never attainable in real life.

But in a corner of his mind the images of a bloodbath continued to manifest themselves with the relentlessness of an unscratchable itch.

Jack knew that he would have no peace until he had made the blond man pay in equal coin for the sins he had committed.

DAVID ALEXANDER

Nine

*T*he brainchild of Allen Dulles, its first director, the headquarters of the Central Intelligence Agency had been deliberately intended to suggest the benign atmosphere of a college campus.

Apparently, the Eisenhower-era architects had succeeded in realizing the director's vision of an outwardly cheerful oasis whose main purpose lay in waging dirty clandestine operations behind the Iron Curtain against the deepening crisis of the early Cold War.

Since that time, the sprawling complex of white, low-rise buildings on two hundred nineteen wooded acres nine miles from the heart of downtown Washington has since become known to insiders as "the Campus."

Bracketed by huge blacktop parking lots, the CIA's two million square-foot Headquarters Building is reached by a private access road branching west from Route 123, a spur of the Washington Beltway as it snakes through the well-to-do suburban communities of Arlington, Falls Church, Maclean and Fairfax, Virginia.

CHAIN REACTION

Every morning and evening, with clockwork regularity, the more than fifteen thousand personnel who work at Central Intelligence Agency headquarters drove to and from the CIA Campus. Though its location is well known, it is isolated enough to attract few curiosity seekers or demonstrators, and those who roll toward the security checkpoint at the entrance gate to America's citadel of espionage have come to regard their vehicles as the closest thing possible to the safest place on earth, and the last place on earth they would go to die.

■

The autumn skies were crisp and clear and the Virginia hills resplendent with brilliant fall foliage. Skeet Parker, a civilian staffer employed full-time at the Directorate for Science and Technology as a photographic analyst for the CIA's National Photographic Interpretation Center, turned his blue Toyota sedan from State Route 7 onto Route 123.

As he approached the turnoff onto the Campus' private access road, Parker was faced with the familiar traffic congestion. Cars were stacked up in a double row due to vehicles ahead passing

through the bottleneck at the entrance
gate before entering through CIA
security checkpoints.

Parker's mind was not on the traffic
situation this morning, however. The
technical intelligence analyst was
perplexed by the inactivity in the wake of
his assessment, or "brief report," to the
office of the Deputy Director for Science
and Technology concerning the discovery
of overhead surveillance data from the
covert Cerberus spy satellite, one of an
array of high-definition space imaging
platforms in geostationary low earth
orbits.

Bureaucratic stonewalling and inertia
aside, the data clearly had potentially
far-reaching implications and should
have resulted in a follow-up by Agency
assets on the ground.

After repeatedly pressing his superiors
in the office of the DDS&T to act on the
intelligence, Parker had drafted a memo
and sent it to the Deputy Director
himself, calling attention to what was, in
his opinion, a significant threat to
national security. Though it was against
unwritten Agency protocols to do this,

Parker believed that he was left with no other choice.

Traffic began moving again and Parker slid into one of the two parallel queues of slow-moving vehicles. Rolling at a crawl toward the main gate, Parker had no idea that his memo had been compromised, and that the DDS&T had no inkling of the danger about which it had warned.

■

Two car lengths down the road, a brown Ford minivan with smoked windows moved at a sedate thirty miles per hour and stopped just short of the turnoff onto the CIA access road.

In the compartment behind the driver a short man with powerful shoulders took deep drags on an unfiltered cigaret while he carefully wrapped black cloth electrical tape around two plastic Mecar banana clips. Each contained forty 7.62 millimeter bullets in such a manner as to place each ammunition magazine at approximate right angles to the other.

He had already assembled two double clips containing a combined total of eighty rounds. When he was finished with the third clip, he snapped it into the receiver well of the Avtomat Kalashnikova rifle that had lain on the juddering floor of the moving vehicle.

"Get ready," the driver said to the man in the back in their guttural native language as the van approached the end of the queue of vehicles moving at a snail's pace toward the CIA campus security checkpoint.

The gunman unsafed the weapon and cranked a round into the AK's firing chamber, propping the weapon across his knees. Flicking the cigaret to the floor he stamped it out and stared at the wall of the van with blank intensity.

■

Parker was barely conscious of what was happening as he stared absently ahead at the familiar sight of the uniformed and federally approved rent-a-cop checking identification at the gate. He drained the cold, too-sweet dregs of the coffee he had bought at a convenience store near his Falls Church home.

Suddenly at the extreme edge of his vision he saw a brown streak come to a full stop and heard the earsplitting squeal of tires. Only when another shape detached itself from the van and hurtled toward him with long, loping steps, did Parker register that the man was carrying a rifle.

When the running man stopped at his car, Parker knew he had been set up. In a flash the ringing silence that had met his ominous findings connected with the deadly sweep of the gun muzzle being trained on him. Coffee spilled into his lap as he dropped the cup and reached for the door handle, desperately trying to jerk it open.

Parker only managed to crack the door ajar.

Standing spraddle-legged in front of his windshield, the gunman propped the AK on his shoulder and squeezed the trigger. Parker's last earthly sight was the contorted face of the gunman behind the sudden blossom of yellow flame that issued from the weapon's flash-suppressor-equipped muzzle.

The impact of the military caliber rounds shattered the windshield as they walloped into Parker at nearly point blank range.

His head and face sustained multiple hits and the trunk of his decorticated body shuddered violently. A dozen more rounds punctured his chest and abdomen, passing through the upholstery and piercing the chassis of the Toyota.

One of the rounds entered the gas tank and the rear of the car exploded in a fireball as the bullet's heat ignited the extremely combustible mixture of high-octane gasoline.

By this time the shooter had turned and raked the vehicle on the other side of Parker's burning and bullet-riddled Toyota with more rapid bursts of automatic fire.

Pulling out the first clip, he expertly flipped it over and inserted a fresh magazine and in a matter of seconds was firing into another car down the line. He continued moving along the queue, firing at random into the vehicles on the CIA access road until his last clip of heavy caliber bullets had run dry.

Turning, the gunman fled toward the van and jumped inside through the open side hatchway door, sliding it shut behind him. The driver goosed the accelerator and the van rode the shoulder in the opposite direction throwing off gravel, until all four wheels were on blacktop again and it sped off around a bend in the road.

It had taken no more than eighty-five seconds for the gunman to kill over a dozen people in a lethal spasm of seemingly random, and apparently senseless, violence.

DAVID ALEXANDER

Ten

*I*n Paris the leaves of the horse chestnut trees along the chic boulevards had finally begun to drop. Autumn had arrived with surprising swiftness after summer's long overdue departure. Rain, the color of mercury and as cold as outer space, was now falling in heavy, steady sheets. Overhead, the sky was gathering itself together, bunching up like a gigantic charcoal fist, preparing for another strike on the city cowering beneath it.

Vanesco jogged along the Quay Voltaire with the river Seine on his right and late morning automobile traffic passing on the broad boulevard to his left in an easy, regular stream. The weather had driven away most other pedestrians and he enjoyed the exhilaration of the cold raindrops that stung his face and icily numbed the exposed scalp of his uncovered head through his now closely cropped blond hair.

Directly ahead of him the Art Deco Alexander Bridge rose above the sluggish river, guarded by time-stained verdigris statues of the goddess Victory wielding gleaming gilded swords.

Turning right onto the bridge, Vanesco stopped and pretended to look downriver toward the Ile de la Cite while in fact he scanned the pattern of pedestrian and automobile traffic for signs of surveillance. His morning run had taken him on a zigzagging route through downtown Paris in an effort to expose any reconnaissance activity that might have been mounted against him.

At the center of the bridge, on the top of the balustrade that bore a verdigris patina, Vanesco spotted freshly incised words amid the jumble of graffiti scratched into the surface of the railing.

Amid the older, darker scratches, two freshly carved initials clearly stood out. To a casual observer -- had that observer taken notice of it at all -- the initials A.M.D.H. would have meant nothing. To Vanesco it was the recognition code that he had long awaited; Army Museum, Detaille Hall.

Since his arrival in Paris he had been coming to the Alexander Bridge twice each week at different times of day to look for the appearance of the code string. Since going to ground after the New York operation, he had informed *al-Qaid* through covert channels that he would not be returning as originally ordered.

The international political climate had changed drastically in recent years and Vanesco could no longer be completely certain that the Arabs would not give him up to the Americans or their surrogates. They might even kill him outright, especially since he was a hired mercenary and not one of their fanatical brethren killing only for the love of Allah and the promise of an afterlife of eternal bliss.

Instead, he had offered his paymasters the prospect of a new and bolder operation, one that would make the violence of the past exercise seem like a trifle in comparison. Vanesco was confident that his plan would find strong interest, if not approval, since it had a number of other ramifications that would interest other players on the global scene, both in the Mideast and elsewhere.

Now Vanesco had been given at least part of the answer. The recognition code was nothing more than an indication to him that his message had been acknowledged and that he was to proceed to the contact point that it had designated.

Vanesco placed his foot straight up on the balustrade and leaned forward to touch his toes. He repeated his runner's stretching exercise on the other leg and then turned back toward the street, jogging across the wide boulevard toward the open greensward flanking the Avenue Du Marechal Gallieni, dotted with stands of lime trees, on the other side.

The gilded lead dome of the Hotel L'Invalides gleamed under a dull gray sky in the near distance. Vanesco slowed his pace to a walk as he gained the other side of the street and headed toward the building complex, stopping every now and then to perform more limbering exercises which permitted him to screen the area for tails.

Because he was aware of the reputation of the French counterterrorist warfare unit, Groupement d'Intervention de la Gendarmerie Nationale, known by its acronym GIGN but commonly pronounced as "Gigene," Vanesco was especially wary of pursuit teams.

The small Heckler & Koch squeeze-cocking automatic pistol tucked away in the fanny pack he wore would be effective against one or two assailants, but not against a competent hit team with an operational plan. Knowledge of his behavior patterns, gained through days of covert stalking, could give the opposition a tangible edge.

Seeing no evidence of a tail, he continued walking until he reached the ramparts of Invalides where ancient cannon facing outward guarded the approach to the seventeenth century hospital and present headquarters of the French armed services.

Entering the cobblestone courtyard through the main gate, Vanesco walked past the well-tended topiary into the wide flagstoned courtyard of honor, the Cour d'honneur, guarded by the immense statue of Napoleon Bonaparte.

Napoleon's Tomb was located in the chapel beyond the Invalides forecourt but it was not his destination. He turned instead into the entrance to the French Army Museum and walked into the west wing housing Detaille Hall, where the museum's equestrian gallery was situated.

CHAIN REACTION

Vanesco stood looking at a glass display case containing an assortment of deadly seventeenth and eighteenth century handguns, one among them bearing a swiveling barrel for automatic burstfire, when a nondescript-looking man sidled up to him holding a Nikon digital camera in his hands.

"Mind stepping aside so I can get a picture?" he asked in French.

"Not at all," Vanesco replied.

The man snapped off a few shots of swords, pistols and other military artifacts in the display case and thanked Vanesco before moving off.

Vanesco returned to his inspection of the display, watching the man with the camera slowly circumnavigate the equestrian gallery as he stopped and snapped a few more photographs of mounted cuirassiers in full battle dress astride their horses. He then left the gallery entirely.

Vanesco felt inside the left pocket of his hooded sweatshirt and touched the slip of paper that had not been there when he had entered the museum.

The man had been good: Vanesco had not even felt him make the brush contact.

DAVID ALEXANDER

Crossing into the Colors and
Standards Hall with its dioramas and
large wall paintings by des Batailles
depicting scenes from Louis XIV's
campaign in Flanders of 1672, he
continued to amble through the exhibits
on the museum's ground floor, then
returned to the main lobby and went out
the door into the Invalides forecourt.

■

Hours later Vanesco had returned to
the two-room flat in Montmartre which
was owned by the woman with whom he
was living in Paris. He had met her in
Rome the previous summer and, posing
as a freelance writer, had cultivated the
relationship with an eye toward using the
girl as a courier or as the provider of a
place in which to go to ground.

An overseas phone call prior to the
strike in New York had confirmed that
she would be available were he to come
to Paris -- as he'd said he planned -- and
Vanesco was assured of a safe house
should the operation turn sour. Though
the flat was within easy walking distance
of the Seine, the long delay had been
necessary to return via a circuitous route
designed to expose surveillance.

CHAIN REACTION

After leaving the precincts of Invalides, Vanesco had entered the Paris Metro at the Louvre-Palais Royal stop and taken the train in the opposite direction of the flat, ending up near the Eiffel Tower after a meandering ride on several subway lines.

Making certain that Juliette was not at home, he took the coded message from his pocket and began the process of decoding using a one-time encryption pad. It took him only a few minutes to decipher the message.

Vanesco experienced a wave of exhilaration as he scanned the clear text. With a slight modification or two, his plan had been approved. He was sanctioned to proceed with it immediately and full resources and infrastructure were to be made available to him in order to assure its success.

Hearing the sound of the door slamming on the street entrance below, Vanesco hid the Walther machine pistol he had placed atop the table for easy access and put a match to the decrypted message, then dropped it into the ash tray. A few minutes later, he heard the sound of a key turning in the lock and the door of the flat opened inward.

Juliette came in carrying two large plastic bags filled with groceries in her arms. She was dressed in oversized sweater and jeans in that casual, almost sloppy style effected by French women of all ages, and in his opinion difficult for females of any other nationality to credibly duplicate.

Her dark blonde, almost reddish, hair cascaded down her back in a carefree manner that nevertheless accented her large, pale-blue eyes, slightly upturned, almost patrician nose, and full, sensuous mouth. The scent of Juliette's perfume began to pervade the air in only a few minutes.

"Did you have a good run today?" she asked the bearded blond man who she believed was an American poet living in Paris on a grant from a prestigious arts foundation based in Seattle.

"Great," he said, poking through the bags she had deposited on the kitchen table. "I see you've been giving the Parisian grocers a good business day."

"I've been all over the quarter," she acknowledged, still sounding somewhat out of breath from having hurried up the flight of steps. "Look, Paul, I brought you some of that wine you like."

Vanesco took out the clear plastic bottle of red table wine and twisted off the screw cap while he went to get some glasses, then poured each of them a glass. When he returned to the table, Juliette had lit some colored candles she had bought.

"Cheers," he said, as they clinked glasses and downed the wine, thinking that it would be a shame to kill somebody as beautiful and companionable as Juliette, though her death was as inevitable as it was unfortunate.

As he sipped the tart, fruity wine with slightly woody notes, listening to the Bach concerto that Juliette had just put on the stereo, he promised himself that when the time came to kill the French girl, he would not make her suffer. He would do it as quickly and as humanely as possible. Juliette would go out easily, he promised himself. She would die without pain.

On impulse, he reached out and clamped his fingers around the burning wick of one of the candles Juliette had just lit, snuffing out the flame.

"What did you do that for, Paul?" Juliette asked.

"No reason, *ma cherie*," Vanesco told her with a smile as he poured her some more red wine, "no reason at all."

Eleven

*K*eller did not return the flawless, neon-bright smile flashed by the pretty female flight attendant strategically positioned at the forward access hatch of the Air France 747 jumbo jetliner, now debarking its business class passengers. He had spent the last nine uncomfortable hours on the plane. His mood was surly as he stepped onto the sloping, carpeted floor of the jetway at Orly International Airport.

Speeding across the Atlantic Ocean at a cruising altitude of some thirty-five thousand feet and an airspeed of approximately four hundred sixty miles per hour had not been good for the vicious hangover he was still nursing from last night's bout with the bottle. Nor had the ibuprofen tablets he had swallowed on the flight done very much toward stilling the malicious throbbing in his temples or cooling the diabolical fires that flared behind his irritated eyes.

All that Keller could think about right now was getting into a shower and sweating out the poisons in his bloodstream.

DAVID ALEXANDER

■

Inspector Rene Denard of Interpol's Paris bureau was waiting for Jack at French Customs. Keller recognized Denard immediately -- a head taller than most others, with a face that resembled the young Chevalier's, he was the type of individual who stood out in a crowd -- and nodded toward him.

Denard's clear blue eyes roved searchingly across Jack's face as the two men shook hands, noting the gaunt, unshaven cheeks and the angry red lines around the pupils.

"My God, Keller, you look like pure *merde*," Denard said with genuine shock, though well aware of the circumstances that had brought Jack to Paris.

"What you see is what you get," Keller returned with a graveyard smile. "I had a slight collision with a bottle of ninety-six proof rye last night. That was a mistake, though it had seemed like a good idea at the time."

"I understand," Denard answered as they walked through the airport terminal toward the blacktop parking area outside, emerging into a clear, crisp autumn day. "You've taken your friend's death pretty hard."

"That's true," Keller confessed, "but it's only a part of the picture." He glanced aside for a moment and added, "I won't bore you with the personal details. You can figure most of them out for yourself."

"A cop's life, *mon ami*," Denard answered, knowing what Keller meant. Alcoholism, divorce and a creeping sense of futility were only some of the occupational hazards that went with the profession. "Everywhere the same."

"Don't worry, though," he assured, turning to look Denard squarely in the eyes. "I can hold up my end."

"I never was in doubt of that," Denard replied with a smile as he gestured toward a man in plain clothes with dark, Spanish looks and the face of a born cutthroat, who leaned against an unmarked vehicle a dozen yards away.

The man flicked away the cigaret he had been smoking with a snap of his fingers and climbed into the car, driving it to where Denard and the American cop stood waiting.

Keller leaned back against the seat cushion, feeling jetlagged and hung over as they cleared the Orly environs and turned onto the Peripherique motorway in the direction of Paris.

Following the car at a discreet distance was a silver Renault, indistinguishable from many of the other cars on the expressway, the driver's practiced eyes never losing sight of the unmarked police vehicle.

■

Neither Keller nor the French cops spoke as the car proceeded along a broad boulevard past narrow, twisting streets sloping down from the heights of the Montparnasse quarter.

Each man was lost in his own inner thoughts. Jack's hangover and jetlag were temporarily forgotten as he studied the time-stained ochre buildings as the car swept past them, their black, lozenge-shaped lead rooftops dotted with dormer windows and bristling with red clay chimney pots.

Memories began to well up from deep inside him, crowding out the present, overlaying the scenic vistas with specters that loomed out of the shadows of the long-buried past.

Keller thought back to his last sojourn in Europe, working for the Agency. In those days he had run covert networks of anti-drug and counterterrorist strike units throughout France, Italy, West Germany and Belgium in a secret multinational campaign, overseen and largely financed by the CIA to stem the flow of narcotics along major European pipelines.

The drugs flowed in from the places like Odessa on the Black Sea, where organized crime had taken over post-Soviet national governments. The traffic netted billions in illicit funds annually, with a portion of it flowing into the coffers of international terrorist groups, many of which, under cover of political motives, were actually arms of global criminal organizations.

Officially, Keller had been assigned to a minor diplomatic position at the US Consular Services Department, his nominal title an agricultural attaché. Unofficially, it was a far different story.

Keller's true assignment was to engineer and implement covert interdiction operations against what he had always referred to in his mind as "the Fifth World."

If the Third and Fourth worlds represented underdeveloped countries, than the Fifth represented the invisible government of highly organized and globally linked criminal cartels whose aims were as much political as entrepreneurial.

The organizations that trafficked in cocaine, heroin, grass and other narcotics did not exist in a vacuum, and could not carry out their day-to-day activities without sanction -- sometimes tacit, sometimes overt -- from national governments.

This basic fact of life put them in league with terrorist and insurgent groups who, though primarily politically motivated, nonetheless required a constant supply of arms and ready cash. The end-result of these connections was a worldwide network in support of global acts of international violence.

Keller had run SLAM teams which launched search, locate and annihilate missions against the organized drug and criminal fraternities. But it ultimately became clear to him that the shadow war he waged could never be won.

He had learned that some of his assigned targets were non-terrorist and political, linked to the Agency's strategic, albeit covert, objectives. The CIA itself was behind many of the same organizations that it outwardly fought against. It was like facing the head of the Medusa. You killed off a few of the writhing snakes that sprouted from it only to see new serpentine offshoots take their places.

Keller's moment of truth arrived in the aftermath of a well-coordinated terror strike in a large city in India, when he'd discovered that some of the 'terrorist cells' were in fact being covertly funded by the Company in what the spooks called a circular operation.

Except for a few key players in the deadly game, the terrorist cadre themselves were neither aware of this fact nor of who was actually running them.

The CIA was using middlemen as cutouts in a grand deception scheme in support of which it sent out killer surrogates, then activated Keller's SLAM teams to take out the terrorist shooters in turn.

The global circular operations were tactically brilliant, maximizing deniability to the fullest.

DAVID ALEXANDER

Trapped amid the vicious cycle of kill and counterkill, and fighting a surreal shadow war without foreseeable end, Keller had decided that he wanted out, but he knew that leaving the fold was a thing far more easily said than done.

His only recourse had been to play his hole card. He had compiled enough documentary evidence to protect himself from Agency reprisals, and made certain the spooks knew it was in the hands of those who would disseminate it in the event of his death or disappearance. But he also knew that the spooks' lethal game was still very much in play.

Every time he read a newspaper or watched televised reports describing some new outbreak of international violence, he recognized a writhing tentacle of the Medusa. As he saw the reflection of his own haggard face in the glass of the car window, half-remembered images from his nightmares back in New York suddenly came back to him.

He had dreamed of the Medusa, its multiple snake heads writhing and hissing as they opened their mouths and bared their sharp, recurving fangs to sink into his flesh and inject their paralyzing venom into his bloodstream.

Jack realized that his subconscious was warning him of the Medusa's presence in the strike on Grand Central Station. Now he wondered as well if his presence there just as the strike went down had been as coincidental as he had at first assumed it to have been.

It seemed farfetched. But Jack was no stranger to the Byzantine machinations of which the spooks were capable. And he had long ago ceased to believe in coincidences.

■

"What's going on up here?" asked Keller as they passed a long line of people queued up in front of a large building.

"The Louvre is having a big Impressionist show today," Denard informed him. "I've gone myself. You might want to have a look for yourself. I can highly recommend the Kandinskys, Cézannes and especially the Monets"

"My interest in art is confined to bullfight posters, I'm afraid," Keller replied. "But if I get an itch for culture, at least I know where I can go."

DAVID ALEXANDER

The car passed over one of the minor Seine bridges and rolled through the expensive quarter on the edge of the Right Bank. Keller was struck with the many differences between Paris and New York, the absence of grime and the sense of impending catastrophe that seemed to hang over the city like an ever-deepening cloud as time passed.

Paris had seen its share of terrorist bombings and murders too, but it had recovered, just as it had from the centuries worth of bloodshed on its streets.

In New York, the constantly escalating violence had no name and no face. The presence on the streets of coke, heroin, crack and other hard drugs alone could not account for it, nor the massive recent influx of minorities and the ensuing clash of mismatched cultures. It was as if a bloodthirsty specter haunted the streets and relentlessly stalked the subways, as if the city had been cursed, damned for the rest of eternity to enact an obscene, diabolic ritual of death, destruction and endemic fear.

"Here we are," Denard said at length as the driver pulled up in front of a small hotel in the Montparnasse district. "I can have Toussont take your baggage for you if you like."

"I'm still healthy enough to carry my own, Rene," Keller said with a smile at Denard and a nod at Toussont.

"Fine, then," Denard replied. "Tomorrow morning, nine o'clock sharp. My office. Be prepared for anything. I know you have not come here merely to eat truffles, and I can promise you I will help you in every way possible."

Keller shook hands with Denard. "Thanks," he told the Inspector. "I don't have to tell you I appreciate your help."

"Speaking of eating," Denard added, gesturing with his thumb at a shuttered restaurant window, "if you want a decent meal, try Le Indochine across the street for dinner sometime. The owner's a friend of mine."

Keller crossed the street and pushed his way into the hotel lobby through the glass entrance doors, catching the eye of the concierge as he strode to the front desk.

■

DAVID ALEXANDER

The silver Renault ground to a slow halt a few car lengths from the hotel's entrance and the driver killed the engine.

The driver's eyes scanned the street in the rearview and then studied the hotel through the windshield.

No difficulties had been anticipated, but a Glock automatic pistol lay beneath the seat in case unforeseen situations arose, as they sometimes did despite even the most thorough precautions.

The driver continued closely watching one of the windows on the hotel's fourth floor. Soon it was opened and Jack looked out briefly. Then he shut the hinged glass panes and pulled the drapes closed.

As the driver's eyes flicked from the window to the street, Jack slipped off his shirt and went into the toilet to draw a hot bath. Coming back out he began unpacking, shaking two more red ibuprofen tablets from the small plastic bottle and swallowing them with some Vittel water from the room's courtesy bar.

On his way to turn off the tap he caught sight of his reflection in the bureau mirror.

CHAIN REACTION

The puckered pink-white scar that snaked from his navel all the way up his right chest and terminated just below his heart, a souvenir of a run-in with a knife-wielding crackhead, was prominent against his pale skin.

His gray eyes focused on his haggard face, and the hollow eyes that stared out from sunken sockets, like live coals aglow in a matrix of cracked putty.

"Denard was right," he said aloud. "You look like pure shit, old buddy," and then he returned to the bathroom.

■

On the street below, the driver of the silver Renault continued to watch the window with the attention of a hunting hawk, and waited patiently for the early autumnal darkness to arrive.

Twelve

*T*he Range Rover navigated the treacherous mountain passes of northwestern Afghanistan.

The driver was armed, as was the professional gunman from Kabul sitting beside him.

The passenger riding in back was armed as well, but his familiarity with weapons was as limited as his familiarity with the stark terrain that seemed to him like a more arid version of that found in his native southern Colorado.

He was a maker of policy and a spinner of webs. Muscle was the specialty and the province of others. He merely directed those who plied the force option where their talents were most expedient.

One of the directions in which he had turned his own special talents had been the CIA campus where a competent and deniable shooter team had been dispatched to deal with some loose ends that had recently come unraveled.

The junior-grade intelligence analyst attached to the Directorate of Science and Technology had been raising quite a lot of ruckus over the overhead surveillance imagery. He needed to be dealt with in a manner that was both swift and which sent a message to others who had similar aspirations. He had been warned to desist, but had ignored the warnings despite the peril that he must have certainly known his recalcitrance would put him in line for.

The passenger was relieved to see his destination suddenly come into view.

The stone edifice seemed to loom out of the rocky landscape. The ancient caravansary had been standing for hundreds, perhaps thousands, of years, used by the nomadic tribes that traveled the legendary Silk Road throughout the nations of northwestern Asia. It had been partially destroyed during the Soviet invasion, and haphazardly rebuilt by the Taliban, but it still served its time-honored purpose as a meeting ground for the disparate clans of a primitive brotherhood.

A number of vehicles of various types had already arrived at the caravansary. The passenger knew that they were waiting for his arrival. The Range Rover rolled to a stop. The driver killed the engine and set the parking brake.

His Pakistani bodyguard emerged from the vehicle first, scanning the area with alert eyes, his bullpup autoshotgun clutched in a combat grip. Only when he was satisfied that there was no recognizable threat did he open the door and signal the passenger to get out.

Inside the caravansary were an assortment of individuals whose features and modes of dress belied their nationalities and ethnic backgrounds. In very much the same manner as the rough nomadic traders who had converged on this spot for centuries, they were united by ties that transcended nationalities and by a sense of common purpose and shared destiny.

In times past those who met here were called Gypsies, wanderers, nomads. This group too had a name, but it was one never spoken, like the true and hidden name of God.

■

The merchandise was stored in two immense containers made of ballistic carbon-fiber composite which lay on the packed dirt floor of the caravansary.

CHAIN REACTION

The merchandise was a kind of Frankenstein's monster, a patchwork of assorted technologies derived from a variety of sources. It had originated as an American gift to the Shah of Iran shortly before his overthrow by the Islamic fundamentalists led by the Ayatollah Khomeini.

For over a decade thereafter, it had lain in a heavily guarded and highly secret storage facility in Tehran, which was watched over night and day. The facility was mined with explosives so that it could be blown to kingdom come if there was ever an attempt to retrieve the merchandise.

When the predicted attack came, launched by Delta Force under the Carter Administration in the name of freeing the US embassy hostages, a combination of events caused its sensational failure and the downfall of the President who had sanctioned it.

Amid threats by Iran to make the nature of the merchandise known to the world at large in the wake of the bungled Delta Force mission, the Republican opposition sent soon-to-be CIA Director William Casey to a clandestine meeting at the Hotel Raphael in Rome in late September of 1979.

There, a promise to release the hostages after a Reagan victory was given by the Iranian representative in exchange for a guarantee on the part of Casey that the Reagan Administration would pursue negotiations based on a covert backchannel.

The backchannel was opened shortly after Ronald Reagan gained office in 1980, and progressed to the visits by then Secretary of Defense George MacFarlane and his young protégé, Lieutenant Colonel Oliver North, in the middle of that decade.

It was the merchandise that gave Iran the leverage to siphon billions of dollars worth of illicit arms from the United States by a variety of stratagems throughout the eighties.

The fact that it was the merchandise sitting on the floor of the caravansary, and not the need to finance the Nicaraguan Contras that lay at the heart of the ensuing Iran-Contra Scandal, was a revelation that was known only to a handful of Washington insiders privileged to have been party to secret testimony by North and others involved in the Iran-Contra conspiracy.

The Iranians had made vague promises about disposing of the merchandise in accordance with the wishes of the White House and other interested parties, but had never honored these commitments.

The theocrats in Tehran realized that as long as they retained possession of it they had a powerful strategic hand to play. One thing they did not have, was the means to fully realize the frightening potential of the merchandise. Had the Iranian Revolution occurred a matter of weeks later than it had, they might have won the prize in its entirety. But it did not and so in turn they had not either.

As a consequence, the merchandise remained in its heavily protected warehouse as years began to pass.

The fact that Saddam Hussein had pledged his support of United States efforts to secure what it considered its property upon gaining victory, contributed to Washington's support of Baghdad and its turning a blind eye to the genocidal war waged against the Kurds by Saddam's regime.

DAVID ALEXANDER

Saddam, like the Iranians, believed that his knowledge of the merchandise could prevent then President George Bush from mobilizing against his annexation of Kuwait in August of 1990, but he was wrong in this assumption. By that time the Soviet Union had crumbled and one of the greatest dangers of exposing the merchandise was nullified in one fell swoop.

But the deterioration of the Soviet empire placed both the Iranians and the merchandise still in their possession in an entirely new light. With Iraq now declared the enemy, ground was broken toward rapprochement with Iran, whose fanatical old guard was replaced with somewhat more secular leaders after Khomeini's death.

As the Soviet power center based in Moscow lost its iron grip on the far-flung satrapies of the former communist empire, islands of high technology were being formed by the receding waters of Soviet dominance. Iran's agents were everywhere in the former republics, buying up with hard currency the technological skills and the technological hardware to render the merchandise usable. In the decades since the Soviet collapse, the Iranians had set up developmental and testing facilities amid the chaos and endemic crime in the former republics.

Though they knew full well what the Iranians were doing, members of the sodality based in Washington turned a blind eye to what was happening. They had plans of their own.

For the first time in nearly forty years there existed a convergence of political purpose and strategic vision on the part of elements of the sodality. The merchandise was key to its ultimate fulfillment.

The final covert action taken because of the merchandise came with the shootings outside the entrance to the CIA Campus on Route 123. The Iranians had been careless, exposing the merchandise to view of an advanced Cerberus-IV spy satellite. The Cerberus could transmit crystal-clear imagery using synthetic aperture radar which could penetrate even the heavy cloud cover that had darkened the skies when they had briefly brought the merchandise into the open before transporting it to the present meeting place.

There would be no more such mishaps; that was the purpose of the passenger's visit to the caravansary today. From now on the mission would be handled with professionalism and its millennial consequences assured. The maker of policy, the spinner of webs, was about to take over.

■

Using a telephoto lens and a Nikon digital camera with an image-stabilized shutter system, the man lying prone in the shelter of craggy cliffs miles from the caravansary shot off frame after frame.

Beside him, his partner kept watch, armed with a Krinkov AKR, the short-barreled variant of the larger Kalashnikov rifle.

Both individuals were wearing camos in a "chocolate chips" desert pattern and had taken other steps to mask their appearance, including painting their faces with streaks of brown and black greasepaint. Due to their preparations they were virtually invisible against the rugged landscape.

CHAIN REACTION

The cameraman finished shooting the frames and put away the camera in a nylon rucksack that bore a pattern identical to that of his clothing. He had collected enough intel product. The Russian border lay only twenty miles due north. Once across it, the intel product would be downloaded and digitally processed, and then perhaps the identities of the men who had gathered in the remote spot below would be known, and their purpose understood by those who had tasked them with the mission.

DAVID ALEXANDER

Thirteen

*K*eller had placed a call to a phone number in Paris that he was not surprised to discover was still in service.

The owner of the number, known as the Flower Man, was useful to far too many parties to have been allowed to go out of business. Keller identified himself at the gruff "*Alouez*" and asked if the items he was interested in were available.

Told that they were, a time and a place was arranged for the cash-only sale to be finalized.

Keller hung up. Through drawn blinds he glimpsed the slim, pale yellow crescent moon riding scudding gray clouds above the gabled black rooftops of the ochre-walled buildings across the gloomy, narrow street. Darkness would come quickly.

Keller had put on a black turtleneck shirt and a pair of heavily laundered black jeans held up by a leather Garrison belt identical to the kind whose heavy iron buckles had won him more than one fight in the concrete school yards of Brooklyn.

CHAIN REACTION

Before leaving the room he arranged a series of "telltales" in case the room was searched in his absence. Who might search the room and why they might do it did not matter to any great extent. There were any number of those with motive and opportunity, including his good friend, and former Gator Force co-combatant, Denard.

Keller made the first telltale out of a shred of foil from the wrapper of a chocolate bar he'd taken from the courtesy cooler.

He unobtrusively tucked the foil strip inside the lock of his attaché case where the careless insertion of a key would easily knock it loose.

Plucking a paper match from a book provided by the hotel, he carefully held it between the edge of the door and the jamb opposite the doorknob. He closed the door until it caught, and then he closed the door fully.

Anyone entering the doorway while he was out would be sure to dislodge it, and the single match stick would be hard to notice on the carpeted floor.

Keller left his plastic key card with the deskman and went out into the street.

DAVID ALEXANDER

It had already grown dark and a fine
rain, the kind they called "angel spit"
during his boyhood in Brooklyn, was
sifting down through the chill night air.
He thought about taking a cab to his
destination, considered walking and
dismissed both ideas in favor of the Paris
Metro -- which he enjoyed riding because
the stations were clean and the trains
usually ran on time.

■

The driver of the silver Renault
waited a few minutes until Keller was
completely out of sight. The sudden
appearance of a large, noisy group of
American tourists which had just
emerged from the airport bus that had
stopped across the street provided the
perfect opportunity to search the cop's
room.

The concierge was harried by the
twenty-odd natives of Cleveland, Ohio,
who had descended on the hotel as part
of a Rotary Club travel junket.

None of them spoke French and each
of them was directing questions at the
hapless deskman at the same time,
oblivious to his discomfiture. This and
the large number of people milling

around the small hotel lobby prevented him from noticing the driver, who slipped in on the heels of the last members of the group and quickly negotiated the lobby. In seconds the driver was out of sight in front of the elevator, located in a blind spot from the vantage point of the desk.

Less than a minute later, the driver had emerged onto the fourth floor, scoped out the corridor and connecting stairway, and was assured after a few moments that the hotel chambermaid was occupied cleaning rooms on the floor below and would not be around for some time to come.

Satisfied that the area was sterile, the driver proceeded toward the room Keller occupied and extracted a set of professional burglar tools from a coat pocket. Working quickly using a snake pick and tension wrench combination to pop the lock, the driver soon entered the room.

In less than ten minutes the search would be completed and the driver back out on the street.

■

DAVID ALEXANDER

Keller emerged from the Metro stop near the Louvre and walked the short distance beneath arcaded storefronts to the quayside of the Seine.

Consulting his digital wrist chronometer, he realized that he had arrived early.

His destination required some deal of walking, but Keller estimated that this would take him only a few more minutes. He decided to cross the Royal Bridge over to the Left Bank and proceed along the Quay Voltaire.

The cool, drizzly night had brought out solitary strollers and couples and the booksellers who did business along the river had not yet closed up their stalls. Keller turned left at the foot of the bridge and continued walking in the direction of la Cite, the large island in the center of the Seine on which Notre Dame was located and which had been the nucleus from which Paris had spread outward over the centuries in concentric circles.

He eventually neared the Carrousel Bridge which crossed the city island. Before reaching it, Keller turned and walked down a flight of lichen-encrusted stone steps toward the bank of the Seine.

A houseboat called the Leo was moored there, offering for sale an assortment of potted plants displayed on its deck. A small brown mongrel dog wagged its tail and yapped playfully as Keller approached the boat, where a man with a weather-beaten face sat drawing on a meerschaum pipe.

"Can I help you?" asked the Flower Man in French.

"I phoned before about the tulip bulbs," Keller replied in English. "You said they'd be ready."

"Ah, yes, the tulips; the lovely, lovely tulips," the man replied with a pleasant smile, drawing on his meerschaum pipe. "Several exciting new varieties have been developed recently. I have a fine selection inside. Should I bring them out or would you like to go inside to inspect them?"

"I'll come inside," Keller said.

Once they were inside the small cabin, the pipe-smoker brought out an outsized hard shell case in whose foam-padded interior were nestled a small assortment of automatic pistols. Keller recognized all of them as quality merchandise, from the Colt Mark IV to the larger-framed Detonics handgun.

"Haven't seen your face in Paris for a long time, Keller," the Flower Man said, now in English, with a hint of Chicago in it. "Is something up or is this just a pleasure visit."

"Like they used to say in the military," Keller replied, "'If I tell you, I've got to kill you.'"

"Same old Keller," declared the Flower Man, shaking his head, "as big a prick as ever."

"Any of these have histories?" Keller asked as he selected the Colt and held it up to the light, feeling the heft of the small yet powerful handgun.

"As always, everything I sell is factory new," the pipe-smoker answered seriously and a little testily, "and completely untraceable. The gun is 'cold.'"

Keller ejected the Colt's high-capacity magazine and satisfied himself that it was not loaded. He snapped the ammunition clip back into the mag well and thumbed back the hammer. With the gun unsafetied, he aimed it two-handed at the pipe smoker and pulled the trigger, which fell on the firing pin with a loud metallic click.

"Bang, you're dead," Keller said with a smile.

∎

The weapon had cost Keller twenty-five hundred US dollars. Although the price included a hundred rounds of Glaser Safety ammunition, bullets that would be hard to come by through normal channels under the circumstances, Keller had still been clipped by the arms merchant, who had probably paid him back for not being friendlier. Forget about the fact that talking to the Flower Man was the same as having unsafe sex. He was in bed with everybody, and anything you passed on to him, he passed on to them.

Whether or not Keller would be able to fob off the unauthorized purchase on the New York police department via his expense account under some pretext or other, the gun was an insurance policy that made Keller feel much more secure.

As far as the local gendarmerie went, Denard could not care less about the strictures that had been imposed upon

Keller by the Mayor's Office back in New York. He would keep his mouth shut.

Furthermore, if anybody needed to be dealt with the hard way in the line of Keller's unofficial duties in Paris -- preservation of urban dignity and ethnic diversity aside -- it would be that much easier to make one and one add up to four if Keller's weapon were technically a nonexistent and unsanctioned commodity.

With the acquisition of a reliable handgun having been taken care of, Keller's next problem was a far more pleasant, though in some ways more difficult one: where to go for dinner. The walk through Paris in the brisk night air had made him hungry, and he was looking forward to enjoying a good meal and some tolerable wine.

In pursuit of a restaurant, Keller spent some time walking through the exclusive quarters abutting the Seine. He found the eateries here overpriced, crowded and generally unappealing. He decided to ride the Metro back to the hotel and take Denard's advice about the place in his own neighborhood, where he had also spotted a number of other restaurants earlier.

Going into Le Indochine, the Chinese restaurant Denard had recommended, Keller dined on a mixture of Thai and Cambodian cooking. That and the strains of *lamtong* music playing from the speaker system sparked memories of his four-year tour in Southeast Asia, courtesy of Langley. Apart from the fact that the food was exceptional, it was a good choice because of its quirky ambiance that was a mixture of Bangkok chintz and Parisian froufrou. Here was precisely the kind of cooking he had developed a taste for back in Phnom Penh in the late-nineties.

Calling over the manager, Keller discovered that Denard had apparently mentioned his name.

"My friend the Inspector did indeed mention you might be dropping by," said Von Simonh, a compactly built man sporting a thin mustache, after confirming Keller's suspicions that he was originally from Phnom Penh and stating he owned the restaurant.

"The food is excellent," Jack said.

"Thank you, sir," Von replied and accepted Jack's invitation to sit down. The restaurateur caught the eye of one of the waiters and spoke a few words in rapid Cambodian French. Jack recognized the word "rouquin," Khmer Army slang for the French red wine that he remembered flowed especially freely during the Cambodian Fetes des Eaux festivities held in November. In a matter of seconds a carafe of wine and two glasses had been set on the table.

"I have been informed that your acquaintance with Denard began in my native country," he said as he filled their glasses.

"That's right," Jack affirmed, lifting his glass and offering a toast. "To le Terre Rouge."

Von smiled and echoed the toast, perhaps remembering the uncharacteristically red soil of Cambodia, a soil that suddenly changes to a deep, bright red just within the borders, and which holds a special nationalistic symbolism for the Khmers, who will not farm brown soil.

As they talked, Von told Keller that his family had run one of the biggest restaurants in Phnom Penh but that most had been murdered by Pol Pot's communists after the Khmer Rouge took over. He also revealed that Denard, then a former French Foreign Legionnaire drifting through Indochina and eager for combat, had befriended him and had later helped him escape the genocidal Reds.

Though Von did not say so, Keller got the distinct impression that the restaurateur was Denard's informant about goings-on in the large Indochinese community in Paris.

Von tore up the check that the waiter had placed on the table, refusing to accept Keller's money after the meal had been eaten and the wine drunk. They shook hands and Keller went out into the night. Partly hidden behind white lace curtains, the owner of the restaurant watched Keller cross the street until he was no longer in view.

His face wore an enigmatic expression as he returned to his small office behind the register desk.

■

In the hotel lobby, Keller picked up his key and rode the elevator up to his room on the fourth level. As soon as he came inside he discovered the telltale he had placed by the door.

DAVID ALEXANDER

The fallen match lying in an obscure corner near the wall meant that someone had come into the room in his absence. Sitting on the edge of the bed he picked up the attaché case and held it propped edgewise on his calves while he inspected the lock. The foil had been displaced, meaning that the attaché case might have been opened.

Keller had hung the "Do Not Disturb" sign on the doorknob and despite the unmade bed, he picked up the phone and rang the front desk. "Could you tell me if the maid has entered the room while I was out?" he inquired.

A few minutes later he had been given his answer.

"No Monsieur," the concierge told Keller. "Nobody has come to your room. Why do you ask? Is there some problem, perhaps?"

"No, nothing," he replied. "I guess I'm just a little paranoid. Good night."

"Good night, sir."

Feeling suddenly warm, Keller removed the turtleneck and threw open the dormer windows. Leaving the windows open but with the privacy drapes pulled closed, he made sure the door was locked and removed the weapon and ammunition from the plastic grocery bag he had carried from the houseboat on the Seine.

Hand-rolling a Bull Durham, Keller sat on the edge of the bed and cracked open the box of Glasers. One at a time, he thumbed each high-ballistic bullet into the three galvanized steel magazines that had come with his purchase, sliding the first loaded clip into the mag well with the Colt in the retracted position with the breech open.

The clip held fifteen rounds, but Keller slid a sixteenth round into the chamber to beef-up its capacity before carefully hitting the release catch to slide the receiver back into position over the barrel. He did not thumb down the hammer, but instead merely flipped up the safety to carry the weapon cocked and locked.

Smoking his cigaret, Keller lay down on the bed with the gun beside him and listened to the November rain incessantly pattering down against the roof outside. Before he realized what was happening to him, he was fast asleep and oblivious to

the crack of sudden thunder that split the
air.

Fourteen

"*K*ostikov ... Covington ... Shia Qiang...." Antonov repeated the names as though they were a mantra which could bring peace to his troubled mind. "Hanafi ... Ahmadinejad...."

But the names induced anything but a tranquilizing effect. How on earth could they, when they belonged to some of the most dangerous men on the planet?

Uplinked from the camera via Bluetooth to a secure satellite phone, the surveillance photographs taken earlier that day in Afghanistan were received in the form of coded telemetry by the Thirteenth Directorate of the FSB.

The headquarters of the Federal Security Service, located off the Moscow Beltway, bore a strong architectural and even geographical resemblance to the CIA headquarters complex in Langley, Virginia.

Internally, on the level of policy and procedures, the resemblance had become even more pronounced in recent years due to the wholesale restructuring of the FSB along the lines both of its American counterpart and the secret intelligence services of other western nations.

In fact, the new FSB had become in certain ways less doctrinaire and less vertically integrated than its original American counterpart. In internal organization, procedural style and strategic mission, the FSB resembled more the early CIA of Wild Bill Donovan's tenure than it did the increasingly more rigidly structured, corporate-style scheme of things that came to prevail at Langley.

Because of this and other factors, the FSB's External Intelligence Service (SVR) had been attempting to bring to its American opposite number vital information on events taking place in Iran.

In addition to remote satellite imaging, agents on the ground had reported disquieting rumors concerning a large-scale operation with highly negative implications for global security. The operation was based on a power play patterned on a recent incident at a small town in the Urals. There, four heavily armed men had received the equivalent of ten million dollars in ransom for hostages they had taken and a flight to Iran.

Colonel Vladimir Antonov sat at his desk and sipped coffee long since grown cold while he studied the digitally enhanced photographic printouts in front of him, each with an accompanying data sheet which provided analytical commentary on every frame in the series.

The cameraman had managed to snap pictures of many of the participants in the meeting held at the caravansary, and through computer enhancement techniques positive identification had been made in the case of many of them.

Members of the intelligence and military establishments of the United States, his own country, Iran, Libya and other national groups were all present at the clandestine gathering. All of them, according to the database kept current on the organization's server, were known to have reactionary leanings.

One in particular stood out among the others.

Caught emerging from an all terrain vehicle was a famous -- and in some eyes, notorious -- former chief of the CIA's covert action directorate. Antonov knew his name and history by heart. Sylvain Covington had been instrumental in setting black operations policy through two presidential administrations, reaching unprecedented power during the Bush presidency. He had recently retired from the Agency, but was known to still be active behind the scenes.

Surveillance photos taken the previous day by the same team in the Khyber gave strong evidence of the reason for the convocation. The ballistically protected canister exposed on the ground had been the subject of intensive debate in the analytical section. However the consensus was that it contained an item of special technology long missing from the inventories of those whose responsibility was to keep track of such things.

The photographs shot in the desolate Afghanistan hills confirmed that events were beginning to snowball, and that the reactionaries had judged that the time was right to make a bid for power.

That the neo-fascists opposing President Valentin Zondvick had sent Lev Kostikov to the meeting was no surprise. Nor was it surprising that the mainland Chinese had sent Qiang, or the Libyans Hanafi, or the Iranians Barzan Ahmadinejad, the first cousin to the current Iranian President.

The presence of Covington, however, came as a shock. It clearly indicated that sanction at the highest operational levels in American covert intelligence had been given. The situation was fast approaching meltdown and direct action would soon prove necessary.

But despite the warnings that Antonov had sent through his backchannel to receptive quarters at Langley, the Americans were silent. Powerful behind-the-scenes interests were undoubtedly making themselves felt. The channel was at this point, to all intents and purposes, dead.

Antonov leaned back and poured himself a fresh cup of black coffee from the silver carafe on his desk and stared out the window, his thoughts as somber as the monotonous landscape and the modern highway beyond, where early morning rush hour traffic streamed toward central Moscow.

Kostikov, Covington, Shia Qiang ... the Libyan intelligence colonel, the

Iranian head of covert operations for MOIS, their secret intelligence service, formerly SAVAK, now nicknamed "Shawarma" for a sandwich of many layers. It was a veritable witches' Sabbath. The only thing missing was Beelzebub himself.

It was now up to their agent in place to secure mission closure, if this was possible, or risk the ultimate disaster; a return to totalitarian rule by a fanatic oligarchy of unprincipled men.

Fifteen

*T*he French Gendarmerie Special Intervention Group, GIGN, had been thorough.

Acting through informants in the international terrorist underground, a positive confirm on Vanesco had been made shortly after his arrival in Paris by a member of the covert tripwire force that had been deployed throughout the city to watch for his presence.

Since the first sighting, Vanesco had been kept under constant and careful surveillance until such time as higher echelons would determine what should be done about him.

French policy regarding terrorists was selectively hard and soft, depending on the prevailing political climate. Though they had taken a stern line on certain cases recently, a new Presidential administration with leftward leanings was in office and there was no telling how it might act in this sensitive situation.

The indecisiveness of the French had been a mistake, because it was only a matter of time before a professional of the caliber of Vanesco burned the surveillance that had been placed on him.

It had happened during one of his daily exercise runs through the warren of streets behind l'Opera.

Turning from the crowds on the Boulevard Haussmann in the vicinity of the Galleries Lafayette where he had been walking for awhile onto one of the narrow lanes extending toward the river, Vanesco had unexpectedly glanced behind him. A man in a windbreaker suddenly performed an about-face to finger a magazine hanging from a rack at a small kiosk.

The action was artificial and had instantly put Vanesco on the alert. Now suspecting that he was being followed, he soon became aware of another shadow, this one a woman. Before he had finished his jog, he had identified the entire five-member surveillance team that had been monitoring him.

From then on it became only a question of when and how to make his escape from Paris, as well as when and how to deal with Juliette. She had become a messy liability. One that needed to be cleaned up.

CHAIN REACTION

■

The building that housed the headquarters of the Paris branch of Interpol was located at the end of a cul de sac opposite a gurgling water fountain flanked by marble cherubs and across the street from an academy dedicated to the study of avant-garde filmmaking.

Like many of the buildings in Paris, the Belle Epoch four-story structure, a former chateau of blooded French nobility, looked far less imposing on the outside than it was on the inside, and its bland facade belied the activities that took place within its deceptively nondescript walls.

Keller had taken the wake-up call from the desk and ordered breakfast sent up. A petit French girl arrived bearing a tray on which he found a stainless steel carafe of hot black coffee, some soft rolls, two croissants, square foil-wrapped pats of butter and an assortment of jams in small, single-serving jars.

The coffee was every iota as undrinkable as Keller had expected it would turn out to be. He had once heard the claim that bad coffee was standard hotel operating procedure. It kept the guests from inundating the poor slobs in the kitchen with requests for seconds.

He had rolled and lit up his first cigaret of the day when the phone again jangled.

"A Deputy Inspector Toussont is here for you, sir," said the deskman. "He says that he has been sent by Inspector Denard."

"Tell him I'll be right down."

Keller had stubbed out his cigaret in the bedside ashtray and slung the harness of his shoulder rig around his shoulder. Throwing on a sport coat, Keller took a quick look around the room and left.

Keller remembered Toussont as the same man who had driven him to the hotel on his arrival from Orly. Denard's man expertly navigated the slow-moving and often gridlocked rush hour Paris traffic and smoothly angle-parked in front of the building.

Keller was quickly cleared at the security desk and issued a clip-on name tag spat out by a small printer. Denard had an office on the second floor off an L-shaped corridor occupied by a secretarial pool.

CHAIN REACTION

The office was a nondescript medium-sized room with white walls and a Masonite drop ceiling lit by fluorescent panels. Its single saving grace was a spectacular view through a tall window on the side of the building of the Paris skyline looking north toward the Eiffel Tower and the Champs de Mars with the modernist skyline of La Defense in the background.

The door of Denard's office was open. The Inspector awaited Keller's arrival inside his office in shirtsleeves and suspenders.

"Some coffee?" he asked. Keller noticed he already had a steaming mug at his side and a plate with a half-eaten pastry sitting next to it.

"No thanks," he said.

"Very well, then we'll get straight to business," Denard said, motioning toward a chair. "You will be interested to know, I am sure, that we have your man under surveillance."

Keller's eyes narrowed and a muscle on his jaw tensed.

"For how long?" he asked.

"Only since yesterday, and only within the last several hours have we conclusively identified him," Denard explained. "Don't worry, we have not been holding out on you, Keller."

Keller relaxed somewhat.

"What's the game plan?" he asked.

"A raid is planned for today," Denard replied. "The antiterrorist unit, Gigene, will take the point. A command post has been set up near the mission zone. I have only to finish up a few minor chores and we can leave right away."

Keller thoughtfully stroked his chin as he blew smoke through his nostrils. "How certain are you that he hasn't exposed your surveillance? That he isn't false-flagging your people?"

"Completely certain," Denard asserted. "With all deference to your recent difficulties in the US, we in France have been living with terrorists and their brand of tactics a good deal longer than you have. Believe me, Jack, we are old hands at this dreadful business."

"I didn't mean to question the abilities of your operations people," Keller deferred, "I just want to make sure that it's us who gets to say 'Doom on you' and not him."

CHAIN REACTION

"'Doom on you?'" Denard repeated, inclining his head to one side. "I don't understand."

"It's a corruption of the Vietnamese phrase '*do-mai-ngieu*' which roughly translates to something like 'fuck your mother,'" Keller explained as he placed the cigaret to his lips. "That's right," he suddenly remembered, and snapped his fingers, "you mainly operated in Laos and Cambodia where the locals spoke French."

"That's right, Jack," he replied. "And remember, we Frenchmen never go out of our way to learn the other guy's language. You're lucky I'm talking English to you right now."

"You're a gentleman and a scholar, Denard," Jack said.

Denard swallowed the final piece of pastry he had been munching and smiled broadly, nodding his head as if savoring the phrase he had just learned along with the meal.

"Anyway, I can assure you, Jack, that it is us who will be saying 'Doom on you' to our friend Vanesco. Of that you may rest assured."

He took a swallow of the by now rancid brown fluid left in the cup and tossed the empty paper plate into the trash receptacle beside his desk.

■

Juliette gasped as she began to climax and her face twisted up in a mask of sexual pleasure.

Her enjoyment was heightened by the excellent grass that her boyfriend Paul had scored earlier that morning in the student's quarter near Sacre Coeur where the drug dealers hung out. Even though Paul himself never touched pot, he had claimed that he enjoyed watching her get turned on, and besides it always made her hornier.

Paul thrust harder and faster as her climax intensified and she threw her arms around his powerful shoulders, digging her fingernails into the thick trapezius muscles behind the shoulder blades.

She was coming in earnest now, the smaller climaxes building to the final mega-orgasm that she sensed arriving with the speed of a runaway express train. Suddenly it was fully upon her, lighting up her nervous system as she felt Paul explode inside her at the final moment of total ecstasy.

CHAIN REACTION

"You certainly don't leave any loose ends lying around," she said to her lover, shortly afterward, kissing him on the mouth while she stroked his hairless, muscular chest. "I wish you would smoke with me just once, though, it would make it that much better I'm sure."

"Can't." Juliette's boyfriend replied, "It would blow my physical fitness program. Maybe my cock might even fall off."

"No, anything but that!" she said with a laugh.

Paul got up from the bed and nakedly went into the bathroom, hearing Juliette say that he was crazy to talk like that in her French-accented English.

Half-closing the door behind him, Vanesco turned on the bathtub tap then withdrew the ratchet knife that he'd hidden in the pocket of the terry cloth robe slung from the hook behind the door and silently flicked open the eight-inch serrated blade with his thumb.

It was time for Juliette to die.

She had seen more than was good for her to know, and there was no way to deal with that than closure.

DAVID ALEXANDER

Though he had been careful to say nothing that might have compromised him, Vanesco could not be sure that he had slipped up in other ways. Even the wrong words spoken in his sleep and recalled under questioning by Juliette could spell his downfall.

Vanesco had grown to like her in the time they had spent together. She would die quickly and painlessly. Slitting the jugular would almost instantly end her life.

"Juliette, honey," he called out, positioning himself just behind the bathroom door. "Come here a minute, will you? I'm in the tub and I need you to reach me down a bar of soap."

He heard Juliette call back, "Be right there, *mon cher*," and soon heard the sound of her footsteps approaching.

Immediately as the door swung open he grasped her by her long dark hair, pulling her head back, and in a single swift movement sawed the razor-sharp cutting edge of the blade across the base of her throat.

Juliette struggled for a moment, her wide eyes staring at him uncomprehendingly, and then went ragdoll-limp. Blood was pouring out of her, gushing onto the tiled bathroom floor, spurting onto the towels hanging on the rack and staining the plastic shower curtains.

Vanesco let her body sag to the blood-spattered tiles of the bathroom floor, showered off the blood covering his naked body, shrugged on the terry cloth robe in which he had hidden the knife, and stepped out into the main living area of the two-room flat. Dressing quickly, he climbed into a long woolen overcoat and placed a soft, snap-brimmed felt hat on his head.

He would leave the building carrying nothing except for the number of the secret Luxembourg account in his head and the small nine millimeter Walther machine pistol concealed in one of the overcoat's deep side pockets.

Sixteen

*T*he operational command post had been established on the top floor of an apartment block midway down one of the streets extending from a four-way intersection at Place Blanche.

By act of Parliament similar to the US PATRIOT Act, the French security services had been granted sweeping powers in carrying out anti-terror operations. The occupants of the flat had no choice but to let Gigene take over and accept a stay at a first-class hotel courtesy of the government as their sole compensation.

Keller's first impression of the operation was that it appeared to have been professionally mounted. Trestle tables had been set up on which an array of computerized communications and surveillance equipment had been installed. One of these was a laser-based audio surveillance device that could eavesdrop on and record conversations inside a room by detecting and amplifying the faint vibrations of human voices against the window pane.

CHAIN REACTION

Denard introduced Keller to the Chief of Operations. The man running the show was a full colonel in the French special forces named Valery Thibodeaux. Keller had heard of Thibodeaux, whose name had been mentioned in connection with a successful raid on a jetliner held by a militant offshoot of Iranian Hezbollah in Algeria some months before.

"A pleasure to meet you, colonel," Keller said, gripping Thibodeaux's hand in a clasp as tight as his own. "I've heard a lot about you."

"And I about you, lieutenant," he returned.

Gesturing toward one of the apartment's high dormer windows, he explained the tactical situation in concise terms.

"We have the building in which our friend is located staked out. A team is on the roof ready for orders to abseil down. Another team, in plain clothes, is positioned on the street and we have more people inside the building as well."

Noticing a pair of binoculars set up on a tripod, Keller peered through them. They were trained on one of the windows of Juliette's flat. Since the blind was partially raised, Keller could see into the room, but the viewing angle was not the most favorable one. He could only get a look at part of a sofa and a framed art deco poster hanging on a wall.

"When will you take him?" Keller asked, having completed his observation.

"We could have moved at any time this morning, but we were waiting for you," replied the colonel. "Of course, had a contingency arisen we would have acted sooner. In any case, now that you have arrived, let us proceed."

A sudden tension gripped the room as Thibodeaux picked up a small black transceiver unit and placed the commo set to his ear. "All units," he announced. "The condition is 'Green.' Confirm."

Keller and Denard waited in anticipation as each unit leader confirmed the strike orders.

Moments later, well-rehearsed and intricately choreographed acts of violence occurred with seamless precision. The roof team abseiled down on nylon climbing ropes and kicked in through the apartment windows, their Heckler & Koch MP5/10 submachineguns tracking the interior of the flat for targets even before their boots had touched the floor.

At the same instant as the first man had gone through the window, the team stationed in the building corridor outside the door used a lock-popper -- a small charge of plastic explosive -- to blow the wooden door clean off its hinges. They bolted into the room, their own H&K submachines tracking for target acquisition.

It took less than an eighth of a second for the well-trained team to determine that the main room was empty. They immediately moved to the pre-planned backup procedures that they had practiced on endless drills at training mockups in France and elsewhere.

While one element secured the main room, other team members of the assault group swept into the kitchen and bathroom, where they immediately discovered the bloody corpse lying on the tiled bathroom floor.

■

"What is it?" Keller said, glancing from Thibodeaux to Denard as the voice of the squad leader crackled over the transceiver unit. Though he could not understand every word of the rapid and inflected French being spoken, the looks on the faces of both men were anything but jubilant.

"They found a body of a girl," Denard apprised Keller after a beat. "Her throat was cut. There was no sign of Vanesco."

Keller gritted his teeth and began pounding a wall. Most heads in the room turned in his direction.

"Damn it!" he cursed as he smashed his fist into the wall.

"Easy Jack," Denard said, placing an arm on his shoulder. "These things happen. We'll find him yet."

Keller shook off the Frenchman's placating hand.

"You had him and you let him slip right past you!" he shouted, his eyes sweeping the room in open accusation of everyone inside it. "All of you fucking 'experts' with all your hot-shit million dollar equipment and you couldn't even catch one lone man. You're fucking useless, all of you."

Keller threw open the apartment's door and stormed into the hallway. He leaned against the dirty sill of a flyspecked window that afforded a dingy view of the round-cornered lead rooftops of the grubby Parisian quarter.

Somewhere out there the man who had murdered his friend and the loved ones of hundreds of other people was free. Now Vanesco had spilled innocent blood again. And he could do nothing about it.

Denard and Thibodeaux both came out of the command post and approached Jack along the hall.

"I apologize for my outburst back there," Keller said to them, having cooled down a little by then. "I know shit like this happens. It's hard for me to be completely rational right now."

"Forget the apologies," Thibodeaux answered, his jaw set. "You're absolutely right. We should have gotten the bastard. I can promise you that there will be a full review of the operation, and whoever is at fault will pay the consequences, up to and including myself."

■

Keller said little as he was driven back to his hotel by Toussont. The day was leaden and the sky overhead was darkened with thick clouds. Keller had a few long distance phone calls to make, but he realized that essentially it was all over but the shouting. At least as far as Keller was concerned, the chase had ended.

He had conducted his investigation, come within an ace of capturing the blond man, and had blown it all in the end, and that's the way it would have to go down.

He was too preoccupied with his thoughts to notice the silver Renault that had stopped near the hotel. Or take note of the fact that the driver watched intently as he entered through the lobby doors.

Seventeen

*K*eller had the IsatPhone chocked between his shoulder and his chin.

"Yes, that's right," he was saying into the GSM 900's mike over the secure Inmarsat uplink to New York, "the Frenchies fucked up beyond all belief."

In New York it was eight o'clock PM. A broken pattern of lighted windows in the blacked-out skyscrapers of Midtown formed a glittering mosaic against the dark night sky.

As he listened to Keller's report, Abernathy took an antacid tablet from a paper-wrapped roll and popped it into his mouth to quiet the ulcers that job-related stress had fertilized like malignant weeds in his stomach. He had been working late and the stress had brought on another painful gastric flare-up.

"And you're telling me he just breezed right past them?" Abernathy commented dourly.

"The dust hasn't settled yet, but that's my guess," Keller affirmed. "From personal experience I can tell you that anyone really skilled at E and E -- escape and evasion -- tactics can never be assumed to be anyplace where they can't be directly observed. Vanesco could have false-flagged the Gigene people in any number of ways."

Abernathy quickly considered and assessed the situation. From his perspective the news was not good. But on the other hand it was not entirely bad either.

On the one side the terrorist had gotten clean away. But on the other, it was not the fault of the NYPD, whose representative had warned the French from the very first about the possibility that their quarry had scoped out the surveillance put on him.

The media hacks in the office of the mayor could do a lot with that angle. By painting the French as disdainful incompetents -- who in a characteristic display of Gallic hauteur had refused to listen to measured professional criticism -- they could give the mayor and the commissioner the high moral ground.

"We'll get that fuck eventually, Keller, but for you it's over in Paris," Abernathy said. "Tie up whatever loose ends there are and catch the soonest available flight back to JFK. We'll schedule a meeting at the commissioner's office the minute you get back."

Keller swallowed the last of the wine he'd poured himself before making the long-distance call. He thought about refilling the glass as he eyed the half-empty wine bottle standing on the bedside table.

Deciding that he'd had enough, he said, "I've already booked a seat on the redeye, Flight 702. I should be landing at JFK at about five PM, your time, tomorrow."

"I'll have a car waiting to pick you up," Abernathy told him. "Don't take it too hard, Keller. You went the distance and that's all anybody had a right to expect. See you tomorrow."

"Yeah, I went the fucking distance, alright," Keller repeated as he signed off and decided to pour himself another bathroom tumbler full of wine after all.

■

Keller heard someone grunt close to his ear and snapped awake, realizing that he had been crying out in his sleep.

It took another second or two for him to tune in on the persistently ringing telephone on the small bed stand just under his elbow and the fact that the room was now engulfed in near-total darkness.

"Yeah, what is it?" he said, slurring his words as, drugged with sleep, he picked up the receiver.

There was a long, measured pause during which Keller heard nothing. He was about to hang up when a voice said in thickly accented English, "We have information concerning the man you missed today. Be at Place de Meudon. One hour. We wait ten minutes and no more."

The line disconnected with a click and Keller heard a dial tone. He slid the receiver into the cradle and picked his watch off the top of the bed stand where he had propped it to serve double duty as an alarm clock. The backlit digital dial showed that it was a quarter past one in the morning.

Keller switched on the reading lamp bolted into the wall over the headboard and stumbled toward the bathroom. He had apparently blacked out sometime in the early evening. The combination of mental fatigue, physical exhaustion, creeping middle age and full-bodied red wine had done it to him.

From past experience Keller had a fairly good idea of the distance from the hotel to the location mentioned by the caller. The square he pictured lay on the other side of town in the Twelfth Arrondissement. It was a seedy district behind the Eiffel Tower where there were a lot of narrow, winding streets and tiny pocket squares bearing picturesque names and moldering statues.

Place de Meudon was probably one of those small squares he had in mind. Keller quickly calculated that it would take him a rough half hour to reach the destination. That meant he had only minutes in which to decide whether to take the chance -- the very probable chance -- of walking into an ambush or dealing Denard and his crew in on the anonymous tip he had just received.

He rolled a cigaret, thinking about the pros and cons as he sifted tobacco between the rubber rollers of the machine from the cellophane humidor pouch. Once or twice his hand reached for the phone. But Keller never touched the handset.

DAVID ALEXANDER

He realized that he had made up his mind the instant he'd heard the caller's message. If there was any chance of gaining information on that smirking blond bastard, then Keller was not about to look it in the mouth and check its teeth for wear and tear.

The vaunted French counterterror specialists had fucked up. In Keller's opinion their reputation for competence was grossly overrated. They had taken their best shot and they had come up empty. Now it was Keller's turn at bat. He was going to do this his way from now on.

Keller dressed and tossed the two extra clips of Glaser ammo into his pockets after shrugging on the shoulder harness in which the gun was holstered. For good measure he dropped a handful of extra ammo into his pants pockets before leaving the hotel room.

Finding a cab posed no problem, even at the advanced hour. They were plentiful on the broad boulevard that ran past the hotel, winding down from the neon-lit warrens in the Pigalle Quarter where the action was on till sunup every night.

CHAIN REACTION

"You know where the Place de Meudon is?" he asked a cabbie in street French.

"*Oui, Monsieur. Vraiment,*" the cabbie said, and nodded as the small vehicle sped off into the neon stream of glowing red taillights rushing toward the city center.

■

A vein running down Keller's left cheek throbbed as he walked along a deserted street and turned a windy corner past the corrugated steel shutter of a closed-down tavern. He had asked the cabbie to inform him when they were within a block or two of the Place de Meudon.

"Point me toward it," he'd instructed as the cab pulled short at the curb.

"Around the corner. Walk straight one block," the driver told him, embellishing his verbal directions with a variety of hand gestures.

Keller nodded and paid the hack driver, then got out and walked. He heard the cab drive away and disappear in the pre-dawn gloaming.

On his own now, he realized he was alone and vulnerable -- "naked" as they used to say in his days with the Agency.

DAVID ALEXANDER

More than once on the ride over he had questioned the sanity of running down the anonymous phone tip without backup, and realized that it was his own sense of bravado driving him on, and that this was stupid, suicidally stupid, in fact. This thought spun through his mind again as he continued walking, but despite everything, he was not about to turn back.

As he continued down the street, Keller had the distinct impression that he was being watched by unseen eyes. But though he remained as alert as possible, he could discern no evidence of surveillance, which, of course, did not mean that it was not there. By now he could see the pocket square with the equestrian statue at its center directly ahead of him.

Keller continued walking.

A few dozen feet before reaching the square, he stopped short and carefully looked around. He scanned the darkened windows of the silent buildings to either side, but saw no evidence of human presence. The same was true of the street to his left and right and behind his back.

CHAIN REACTION

Taking a deep breath and steadying himself, he walked directly into the square and strode toward the statue.

In the glowing green view field of a starlight scope bolted to the receiver of a high-powered sniper rifle, a shooter perched atop one of the roofs overhead sighted the luminous red target crosshairs on the upper right quadrant of Keller's skull.

The sniper inhaled deeply to enhance his nerve control and slowly began squeezing the precisely calibrated trigger of the deadly, long-barreled weapon.

Eighteen

A sudden clatter made Keller turn in time to see a black alley cat scurry from atop a dumpster filled with trash and disappear between the front tires of a parked car.

In that split-instant something stung Keller's cheek and he heard another sound, fainter and flatter and closer to where he stood. That of metal puncturing.

The realization that a small petaled hole about a centimeter wide had appeared on the bronze flank of the sculpted horse behind him registered its shock in his brain. He knew that a second bullet would immediately follow.

Keller was ducking for cover behind the huge marble pediment of the statue, drawing the Colt from its shoulder harness, as another silenced sniper round impacted with the statue a few centimeters from the first bullet hole.

On the rooftop of the chateau directly across from the square, the shooter cursed and cooked off another shot group. The G3SG/1 was a clip-fed sniper weapon that was equally formidable as a high-powered assault weapon when the need arose.

Due to bad luck, the shooter had lost the element of surprise, but his quarry was still pinned down and still outgunned. A kill might yet be scored.

Keller tracked the Colt in the general direction he guessed the flash- and sound-suppressed fire had originated.

Though he couldn't make out the shooter's position, he took note of a salient fact. Unlike most of the other buildings in Paris, those fronting the square had flat roofs, making them ideal for use as a sniper's eyrie.

It was obvious that the square had been chosen as an ambush site for precisely that reason.

Keller figured he was obviously dealing with a night-vision equipped gunman and also knew that his tactical situation was extremely precarious. Had he been the one planning the ambush, he would have made certain that the sniper had backup positioned somewhere on the ground, ready to close in and finish off the target if the first attempt at taking down the target failed. Keller's only question at that point was why they had not yet made an appearance.

Another flurry of rapid gunfire from the roof angled down at his position, and this time Keller was able to spot the faint reflection of suppressed muzzle flash against the black slate roofing tiles.

He fired off a three-round burst in answer, more to demonstrate that he was armed than in the hopes of hitting anything. The sniper was not only hidden, but the roof was at the limit of the nine-millimeter handgun's effective range.

It was now apparent to Keller that the gunman stationed on the roof had shifted strategy from making a quick, clean kill to one whose sole objective was to flush him out into the open. Once he was exposed and vulnerable in that way Keller would be fair game for both the shooters on the ground and the sniper perched above.

More sound-suppressed automatic fire lanced down from the roof a few seconds later.

And this time Keller saw that his antagonists had finally grown impatient.

CHAIN REACTION

Under cover of the distraction posed by the fire, two men broke from a doorway in the most deeply shadowed corner of the pocket square and opened up on him with conventional semiautomatic handguns.

Keller snapped off a burst in answer, forcing the two shooters to split up for opposite corners of the square. But he was unable to draw a bead on either of them as they tucked left and right in a dodging, evasive dance.

Keller had tried counting off the shots that he had discharged from the Colt, but in the heat of action he was not certain exactly how much ammunition he had expended.

Taking advantage of a brief lull in the firefight, he ejected the magazine and snapped a fresh clip into the Colt's mag well, chambering a bullet.

Soon, more gunfire, this time from three directions at once, greeted him. The bullets ricocheted off the pavement, one of the fragments zinging him on the hand.

Though its energy was largely spent it had started blood pouring.

Keller realized he had no option left but to make a break for it and hope that he could get clear of the square without taking a hit. It was probable that an observer from one of the apartments in the surrounding buildings had summoned the police. But if he stood pat he could be dead in a matter of seconds.

Keller steadied himself with a deep breath, tried to judge the position of the two men hunkered at the corners of the square, and readied himself to bolt.

Headlights suddenly pinned him in their blinding glare.

Momentarily unable to see, Keller raised his hands to shade his eyes as the driver jumped out and produced a bullpup assault weapon, vectoring an incandescent arc of automatic tracer fire into the now floodlighted shadows.

"Get in the car!" he heard a voice yell. "Quickly!"

Though momentarily stunned, the roof-based gunman was now raining steady 7.62 millimeter fire down in the direction of the driver. Keller turned and snapped off a covering burst from the Colt as he ran pell-mell for the vehicle, hammering out more fire midway to the car as incoming bullets sparked against the flagstone pavement.

As Keller gained the vehicle, the woman with the assault weapon raked the square with a final, scything automatic burst, threw her weapon to him, and jumped behind the steering wheel.

Dropping the Colt onto his lap, Keller fired the bullpup through the open window. The woman expertly spun the wheel and sped the vehicle away from the square with the screech of tortured tire rubber echoing off the buildings in the night.

■

They heard two-note police sirens as the driver navigated a maze of side streets with flawless precision driving and the familiarity of a Parisian native.

Still high from the firefight, Keller was beginning to come back down to earth as the adrenaline in his bloodstream slowly metabolized. He studied the driver in the uncertain, flickering luminance that spilled into the car from street lighting stanchions under which they passed.

Her face, though set in tense concentration, was undeniably beautiful in profile, with a small nose, high cheekbones and full, sensuous lips that were slightly turned outward. Her long hair was jet black and hung straight and loose below the shoulders of the well-cut black leather jacket she wore.

"I think we've cleared the danger zone," she said to Keller after they had gone some distance more and the police sirens were clearly receding from the range of hearing.

"Who the hell are you?" Keller asked. "You're not one of Denard's and I don't think you're CIA."

"Does it matter?" she asked. "I saved your life."

"Lady, we could be on our way to hell right now for all I know," he shot back.

A slight smile tightened the corners of her mouth. "Very well. My name is Tatyana Danilovna. You may call me 'Tanya.' I have been assigned by the Russian External Intelligence Service to protect you while in France."

"Okay, you're SVR," Keller declared. "I know your people and my people are supposed to be hotdogs with borscht on the side these days, but why take an interest in me?"

CHAIN REACTION

"I will tell you everything I can, but not this second," she replied as she drove. "At any rate, I am sure your own operational background can supply you with the basic principles involved, in this case that of the 'link man.'"

Keller nodded. He knew what the woman was talking about. In a world where self-interest was always the bottom line, the unexpected help from the Russian *Sluzhba Vneshney Razvedki* meant that his instincts had not been lying to him.

He had walked into an operation as deep and black as a Pennsylvania mine shaft and more full of spooks than a cemetery on Halloween. He was almost certainly once again staring into the face of the Medusa.

The old East-West confrontations might be an on-again, off-again thing, but not the far more ancient struggle between anarchy and order, of a culture of madness against a culture of civilization, of the sociopaths against society itself, and against the hunger of power to sustain itself by growing ever larger, ever vaster, and ever more corrupt.

"We can't go back to your hotel, of course," the woman added. "It would not be safe." As she glanced toward Keller she saw that he was laughing. Her face grew perplexed. "Did I say something amusing?"

"I was just thinking," he replied. "The dirtbag I was after, the guy I want to nail so bad I can taste it, didn't even bother showing up to punch my ticket. Instead, he sent in a couple of errand boys. I wasn't even worth his time."

"How can you be certain of that?" she asked.

"Take my word for it, I'm certain," Jack retorted bitterly. "I know that bastard inside-out. I know his towering arrogance. How he thinks he's better and smarter than anybody else. Yeah, I know him. More than I'd like to."

Tanya said nothing as she continued driving, but wondered momentarily at the wisdom of her superiors, Antonov in particular, for having placed their bets on the American cop.

He seemed hardly the type whom she would want to rely on in the difficulties that lay immediately ahead.

CHAIN REACTION

Inside him, she sensed, there was something broken, perhaps broken beyond all hope of repair.

Nevertheless, she would have to resign herself to what had to be done. There were no other choices left, and, like it or not, Jack Keller was her only remaining hope.

Nineteen

*T*hey sat in the Renault, its ignition off and its engine ticking beneath the hood on the outskirts of a pocket park on the other side of the city near the Gare du Nord railway terminal.

Keller had used a foil-wrapped towelette to dab away the congealed blood from the superficial bullet wound on his left hand, then applied a self-adhesive bandage from a small first-aid kit in the glove compartment.

During the last few minutes he had arrived at what he knew was a turning point.

Keller saw himself faced with two choices.

He could either report what had taken place in the square to Denard's people, have them accompany him to his hotel room where he could retrieve his plane tickets and meager personal effects and be on the scheduled flight to JFK, and put Paris behind him.

Or he could continue on as a "solitaire," acting completely on his own and without official sanction.

CHAIN REACTION

Keller's old European network had long since been decimated by the natural forces of time and attrition. But here and there one or two of the old field "whores" he'd run during his days with the Agency were still around.

As was usually the case, Keller knew that these operational contacts still occasionally acted in a semiofficial capacity for various global intelligence networks including, though by no means limited to, the CIA. There was a danger he might wind up dealing with a double or a triple, but that was an acceptable risk as far as he was concerned.

In addition to an infrastructure that Keller could turn to for reliable intelligence, he also had access to secret contingency funds.

During Keller's long employ with the Company he had busted organizations to whom a million dollars was small change. Vast sums of illicit money had passed through his hands, and had done so with great regularity.

He did not consider himself as a violator of laws, or even of ethics, by having secreted over two hundred thousand dollars in a variety of worldwide numbered accounts. The world in which he'd once moved was a lawless shadow world, one where his employers were in league with the very forces they outwardly sought to destroy.

Parts of his "spooker" -- a term those in Keller's former line of work used to describe these clandestine IRA accounts -- were held in several numbered depositories in Zurich banks. They were old accounts, set up using cutouts, and still, to all intents and purposes, beyond the reach of Washington.

Standard operating procedure called for keeping the sums of a spooker small and widely dispersed, the better to protect their secrecy. With a brief stop in Zurich to secure some of his private contingency funds, Keller could then move on to Venice where he knew that one of his most reliable former operatives could still be found.

Now, as he sat in the car in the darkness that lingered before daybreak, smoking a cigaret with a stranger who had just saved his life, Tanya was saying to him, "Then you must come with me. The Orient-Express is stopped in the Gare du Nord right now. There is always room for passengers with sufficient money to pay extra for a berth."

"Why the Orient-Express?" Keller asked. "Why not some other passenger train, maybe one with a lower profile? There may be people out looking for us."

"The high profile of the Orient-Express is precisely why it is our best protection," she replied. "It is one of the last means of transportation that we would be suspected of using to leave Paris.

"Secondly, the Orient-Express goes directly to Zurich, Vienna and Venice from this station, usually without passport checks at borders.

"Finally, while I believe that you and I might be able to blend in among the wealthy passengers, I believe that the opposition would stick out like sore thumbs were they to venture on board."

"Why do you say that?"

"You answered that question only a little while ago: the low-level personnel encountered thus far could not possibly pass for the affluent travelers on this train."

Keller considered what Tanya had just told him. After a few moments' reflection, he found himself forced to admit that every one of the conclusions that she had drawn was sound.

"Okay, you've sold me," he agreed.

"Excellent," she replied. "Don't worry about money. We will both travel as guests of the SVR."

"There's one last point, though," Keller said to her. "As far as I'm concerned, I'm a solo. I'll take you up on your offer of a ride as far as Zurich where I have access to some hard currency for operating expenses. But after that, we go our separate ways."

Tanya's eyes shot Jack cold green fire as she darted him a sharp sidelong glance.

"However you want it, Mr. Keller," she said, and climbed out of the car.

Twenty

Captain Frank Abernathy stood at the arrivals lounge of John F. Kennedy International Airport in Queens, New York, scrutinizing the faces of the passengers debarking from the jumbo jet that had just landed on a nonstop flight direct from Orly International Airport in Paris, France.

Beside Abernathy stood his driver, Sergeant Ernie Garibaldi.

Both cops had been waiting for at least a half hour prior to the plane's scheduled arrival, having consulted the large, ceiling-mounted computer displays in the airline terminal to ascertain that Keller's early morning flight had in fact departed Paris on time and would arrive on schedule.

But Keller was not to be seen among the first group of passengers off the flight. Abernathy moved to one side so he could get a better look into the interior of the jetway, but still saw no sign of him.

"Something's wrong," he told Garibaldi. "Keller's not here."

"Relax," Garibaldi counseled, "Jack's probably just taking a leak, is all."

"You're a regular fucking riot, Garibaldi," Abernathy said mirthlessly.

He continued to watch with growing impatience as the last of the passengers disembarked.

Finally, shaking his head in consternation, Abernathy approached the departure gate, flashing his gold detective's shield.

"I'm looking for a passenger who was supposed to be on this flight," he told one of the flight attendants.

"What's the name?" he asked.

"Keller. Jack Keller."

"Doesn't ring a bell. But you can ask the captain to check the flight manifest or have a look around."

Realizing that his blood pressure was rocketing into the stratosphere, Abernathy stormed down the inclined jetway with Garibaldi following at his heels like a trained pit bull.

Abernathy declined the captain's offer to check the flight manifest because he had already confirmed that Keller was booked on the flight at the check-in desk before going to the arrivals lounge.

Instead he would search the aircraft, which was a double-decker jetliner whose top level was reached by a spiral staircase aft of the lower first-class cabin.

"You take the top, I'll take the bottom," he told Garibaldi. "And don't forget to check the toilets."

"Right," Garibaldi said and mounted the stairs.

A short time later, it was apparent that what Abernathy had suspected from the first was actually the case.

Lieutenant Jack Keller had not arrived in New York on the plane. A gut check told Abernathy that Keller would not be on the next plane either, and that Keller was likely to turn into a very big problem for the captain, the police department, and probably also for the City of New York.

Twenty-one

*A*s Tanya had promised, there had been no difficulty in obtaining a berth on the Venice-Simplon Orient-Express once the initial reluctance of the trainmaster had been overcome by a liberal application of feminine charm and high-denomination euros.

The trainmaster served the functions of the concierge of a rolling first-class European hotel. He was a tall man with a patrician face, resplendent in a black waistcoat that reminded Jack of a circus ringmaster's, the banked fires of whose dark eyes had lit up when he had suddenly seen the color of money.

"You are fortunate," he said in French-accented English, with the careful diction of those who spoke a language they had not learned from birth and did not use extensively. "There has been a recent departure of one of our passengers due to illness. Because of this I can offer you a very comfortable sleeper compartment at the front of the train."

"Thank you," Tanya said, "you are very kind."

CHAIN REACTION

Jack had merely flashed a sardonic smile at the trainmaster who had just pocketed the equivalent of over five thousand US dollars. He shook his head in dismay as they walked along the dark platform toward the front of the train just behind a red locomotive.

The halted line of gray railway cars was quiet, except for an occasional puff of steam that rose from beneath the undercarriages of some, and most of the compartments were dark and had their blinds drawn. Looking over the train, Keller felt himself suddenly transported back in time to another, simpler, age.

"It's a beautiful hunk of machinery, I'll say that much," Keller told Tanya with genuine appreciation.

"Then you've never traveled on it before?" she asked.

"No. Have you?"

"Yes," she answered after the briefest of pauses. "Once before. To Istanbul."

She turned her head away and Jack did not press her for details.

■

They saw lights glowing in the windows of the bar car and climbed the short flight of iron steps into the railway carriage's opulently appointed interior.

The piano player had long since packed up his synthesized electronic instruments. The only other occupants of the car were a wealthy and sedate seeming older couple, who looked like old money from central casting, finishing off a bottle of iced Taittinger brut in the far corner beneath a mosaic of etched Lalique glass.

"Can we still get a drink?" Keller asked the weary looking bartender.

"Certainly, *Monsieur,*" he laconically replied, his fatigue showing in his voice.

"A double bourbon on the rocks for me," Keller said. He glanced at Tanya.

"I'll have a Ricard," she stated.

With a choice of anyplace to sit, save one, they found a small table midway across the car and settled into the plushly upholstered brocade-covered seats by a window that looked out onto the dimly lit train station.

The bartender brought the drinks quickly, eager to close up for the night and grab some sleep in the cramped compartment behind the galley that he shared with two other train functionaries. He muttered a barely audible

"*Merc*i" as he scooped up the francs from the tabletop.

"I would have pegged you for a Stolichnaya drinker," Jack said, watching her sip the dense yellow liquor. "What is that stuff anyway? Looks like something I once drained from a crankcase."

"It's a French drink, terribly trendy I'll admit," she replied with a smile. "But that should not surprise you. We Russians have been enamored of the French since Catherine the Great carried on a running battle of wits with Voltaire. Our greatest writers have spurned Russian for French. Haven't you ever read Nabokov?"

"Can't say I have." Jack returned her smile as he sipped his bourbon, feeling the slow alcoholic fire spread through his veins. "I try to confine my reading to important stuff, like the sports section."

"Somehow I don't believe that, Mr. Keller," Tanya said.

"Jack," he replied. "Call me Jack."

She went on, "I've a small confession to make. A little while ago I thought to myself that you were a man broken in spirit, troubled at heart, bruised in ego. Now I don't think that's quite the right way to look at you. You're ... you're ... I don't know how to say it in English."

"'Bent,' maybe?" Jack made a twisting motion with his hands.

"That's exactly right, Jack. You are most definitely a little 'bent.' But what I don't understand is why you are that way."

"You've probably been briefed regarding my past and present line of work," he replied, rolling a Bull Durham and licking the gummed edge of the crinkly rice paper. "That should paint the entire picture."

"Not necessarily," she said with a shake of her head that tossed back her long black hair. "Others who have been through worse -- and believe me there is worse -- have not been affected as you seem to have been."

"I guess the bottom line is that it's just like what my dear mother used to tell me," Keller ventured, "'Jack,' she used to say, 'you've got a mean streak in you a mile and a half wide.'"

Tanya said nothing as she looked at him across the rim of her glass. Both fell silent for awhile and Jack noticed that the bartender had doused the lights on the bar and was just about to leave.

"By the way, you were good back there," Keller spoke up. "Damn good. I've seen guys who considered themselves macho to the nines totally blow it under the kind of heat you took in the firefight. I owe you one, Tanya."

Jack noticed that the elderly couple were getting ready to leave too. They moved with the slow, elegant grace of those who had never worked a day in their lives toward the bar-end of the car, passing the table at which he and Tanya sat.

"Good night," the man in the tuxedo said to them, his accent upper-class British.

"The fucking Duke and Duchess of Windsor," Jack remarked sarcastically after they had left and were out of earshot. "You wonder when you look at people like that what goes through their minds. Whether they're really as jaded and apathetic as they appear."

He drank some more bourbon.

"Which brings me around to you. Even though I've seen you in action, I still can't picture you running the Spetsnaz course in camo fatigues."

"Spetsnaz was not open to women during my days of training, nor is it entirely yet even today," she responded, and measuring her words, went on, "nor did I enlist but was recruited a few years ago. Things were again changing in my country, I thought then, and I saw a chance to be of service."

Tanya fell silent, lost in thought, and as Jack watched her he realized to his complete surprise that he was beginning to feel all the telltale stirrings of emotional and physical attraction. He told himself to stop looking at her that way, but knew that his heart had no intention of heeding the prudent cautions of his mind's inner voice.

Concerned that she might see what he was thinking registered in his eyes, Jack looked out the window at the station platform, lit in conical pools of antiseptic blue light spilling from incandescent bulbs.

Suddenly the car gave a savage lurch and the hissing sound of steam came from below. Jack saw bluish clouds of vapor rising on both sides of the window as he heard a train whistle give two short, sharp toots from the head of the platform.

"We're starting to roll," he told Tanya. "Why don't we go up front and have a look at the berth?"

■

The steward assigned to their car was expecting them and he showed them to their compartment.

The berth was spacious and opulently appointed. Its japanned walls were made of parti-colored strips of inlaid polished wood in delicate patterns, and a section of wall doubled as the door to a small bathroom with a sink, though the head, explained the steward, was located at the front of the car.

There was a small table with a functional electric lamp with a pink silk shade that could be propped horizontally just beneath the window or folded down for convenience and two Murphy beds, one above the other, that folded back into the wall opposite the bathroom.

Keller closed the compartment's door and locked it behind them.

"I don't know about you, but I'm beat," he announced. "I'll be happy to bunk on top, if you don't have a preference."

"That will be fine with me," she answered.

"If you need some privacy, I'm going to the head," he told her. "I'll rap once short, twice long, when I get back."

Jack watched the Parisian rail yard slip away through the smoke-stained windows amid the roar of the locomotive's diesel engine and the piercing blasts of its horn. The train had gathered speed and was already chugging at a good clip as a false dawn lit the brooding industrial skyline with a shimmering purple haze.

Jack felt oddly out-of-synch with reality as he negotiated the swaying corridor, holding onto the polished brass handrail that ran beneath the windows to steady himself against the wildly pitching and yawing deck of the car.

He did not permit himself to linger on the incongruity of his finding himself on a midnight train hurtling away from Paris in the company of an exotic woman he had met only a few hours before, nor on having turned rogue and operating without backup or sanction to run down a case that experience and common sense told him would be impossible to bring to a satisfactory close.

Jack knew that for some time to come -- how long he could not say -- he would be operating on nerve, instinct and adrenaline alone, making decisions quickly and letting the consequences sort themselves out. What he did not know, what he could not put into words, was why in the first place he had chosen to act as he was now doing.

But he sensed that it would be better to leave his inner demons slumbering for the moment.

When Jack returned to the berth his recognition code was not answered. He rapped on the door a second time and reached beneath his jacket for the Colt holstered beneath his left armpit. The door opened a split-second later.

"Sorry, I was washing my face," Tanya apologized.

She was wearing one of the soft terry cloth robes that the train provided for its passengers. She had removed some of the makeup from her face and had tied back her black hair into a ponytail. If anything, it made her look more beautiful than she had seemed to him before. "I didn't hear you knock the first time."

"That's okay," he told her. "Now do me a favor and turn around. I'm about to strip down to the altogether and I'm afraid it won't be a pretty sight."

■

Jack lay on his side on the top bunk smoking a hand-rolled cigaret while Tanya briefed him on the operational side of their working relationship. Circumstances had prevented them talking shop until now, and with the racket raised by the sound of the train thundering over the tracks and the music of the built-in radio providing additional noise cover, they judged it to be safe enough to speak in guarded tones.

They had cleared the outskirts of Paris about twenty minutes before. Now they were rapidly moving southward through farm acreage and extensive vineyards that streaked by in the light of the newly risen sun.

"The killer you want is part of a major undertaking by elements of both our governments' intelligence services and high political echelons. The Iranians, in partnership with al-Sharqi, are the third leg of the 'troika,'" she said. "The man who organized the operation in New York has been tasked with carrying out this new operation."

"What part do the Iranians play?" asked Keller.

"They are in possession of one of the best-kept secrets of the Cold War," she replied. Then she briefed Keller on the merchandise that had been given to the Shah and the nature of its disposition over the course of decades.

"It's incredible," Jack said when she had finished. "If they pull it off, Iran becomes a regional superpower, absorbing Afghanistan and the former Soviet Muslim republics, the Russian fascists take back most of the Soviet Empire in the 'near remote' and the wannabe Cold Warriors at the CIA and Pentagon can get on their horses and play cowboys and Indians."

"You don't believe me, then?"

"Oh, I believe you alright," he replied. "It all makes sense in a perverse way that's perfectly logical in a wilderness of mirrors."

"You've read T.S. Eliot, I see?" she commented.

"There you go again," Jack said.

"The phrase 'a wilderness of mirrors' is a line from a poem Eliot wrote called "The Love Song of J. Alfred Prufrock.'"

"Is that right?" Jack remarked. "It's also a line from James Jesus Angleton, a commie-hating, paranoid, director of CIA covert operations who used it to describe clandestine tradecraft in the 1960s. I guess that proves once again that you should never trust anybody."

"I know you don't trust me," she replied. "But in light of what I've just told you, don't you think it would be far better for us to work together as a team?"

"No," Jack said with finality. "I'm not claiming it's logical, but I'm still going the distance alone. Right or wrong, I've made my decision. The chips will just have to fall wherever they may."

Twenty-two

J ack became aware he'd been asleep when he awoke with a violent start. In the seconds it took for him to orient himself, he realized that the train had stopped moving.

The dark green canvas blinds that covered the windows were rolled up. Jack saw that the train was halted abreast of an apple orchard in an Alpine valley bordered by high mountains of sharp-edged black granite whose glaciated peaks were covered with cottony white mist.

"Tanya?" he called out.

Getting no answer, Keller checked the lower bunk. It was empty except for a handwritten note on a sheet of beige V.S.O.E. stationary. "Have gone to the dining car for breakfast. Hope you can join me. Tanya."

Keller splashed cold water on his face and cleaned up as best he could in the confined circumstances of the compartment. After dressing and a quick trip to the head he crossed through three passenger carriages toward the dining car, waving hello to a steward who was shoveling lumps of coal from a bucket into a small furnace near the floor of the car. "A vision from hell," the thought came perversely into Jack's mind.

Tanya waved to him from a table at the rear of the car as she raised a steaming delft china cup to her lips.

"So you're finally awake," she said, "the way you were snoring I thought you might doze through the entire trip."

"I hope I didn't talk in my sleep," Jack replied. "Sometimes I have a habit of telling off-color Borscht Belt jokes."

"Borscht Belt?" she said. "What's that? Not something worn around the waist, I take it?"

"No, forget I mentioned it. Just some bad New York humor."

"I've already ordered breakfast," Tanya said. "The coffee is excellent."

Keller upended his coffee cup and poured it full of steaming black liquid from the silver carafe on the tabletop. "You know your coffee," he remarked. "But it still doesn't beat what comes in blue paper cups decorated with badly drawn pictures of the Acropolis."

"Another example of 'bad New York humor,' Jack?"

CHAIN REACTION

"Unfortunately, yes."

Picking up a menu, Keller struggled with the French descriptions of the culinary delights available from the train's galley. As he was making up his mind between the Poutines Aux Creme Brulee and the Ouvre Aux Jambone, a waiter in white livery came by carrying an oval silver tray on which Tanya's order had been set.

Jack ordered the ham and eggs and rolled himself a Bull Durham while he glanced around the car. Carbon copies of the aristocratic types from central casting he had seen in the bar car back in Paris now occupied the rolling restaurant, sitting with the cold rigidity of penguins clustered on an iceberg.

Tanya was right, he reflected. In this crowd the throwaways they had encountered in Paris would be as conspicuous as a stink tree from the Bronx in a manicured English garden.

Though Jack wore a sport coat, he seemed to be the only man not wearing a tie, even first thing in the morning -- though his turtleneck gave him just enough of an air of respectability, he thought, to pass muster among the

Mandarins. A two-lane secondary road ran past the railroad right of way on one side of the train, while on the other side was the apple orchard that Jack had seen before.

"Why do you think we've stopped?" he asked.

"Earlier I asked the steward assigned to our car," answered Tanya. "He told me that they were hooking up a second locomotive to push us through the Brenner Pass. We're also taking on water and coal for the boilers in each car. Though the Orient-Express is pulled by diesel locomotives, it seems the heating system dates back to the nineteenth century."

"I know," replied Jack with a nod. "I saw a guy shoveling coal into a small furnace on my way over."

"I was also told that we should be arriving in Zurich by around noon," she added. "There's a one hour stopover before the train moves on from there. Do you think that will be enough time for you to accomplish what you need?"

"I suppose it'll have to be," said Keller, who returned the questioning glance given him by Tanya. "What are your plans?"

"I've asked the trainmaster to phone ahead and book a flight from Zurich International to Bonn where I can connect with an Aeroflot passenger flight to Moscow."

Keller again met Tanya's searching gaze. Her large, almond-shaped eyes seemed to fill the universe, drawing him in hypnotically like drowning pools. He began to say something when the waiter arrived with his order, wished him bon appetite, and departed.

"Looks delicious," Jack said as he dug in.

"You were about to say something, weren't you?" she asked.

"Yeah, I was," he replied, looking at her squarely and laying down his utensils. "I was thinking how every man and most of the women in this car can't take their eyes off you. Frankly, I can't either, and that alone makes you an operational liability to me. It's really best we part company in Zurich, Tanya."

Jack tore his glance away and fixed his attention on the food in front of him, for which he had suddenly lost his appetite. Suddenly the train gave a lurch accompanied by the now familiar hissing of steam as the scenery began to roll past their window, paying itself out like a scroll of colored paper.

"Looks like we're moving again," Jack observed.

■

The train gathered speed as it negotiated the steep, tortuously twisting track that snaked through the Brenner Pass which spanned the high Alpine regions between Austria, Italy and Switzerland collectively known as the Southern Tyrol.

The orchards and fields of the French countryside were now long gone, displaced by the stony, pine-studded hills passing hard by the tracks on either side.

Every so often, above the incessant clatter of the train's wheels came the shrill, piercing sound of a double whistle, one from the locomotive pulling the train, the other from the one pushing it from behind, its mournful note attenuated to an eerily spectral shriek by the brooding hills. Twice diesel locomotives pulling long lines of boxcars, hurtling in the opposite direction along the adjoining track, came screaming by at breakneck speeds, rocking the Orient-Express with blasts of high-pressure air.

Jack was now working on a bourbon and soda and his fifth hand-rolled cigaret of the morning. Tanya had been speaking about her skiing trips in some of the small towns that dotted the Alpine valleys. Jack had once skied nearby, just across the South Tyrol in the small town of Martinsbruck, Switzerland, and they learned that they had stayed at the same lodge.

"But I found the Swiss rather cold," Tanya opined. "How did you come to regard them?"

"Actually, I like the Swiss," Jack remarked. "They're one of the few people on earth that are pretty much on the outside what they are on the inside. The Swiss will never bullshit you. They're mercenary bastards through and through, have been since day-one, but at least they make no secret of it."

"That's an interesting perspective," she offered, "though I'm not certain it's one the Swiss would appreciate."

"What really fascinates me about this country is some of the recent history it's been party to," Jack continued. "During World War Two the more fanatic Nazis planned to stage their last stand in these mountains."

"I know," she put in. "The so-called Alpine Redoubt."

"Right," he said with a nod. "Though Hitler and his goons never did get up the nerve to stage their final Gotterdammerung, they nevertheless managed to bury extensive caches of loot, secret documents and other artifacts all over this country. To this day billions in Nazi gold believed to be buried here are unaccounted for."

"There was also very heavy fighting in these hills during the final days of the war," she added. "Hitler was believed to be hiding here. My grandfather while very young was involved in a search by the Russian army for him."

"Is that right?" Jack replied. "You know, it's funny but my dad was involved in mopping up action in these hills in April of 'Forty-five. I guess it's a small world."

CHAIN REACTION

"Look, Jack," Tanya suddenly called out. "On your left."

Jack did, and saw what Tanya was pointing out. It was a high Alpine chalet perched like an eagle's eyrie on the pinnacle of a craggy peak.

"You told me in Paris that you had traveled on the Orient-Express once before," Jack recalled spontaneously. "I don't know if I have any right to know, but I'm kind of curious about it."

She paused for a few moments, then began, "Shortly after my recruitment I was given an assignment. An arms manufacturer who had developed a radically new cannon design had made overtures, through middlemen, to sell the design to the ministry of defense.

"It was to be arranged that I would make contact in the bar car of the Express between Paris and Zurich in order to secure computer data containing the weapon plans for evaluation in return for a stipulated price. I received the flash drive containing the data, passed on the information that the funds had been released to his numbered account, and left the car.

"The train stopped suddenly before we pulled into Zurich. One of the passengers had jumped or fallen off and had killed himself. It was the arms dealer. They had used me to expose him. A hit team must have been on board to carry out the execution. It seems the military had no interest in the weapon but did not want it falling into the hands of anyone else.

"It was my indoctrination. Apparently I had been judged trustworthy because from then on I was placed in the field on a regular basis and given assignments of greater importance."

Jack nodded but said nothing more, and turned his attention to the breathtaking views outside the window. He shook the glass in his hand to mix the melting ice cubes with the diluted booze and took a long final swallow, watching his ghostly reflection hover in the window over the streaking Alpine scenery and suddenly feeling very tired and much older than his years.

Twenty-three

*K*eller and Tanya exited the cab that they had taken at the train station in Zurich that had pulled up in front of the main Swiss branch of Credit Commercial. A glance at his watch confirmed to Keller that if they wanted to make the transaction with enough time left to get back to the train they would need to hurry.

"Wait here," Keller told the cab driver, who nodded in understanding, turned off the ignition and picked up a newspaper which he propped flat against the dish of the steering wheel and began to read.

Keller walked across the tessellated marble floor of the bank lobby, beneath a cathedral ceiling bearing more paintings than the Sistine Chapel. Approaching a teller's window, Jack stated that he wanted to make a withdrawal. The teller handed him a standard form with spaces for the denomination and nationality of the currency requested and numbers of the pertinent account or accounts, then asked him to fill it out.

Within a matter of minutes, Keller had taken possession of seventy-five thousand dollars in US currency in twenty, fifty and one hundred dollar denominations. It was a fairly sizable wad but not too large to fit in his pocket long enough to be transferred to a money belt he was able to purchase at a leather goods shop across the street.

"If we light a fire under our venerable coachman," Keller said as they were about to climb back into the cab, "we might be able to get you to the airport in time for me to reach the train."

"There's no time for that, Jack, and you know it," Tanya replied soberly. "If you don't get back on the train you could be stranded in Zurich for hours, maybe even overnight."

"You're right again," Jack had to admit. "I guess it's so long."

"Yes, I suppose it is."

"Look, Tanya ... I ... "

He groped for words, realizing three things at once: that he had taken hold of her elbow, that she had become very important to him, and that he did not want to let go.

"Yes, Jack?"

She met his gaze for a long moment.
"Nothing. Just good-bye."

He pulled open the passenger door of the cab and held it for Tanya. She silently got in and he shut it behind her.

"Take the lady to Zurich International Airport," he told the driver. "She has a plane to catch."

She turned her face away from him as the cab began to roll down the street. Jack stood outside the bank and watched it turn the corner and disappear. He shut off the part of his mind that was trying to tell him things he did not want to hear and looked around for another cab to take him back to the station.

■

Tanya confirmed that the flight she had booked was scheduled to depart on time and took possession of her tickets at the airline courtesy desk. The fact that the stylishly dressed woman had no carry-on luggage did not seem to phase the uniformed airline employee in the least.

Confident that she had sufficient time before she needed to be at the departure gate, Tanya went to a bank of telephones. She had an important call to make.

From her purse she took a device that closely resembled a pocket digital recorder -- which in fact it was, albeit one capable of playing back a recorded voice message at very high speed to deliver a reliable burst transmission over unsecure telephone lines.

Dialing a twelve-digit coded contingency number that she had memorized, she was instantly connected to a sterile telephone in Moscow. Upon giving the proper two-word recognition code to the female voice which answered, she was connected with General Vladimir Antonov of the FSB.

■

Keller had barely made it back to the train on time. Hearing the doleful sound of its whistle, he raced through the terminal and gained the platform just as the train began to rouse itself like an awakening dinosaur and began lumbering away.

Sprinting ahead to the nearest car, Keller managed to jump onto the platform and mount the iron boarding stairs. Leaning against a bulkhead as the train chugged from Zurich station, he felt his cigaret smoke-damaged lungs burn like fire and cursed himself for having been unable to break his tobacco habit even after years of trying to quit.

He walked toward the center of the train and reached the bar car a few minutes later. The car was packed with rich European snobs and their coarse American counterparts, but Keller managed to squeeze onto a stool at the bar where he ordered a double bourbon on the rocks and rolled another Bull Durham.

She had come into his life only the night preceding the day before and she had left him less than an hour ago, but already he was beginning to feel a yawning emptiness opening up inside of him.

There had been things to do and places to go, so he had been able to keep his emotions under control, but now he was back on the train and part of him expected her to be there with him, and he knew that he had to get a drink inside of him with all deliberate haste or he might start doing things that he would come to regret. Today, tomorrow and maybe even for the rest of his life.

DAVID ALEXANDER

Jack knocked back the bourbon and ordered another round, unable to keep from tuning in on the conversation around him. The piano man -- a jovial Captain Kangaroo type with thick gray hair, bushy gray eyebrows and a shaggy gray handlebar mustache -- was at his electronic melody station belting out a lively rendition of "It Had to be You" complete with synthesized mariachis and an acrid pall of cigaret smoke hanging over the car.

As the train pulled away from Zurich Station, now at breakneck speed, and barreled southward toward the Italian border, and the Lombardy region beyond, Keller began to tune in on one colloquy in particular.

An especially loud Britisher in an expensive silk suit had by now seated himself beside him. He was carrying on with a brassy Australian blonde in a Spandex cocktail dress, claiming to be a wealthy business tycoon and a self-made man who had amassed a fortune playing the Japanese stock market.

As the booze worked its familiar magic, Keller began feeling surly. But he was still sober enough to become aware that if he lingered at the bar, there was a strong likelihood of his putting somebody -- probably the Brit -- up against a wall, or failing a wall, through a window, or failing a window, ass-over-teakettle across the top of the bar. Keller bought an overpriced bottle of Old Grand Dad for companionship and went bravely back to the empty compartment, unwilling to risk the consequences of staying where he was.

■

The Orient-Express had crossed over into Italy a half-hour before and was now chugging at a fast, steady clip through the flat Lombard plains of the Po river valley only a few miles north of Venice, its final destination.

The bottle was one quarter full as the locomotive tooted its whistle and the engineer slowed the train to half its speed. It passed through the somnolent railway station at Vicenza without stopping. Businessmen clutching attaché cases stood on the platform, watching in fascination as the Orient-Express went rushing past, and Keller shot them the finger out of sheer malice.

"Jack, you are losing your fucking grip," he told his reflection hovering in the window glass as he downed another slug of bourbon, "you fucking hear me, Jack old kid, old pal?" adding with a drunken snicker, "but so fucking what if you are Jack, old fuck, old suck?"

Keller had run out of rolling paper and now lit up one of the dead butts he'd stubbed out in the large brass ash tray built into the table beneath the window.

The smoke tasted rancid and seared his lungs as he leaned against the metal window frame, wincing from the gray-blue ribbon that curled up from the cigaret in the side of his mouth. He watched the scenery flash past as the train rolled like a juggernaut through the flood plain of the Po over which towered the nearly perpendicular bluffs of tawny brown stone that made up the Dolomite mountain chain.

Now and then Keller caught a glimpse of a Renaissance fortress perched atop one of the high bluffs, a bulwark against plotting Medicis and warrior Popes. He thought about Cassino, one of the meatgrinder killing grounds that his father, then attached as a corporal to the

CHAIN REACTION

New York Infantry Division, had survived during World War Two. But that was another big house on a high rock in a different part of Italy, closer to Rome than Venice, and it had happened a very long time ago.

The Orient-Express slowed again in order to pass through the small towns of Padova and Mestre. When it emerged from the final station, Keller saw the glittering steel-gray waters of the Venetian lagoon suddenly visible on either side of the Napoleon Causeway, along which the train now sped at a rapid clip as though eager to get where it was going and get Jack Keller out of its system.

A brisk wind whipped at the waters and churned up small whitecaps and howled past the train, screaming a baleful banshee wail of welcome to the city that its bards have hailed with deliberate deceit as "The Most Serene."

Keller poured himself another shot of the giant killer for auld lang syne as the train slowed and pulled into the railway terminal in the city of Venice.

Twenty-four

*T*he frigid wind sluicing down from the wrinkled gray-blue hills rimming the outskirts of the training camp at Tal Mindar, Iran, the one the natives called the *gharbi*, had the caustic bite of corrosive acid flung viciously against flesh.

Wearing a lightweight nylon windbreaker over a crew-necked jersey and sipping hot black coffee from a waxed paper cup, Gregory Vanesco watched the specwar unit he had personally trained run through their third practice drill of the day on the mockup that had been constructed expressly for the purpose of honing their lethal skills to a razor edge of deadly perfection.

Cold and alert, Vanesco's pale gray eyes missed nothing. Any flaw in the performance of the troops instantly registered and was mentally noted for later correction. The team was made up of the best, the cream of applicants from the world's most renowned special forces units.

There were ex-Delta, former Russian Spetsnaz, a slightly crazy but coldly competent killer from one of the Israeli

CHAIN REACTION

Sayeret Motkal "Wrath of God" commando units, a talented shooter from the Iranian Shawarma specwar groups, with a death-wish exceeded only by his lust for blood, an ex-French Foreign Legionnaire, and others, including a few individuals who had learned their skills in the underground armies of terrorist groups like the German Baader-Meinhof and Italian Brigatti Rossi.

They had all been handpicked by Vanesco for their warrior spirit and their ability to perform the demanding mission he would require of his team.

The task facing Vanesco was to take these abilities and distill them into a potent mixture of ferocity, competence and will to win at any price.

Each day's training exercises began sharply before sunup and included a grueling drill on a survival course, target shooting in which every team member cooked off more than two hundred rounds of hollowpoint ammunition a day, and motivational sessions at which the day's errors in performance were scrupulously analyzed and reviewed in painstaking detail.

DAVID ALEXANDER

When the skills of the group had been assessed and their initial sheep-dipping into the training program had been achieved, Vanesco began instruction on the mission simulation range.

The range had been constructed by a contracting firm based in Hong Kong that specialized in building highly realistic simulations of actual mission environments.

The Asian contractor played the field. Vanesco was aware that the firm had only recently completed a simulation range for Delta Force's sprawling compound situated at Fort Bragg, North Carolina, and had incorporated lessons learned in this endeavor in improving the specifications for that used by Delta's chief global adversaries.

The range that had been constructed in Iran had been built from plans based on a series of aerial surveillance photographs taken of the actual installation, located a little over fifty miles southwest of the provincial capital of Dushanbe, in the Tatar republic of Tadzhikistan.

The simulation range incorporated several squat concrete blockhouse structures which had been constructed from a special type of cement-based building material that could absorb bullets during live-fire exercises without fragmentation or ricochets.

These structures were surrounded by twenty foot-high hurricane fencing topped by coils of razor wire. Since a considerable percentage of the actual target consisted of underground bunkers, these too had been duplicated in the simulation range.

The Hong Kong firm had offered the option of remotely controlled weapons that could be positioned on the perimeter to simulate defensive fire, but Vanesco had not taken them up on the offer.

To his thinking there was no acceptable way to duplicate defensive fire except by using live subjects during training exercises. For this purpose he deployed throwaways or "Dixie Cups" that Vanesco had culled from the lowest ranks of the Iranian armed forces.

Since there was no shortage of men deemed weak or untrustworthy whom the Iranians would in time kill anyway, he could be prodigal in positioning his straw dogs and sacrificial lambs on the perimeter, armed with automatic rifles and instructed to keep the invaders out any way they could.

They were doing this just now, as Vanesco sipped his rapidly cooling coffee.

Setting down the cup he raised a pair of high-powered binoculars to his eyes. From his aerial vantage point in a glass-paneled observation booth on a forty foot tower overlooking the training range, he focused his attention on different sectors of the mockup raid on the installation.

His elite unit, garbed in black Balaclava hoods and NATO pattern camouflage BDUs worn bloused over standard paratroop jump boots, carried mini-grenades hanging from load-bearing suspenders. They were also equipped with an assortment of small arms ranging from H&K MP5/10s to Steyr AUG rifles configured for the assault-weapon role.

The unit attacked with speed and precision as they had been taught.

Already there were casualties among the defenders, one of whom died before Vanesco's eyes as a black-masked striker raked a burst of automatic fire across his midsection at close range, ripping open his belly amid a hot spray of blood.

CHAIN REACTION

As Detachment-1 came in on the ground, riding fast attack vehicles of the sort used by US special forces troops to excellent advantage in both Gulf wars, Detachment-2 elements were STABO-dropped directly into the compound, fast-roping from the open hatchway of a hovering Mil Mi-6 Hook assault transport. A dozen troops hit the ground running in a matter of seconds.

The action to storm the compound was intended as a violent spasm of multilayered attack that would disorient, and quickly kill, the opposition forces before they could muster anything more than token resistance.

With most of the perimeter troops dead and the compound taken, and only a single combat fatality reported among his own troops, the second phase geared to take the underground section of the base was already underway.

An array of video cameras positioned along the corridors below the ochre sands of the Iranian desert showed Vanesco that his troops were now sweeping through the installation's subterranean portion and were swiftly securing this sector as well.

Less than a minute later, the base was securely in the hands of the invading force. Vanesco permitted himself a taut smile of satisfaction. The operation had taken less than seven minutes from beginning to end.

His troops were getting better, but there were still some areas that required considerable tightening up. He would drill them again, until they got it right, and if more of them died in the process, that would simply serve as an object lesson to the rest.

BOOK TWO:

CHAIN REACTION

Twenty-five

*T*he Adriatic had stretched out a paw, and like a mischievous alley cat, clawed at the small thing smothering slowly in its moist embrace.

Despite the massive, electronically controlled sea gates installed to keep out the ocean, seasonal swells brought cold surges of water up from the frigid depths that overflowed onto the Venetian streets.

St. Mark's Square was flooded. Duckboards of scrap wood had been spread across the flagstones of the ancient plaza as they had been on meaner streets and alleys throughout the city.

The inhabitants of Venice could be distinguished from the tourists by the rubber wading boots they wore, and by their stoic acceptance of public thoroughfares that had been transformed into miniature streams and lakes by the caprices of the ocean that had mocked them for a thousand years.

Venetians could try to stave off the sea but in the end they were doomed. In time the Adriatic would reclaim its own.

CHAIN REACTION

The city was built on hundreds of mud islands, its streets and building foundations supported by a layer of rubble heaped on rotting pine pilings. Every year the foundations sunk a little deeper into the mud of the lagoon. That the mud would in the end be victorious was a foregone conclusion.

Keller felt a spiritual connection with Venice precisely because she was a city perched on the brink of slow but inevitable disaster. He felt the same way about himself.

Sensing the futility of their situation, the Venetians had from the beginning surrendered themselves to a carnivalesque abandonment of decorum's rules. Keller had long ago given up trying to make sense of the game and lately didn't even want to play it anymore.

During the Renaissance, the Venetian clergy had openly consorted with harlots and sired illegitimate offspring, drinking themselves into a divine stupor in the process, none of which had hindered their ability to conduct the Lord's business on earth.

DAVID ALEXANDER

The descendants of those once-upon-a-time *cortigiani* still plied their ancient trade within hailing distance of St. Mark's church and Venetian merchants still took a perverse and traditional delight in selling authentic antiques which they had fashioned in their workshops only the night before.

■

The number six vaporetto-waterbus chugged and clanked along the Grand Canal between the San Toma and Ca' Rezzonico landing stages.

Jack Keller leaned over the painted steel railing on the upper deck of the boat, smoking a hand-rolled cigaret and staring up at the weathered gray facade of the steeply arched Rialto Bridge that the waterbus had just passed directly beneath, a cold cocktail of rain and sea mist stinging his hot, overtired eyes.

He had spent the last twelve hours sobering up in his room at the Carpaccio, an unpretentious second-class hotel that had been converted after the Second World War from the former servants quarters of a Gothic palazzo on the Grand Canal, and had placed an overseas call to Abernathy in New York, whom he felt he at least owed an explanation for his activities since he had dropped out of sight in Paris.

Abernathy had been more pissed than a Port-o-San at a rock festival.

"Where in fuck's name are you, Jack?" he had insisted on knowing. "Nadelman, who in case you've forgotten is our fearless fuckin' police commissioner, wants your goddamn balls for a hood ornament on his new staff limo. If not for my personal intercession you'd have been fired by now and wanted by Interpol on top of everything else."

Keller had waited until Abernathy calmed down a little and told him that there was no way he was coming back home until he had accomplished what he had traveled overseas to do, which was track down the terrorist leader of the Grand Central hit and see to it that he paid for his crimes, one way or the other.

"The so-called professionals fucked up like rank amateurs," he told the chief of detectives back in Manhattan. "From now on I'm doing things my way. I'll call you soon, Frank. That's a promise."

Keller had hung up before Abernathy could answer.

DAVID ALEXANDER

The vaporetto made a succession of stops along the broad canal as passengers came on and disembarked. Keller's destination was one of the final stops on the boat's route before the vaporetto made a U-turn and swung back along the canal to the giant municipal car park at Piazzale Roma that was the Venetians' single concession to the invention of the automobile.

As the maritime counterpart of a subway conductor pulled open a security gate and attached a thick, braided hawser rope to a huge and weatherworn iron spile on the stage, Keller trudged onto the quayside.

A dense, briny fog of gray, swirling mist hung over the narrow, zigzagging streets, cutting visibility to only a few feet in all directions.

Turning up the collar of his black leather jacket, Keller crossed a humpbacked wooden bridge into a shadowed alleyway that led into a pocket square with an ornately decorated wellhead at its center.

Feeling a little like a laboratory rat in a plastic maze, he stopped for a moment to consider which of the cramped serpentine passageways that led off the square was the correct one to take.

■

Gian Luigi Anjulo was the scion of old stock that dated back to the final Venetian Doge of the Renaissance, Marino Grimani, and like his esteemed predecessor sported a nose that resembled a warty cucumber set in a face that resembled a misshapen eggplant which had somehow grown a shock of bright red moss on its top.

He had inherited one of the minor palazzi in the out of the way Dorsoduro section of town. The ancestral manor did not overlook the Grand Canal but instead faced northward to the lagoon. Few clouds do not have silver linings, though, and what might have been a misfortune and a social disgrace to others had become a source of wealth, power and status to Angulo.

The isolated location of his palazzo, with its dock right on the lagoon, made it the perfect transshipment point for smuggled merchandise crossing the Adriatic from Eastern to Western Europe and vice-versa.

DAVID ALEXANDER

Since Venetian traders had flouted the law since time immemorial, baksheesh to the right parties in the Venetian branch of the Guardia di Finanza, the Italian Customs Service, which had the bewildering task of patrolling hundreds of narrow, twisting waterways in Venice, insured that Anjulo and his band of smugglers could come and go in relative peace and tranquility. For them at least, Venice was truly "the Most Serene."

Angulo's headquarters was a small restaurant, bar and *tavola calda*, whose miserable fare was deliberately intended to keep tourists, curiosity seekers and casual diners away.

It was said that Angulo had personally thrown three cooks into the canal outside the restaurant because they had prepared dishes that did not make patrons immediately vomit.

Its true patrons were the members of Angulo's fraternal order of smugglers, gunsels and thugs. Angulo himself did business from a back room from which a trap door led directly down into the basement of the building. A fast motorboat was always kept there, ready

in the event a hasty getaway was
required.

■

"I don't give a rat's prick whether or
not you are married to my cousin
Bettina."

Anjulo was berating one of his men
who had lost a large shipment of
contraband in the lagoon the night before
originating across the water in Trieste. It
had cost him nearly twenty thousand
euro, and perhaps more. "You, Fazio, are
a piece of shit, and you will pay for what
-- "

" -- *Scuzi, signore*."

The door had opened a crack and
Zuan, the portly bartender -- who
doubled as the hawkeye for the place --
timidly stuck his bald head into the
smoky room.

"Not now, Zuan, I'm busy," Angulo
growled.

"*Mille, scuzi, signore*," Zuan pressed. "*Mille,
mille, scuzi*, but the American outside says he is
an old friend of yours, a signore Keller."

Angulo jumped up, and telling Fazio
he would deal with him later, strode to
the door.

"*Che incredibile! Che meraviglioso!* Keller, it is really you!" he cried, waving his left arm excitedly, recognizing the man who had sat down, and releasing his right hand's tight grip on the butt of the small .38 caliber Beretta pistol in the pocket of his fashionably tailored silk sport jacket.

Anjulo ushered Keller into the back room and dismissed his men, though Keller knew that his bodyguards would always be hovering close by in case of trouble.

"I need your help," Keller said after the preliminaries had been gotten out of the way.

"Tell me how," Angulo responded. "And it is done."

Keller gave Angulo a brief but thorough account of why he was in Venice and why he would not yet return to New York.

Angulo regarded him through slitted eyes as he leaned back in his chair.

"There is something else too, no?" he opined, carefully studying Keller over steepled fingers. "You have a certain look in your eye, my friend."

Angulo's ugly face twisted itself into a shrewd expression. He made a fist and a smile crossed his features as he pounded the desk top sharply with the side of his tightly balled right hand.

"Yes! There is a woman, there must be."

"Yes, a very beautiful woman," Keller replied.

"Then you are a lucky man, *mi amico*."

"I sent her away," Keller answered.

"Then you are a fucking moron, *mi amico*," Angulo retorted. "But come, we won't talk in this shithole. I'm through for the day anyway, and as you know, the food here could kill a buzzard. We go to my place where we drink some good vino rosso, eh?"

Anjulo got up, stuffed a blue steel automatic into the pocket of his black leather jacket and raised the trapdoor on the floor near the desk.

"You still keep a fast boat handy I see," Keller observed.

"She is a brand new one I had custom-made in Milan. I would take her over any woman," he added with a smile. "Mario, Vincente, *andiamocene!*" he called to his stolid-faced bodyguards who looked ready to fight, fuck or die if the safety of their boss depended on it.

Below the flight of wooden stairs was a landing stage lit only by moonlight, and the anemic glow cast by municipal lighting from the narrow alley on the other side of the narrow canal it abutted.

The boat moored to the spiles of the landing was anything but shabby, though. It was a sleek-hulled power launch of a type the Venetians called *motoscafi*, constructed of gleaming lacquered mahogany. Keller knew it would be nothing but high-technology diesel engine beneath the hood and capable of speeds in excess of thirty knots even in rough seas.

"How do you like her, Keller?" asked the Italian.

"You were right," he answered. "The boat is awesome."

They climbed in and Anjulo turned on the electronically fuel-injected ignition. The Chris-Craft engine purred to life with a throbbing undertone of menace as one of the two muscular *bravi* cast off the lines and Angulo idled the launch into the canal.

He took it at slow speed for awhile, and they glided through the murky black waters in the eerie darkness of the Venetian night, passing alleys guarded by bizarrely lit stone gargoyles in which lovers furtively embraced, and beneath decaying limestone bridges fronting small, darkened public squares from

which music and laughter, strangely
warped by Venetian stone, drifted across
the oily black canal water from its
unseen wellsprings deep in the city's
black heart.

Soon they had reached the mouth of
the canal and were out in the shallow
lagoon separating Venice from the Gulfs
of Trieste and Venezia and protecting the
island city from the worst savagings of
the Adriatic Sea.

Angulo pulled out the throttle and the
boat leaped forward like a cheetah
chasing after a fleet gazelle. The engines
no longer purred -- they roared with a
deafening, thunderous cacophony -- and
the boat bounced and juddered as it
tossed up frothing white spray along its
sleek flanks of polished mahogany.

Angulo smiled at Keller and threw
back his head to give out a wicked,
braying guffaw as he clapped Jack hard
on the shoulder and cupped one hand
against the side of his mouth.

"It is good to see you, Keller, you
crazy sonofabitch," he shouted.

"And good to see you, you
unprincipled whore," Keller yelled back

with a gusto that easily matched his host's.

The palazzo was just ahead, lit only by the two caged incandescent bulbs on its landing stage that cast a feeble yellow glow on murky canal water and weathered, time-stained stone. Angulo slowed the speedboat and his men made it fast to the striped mooring pole.

"Watch how you walk," Angulo cautioned, "the steps are slippery and loose."

Keller climbed out of the boat and trod on slick, wet stone stairs eaten away by time and the sluggish acid waters of the dying lagoon.

■

Keller had forgotten how opulently the palazzo was decorated. Its unprestigious location away from the action at the city center in no way diminished the splendor with which its interior was appointed.

Angulo had one of his men go down to the cellar and fetch a few bottles of his best wine. As they sat drinking and looking out at the lagoon through the French doors of the terrace beside a crackling fireplace, Anjulo suggested he move from the Carpaccio to stay with him.

"The view sucks, as you can see," he lamented, "nothing but lagoon water at night and the occasional freighter and supertanker sailing past during the day. But here you can be comfortable as well as protected."

"I'll think about it," Keller promised. "But for now I'll stay put."

"As you like," he replied. "But for tonight at least, you are my guest. In fact, you may be of some assistance to me."

"Just tell me how."

"You know the smuggler's trade as well as I do from our days running guns and other materiel for the CIA. A young associate of mine fucked up badly with a recent shipment. I am forced to make good with a second run early this morning. It would greatly help to have a competent hand along, someone I can trust."

"I'm your man," Keller said after only an instant's concern about the proprieties of a cop engaging in illicit activities, albeit those winked at by Italian Customs.

"Good," Angulo said, adding, "You won't believe the money to be made these days, Jack. Since the Balkans went to hell in a killing frenzy there has been a tremendous need for my unique services. It's a powder keg even today. In fact I am expanding the business. I could use a partner.

"Fuck the police department in New York, Keller. The city is doomed, the Russian mafia, the Chink triads and the corrupt politicians and real estate developers run it. Your horny Spanish mayor, who studies the highway traffic of Paris and the chic boulevards of Madrid when she should be dealing with the problems of your five boroughs -- even she is a crook. Believe me, I know the score. Work with me, *mio amico*. I will make you so rich you will shit diamonds out your ass and piss champagne from the little hole in your long dick."

"Well," said Keller, pouring himself another glass of red wine, "I'll think that one over too."

Twenty-six

*J*ust before sunrise, Angulo's crew slid noiselessly away from the palazzo's mooring platform and into the calm black waters of the deathly still lagoon. The early morning convoy was made up of Anjulo's fast launch at the head of two smaller powerboats equipped with four-stroke Mercury Verado outboards.

They cleared the canal and were out in the lagoon. Keller looked left and caught a breathtaking glimpse of Venice as the first rays of the rising sun bathed the city in a rich wine-colored glow tinged with muted undertones of purple, yellow, vermilion and blue.

The cool air was thick with shrieking gulls performing crazy arabesques above the golden spires of Salute, their shrill chorus suddenly drowned out by the brassy clanging of a bell at the top of the high brick campanile in St. Mark's Square.

Its running lights still on, a passengerless vaporetto-waterbus coasted across the sinuous green canal waters toward the Ducal Palace where multicolored pennants fluttered in a lazy breeze. It cruised past a supertanker from Brazil docked in the artificial deep water channel on the quay directly in front of the ornate facade of the Do Leoni restaurant at the opulent Londra Palace hotel.

Turning to face the bow, Keller sighted the spiral of marker buoys indicating the deep channel to the outer lagoon islands to which the three boats were heading. There were several small islands in the Venetian lagoon, some like Torcello and Burano inhabited for centuries, others containing nothing but ruins, and one used exclusively as the city cemetery.

Keller grabbed for the gunwales as the motoscafo neared the first buoys of the cordon, and Anjulo opened up the throttle full-out as Jack had expected him to. The speedboat leapt across the water with a deafening roar as her powerful diesel turbine engines sent fierce vibrations rippling throughout the reinforced hull.

■

By first light, they had reached a small, rocky island at the seaward edge of the lagoon. Miles in the distance, Venice was now no more than a vague blur on the far horizon.

Keller noticed the ruins of some large buildings on the island, which was otherwise vacant except for a few stunted trees.

"What are those ruins?" he asked Anjulo.

"A Carthusian monastery," he replied, as he throttled down again and angled toward the island.

"The brothers were evacuated during a bad flood fifteen years ago. They refused to leave and had to be forcibly removed. The lagoon rose twenty feet above its normal level. Had they stayed they would have drowned. As you can see, the floodwaters completely leveled the buildings on the island."

As the boat neared the shore, Keller noticed a Boston Whaler refitted with a heavy deck gun that was docked at the seaward side, invisible from the lagoon side until anyone approaching was practically right on top of it.

"Looks like your associates are here already," Keller observed.

"I expect them to be," Anjulo acknowledged. "They are gunrunners with connections to all of the various factions involved in the Yugoslavian underworld; Croats, Serbs, Muslims. They cater to all sides. Our shipment is a consignment of US-made M16A2 assault rifles for which we are being paid in American dollars, gold bullion and Turkish cigarettes, the latter of which you may be surprised to learn is sometimes worth more than all the rest."

Keller dragged on one of his hand-rolled Bull Durhams and scanned the shoreline ahead of him. Though able to detect no sign of human habitation, it was even money that they were being watched with guns pointed at them from the monastery ruins.

He was armed as was Anjulo, and the five men in the two other boats were all carrying Franchi SPAS-12s and SPAS-16s, small automatic shotguns that packed a heavy wallop. Keller decided that under the circumstances the chances of a violent double-cross were slim.

"How do you contact your clients?" he asked.

CHAIN REACTION

"We have a system by which I listen for their regular transmissions at midnight on alternate days on a 60 megacycle frequency. My code name is 'Machiavelli,' who, by the way, happens to be a distant relative."

Speaking in a rapid cadence, Angulo issued orders in Italian and his bravi jumped to it. As a pair of them stayed behind to guard the boats, Angulo, Keller and the three other beefy, shotgun-toting strong-arm types crunched over the gravel-strewn surface of the island.

Before they had drawn abreast of the ruins, a group of men in black leather coats, knitted watch caps and military fatigues emerged from the scattered building rubble. They were armed to the teeth just as Angulo's crew was, but instead of shotguns which had always been the Italian weapon of choice, they ported mean-looking AKs of both long- and short-barreled variants.

Angulo stepped forward as the leader of the Yugo contingent did the same. The two men conversed briefly and then briskly shook hands.

Angulo turned to his group and issued instructions for the merchandise to be offloaded from the boats to the ruins. The Yugoslavian gunrunner did the same, producing several large olive drab nylon barrel bags stuffed with currency and indicating with a wave a stack of cardboard cartons containing Turkish and Egyptian cigarettes.

After another exchange, Anjulo and the head of the other smuggling band traded final handshakes on the deal. Keller noticed that the Yugoslavian leader had been eyeing him suspiciously. He continued casting glances Keller's way as he spoke with Anjulo, and though Keller couldn't make out what was being said, he was certain they were discussing him.

■

As they left the exchange site, Keller asked Anjulo what the glances had been all about.

"Chotek said he didn't recognize you," Anjulo answered with a broad grin, calling the Yugoslavian smuggler by name. "He said you looked like a cop to him."

"What did you tell him?"

"I told him that you were a cop, but that you were also a personal friend of mine, and besides that you were a cop from New York City which made you almost a criminal anyway."

"How did he take that?"

"He said if I vouched for you, then you were okay by him, and that he had a cousin in New York who worked as a superintendent in a building on the upper East Side. He said if you mentioned his name his cousin would show you every hospitality and could easily get you laid."

"Maybe I'll take him up on that one day," Keller ventured.

They climbed back into the boats and cast off again.

By now the equinoctial sun had risen to a low elevation in the powder-blue skies, hanging above the eastern horizon and casting a thin bronze-colored glow on the dark green waters of the lagoon.

It was getting warmer and some of the bite had gone out of the chill breeze that blew in from the sea as they backed out the boats for the return trip. The motoscafo's powerful engine roared to life and the powerboat thundered toward Venice with Angulo at its helm, laughing and joking like a rebel angel whose

DAVID ALEXANDER

hooved feet touched the earth and whose
dark wings kissed the sky.

Twenty-seven

*K*eller was garnering hostile looks from the waiter at Ignazio's Ristorante who had just served him his meal.

"What's his problem?" he asked Angulo as he sprinkled the flaky yellow powder onto the food on his oven-warm plate.

"You're putting cheese on your fish," Anjulo explained.

At a table nearby, two of his bodyguards busied themselves drinking red table wine and consuming heaping plates of semolina pasta a la carbonara so fresh it had been a lump of dough not twenty minutes before.

"So what?"

Keller had asked for a tray of cheese when the fish had arrived.

"Let us say that true Italians frown on this practice," Anjulo replied tactfully.

Keller continued sprinkling, saying, "Everybody puts cheese on fish cakes where I come from."

"Where you come from, maybe," Anjulo said, "but not here."

"From the guy's looks he'd like to bounce my head off the wall," Keller suggested.

"I know of several waiters in more expensive restaurants than this who have gotten violent with patrons over less perceived effrontery. Try doing this at Harry's Bar," Anjulo commented with a laugh. "We Venetians are passionate about food, more so than any other Italians I would say, even more than about women."

"I believe you."

The meal at Ignazio's, a restaurant that Anjulo had deemed superior to all in Venice, was selected in order to celebrate the successful closing of an important deal. The weapons transaction had netted Anjulo a quarter of a million dollars in hard currency.

Anjulo expressed his profound gratitude at having had Keller along with him. He again repeated his offer for Keller to join him as a full partner, admitting that he had taken him along in order to demonstrate how good the business could be for him, though also insisting that his presence had helped ward off trouble.

"How's that?" Keller asked as he chewed a mouthful of his fish under the basilisk eye of the waiter who shook his head disdainfully and muttered oaths sotto voce as he passed on his way to another table. "Everything looked smooth as clockwork to me."

"It was," Anjulo affirmed. "But it might not have been. The double-cross is always factored into the equation. It does not happen often but sometimes things can turn very ugly."

"Well, your men look capable enough to me. I doubt that anybody would want to mess with them without thinking twice," Keller observed. "Just get me the information on that blond bastard who organized the New York hit. That's all I want."

"It's on the way as we speak," promised Anjulo. "I've put out feelers. A day, maybe two at the outside, and you'll know what you have come to Venice to learn."

Keller caught the sudden flash in Anjulo's dark eyes as he spoke.

"What is it?"

"You must promise to be very careful, my friend," he warned Keller. "I've heard enough by now to know that this man is extremely dangerous. You are playing a zero-sum game in which there will be no second chances."

"I understand that. It's been clear all along," Keller said. "But thanks for giving a damn."

■

The main course was eaten and enjoyed, and so was the gelati served for dessert. They were sipping espresso and smoking cigars when the glowering waiter came over and spoke some words in Italian to Anjulo.

"He says a man crazy enough to put cheese on fish must come from New York."

"Tell him he's right."

"You can tell him yourself, Lafcadio speaks perfect English."

The waiter pulled up a chair and said, "You know Brook-leen?"

"Like the back of my hand," Keller replied.

"I have brother live in Brook-leen," he said. "I like to talk to you about Brook-leen, *per piacere*."

Anjulo listened and occasionally joined in with commentary of his own while he drank a

Sambucca *con mosca* -- with some coffee beans on top -- and then said he wanted to leave.

"It's getting late, Jack," Anjulo remarked with a yawn. "I must be getting old. The run out to the island has worn me out."

Since Keller's hotel was only a short distance away, Anjulo bid him good night and left with his bodyguards in train. Keller continued talking with the waiter until closing time, both men avoiding the sensitive subject of combining cheese and fish.

In time it had grown late. Keller got up, bid goodnight to the restaurant's staff, thanked them for the free bottle of anisette they'd parked on the table to flavor his espresso, and left the eatery.

Despite the last Sambuca he'd had for the road which had warmed his stomach as well as fuzzed his mind, Keller quickly sensed that he was being followed, and followed by professionals. Though unable to visually confirm their presence, Keller nonetheless had picked them up on his street radar, a sense that had been developed over the years and which had proved unerring.

DAVID ALEXANDER

The entrance to Keller's hotel was located on a pocket square at the end of the narrow alley-like street on which Keller now walked. The street took a dogleg near a humpbacked iron footbridge and went straight to the square. In order to reach the hotel itself, you went down a shoulder-broad alley that took a zigzag turn before blind-ending about fifty feet beyond the hotel's black iron gate. The only other way in was via the Carpaccio's dock entrance on the canal that ran below the footbridge, and that was inaccessible to him.

The way Keller judged the situation, his best shot at coming out top dog lay in reaching the hotel. Trying to outmaneuver a tail team in Venetian streets would be unwise. The streets formed a labyrinth with hundreds of dead-ends and the opposition might know them far better than he did. On the other hand, it would be hard for the other side to effectively position people in the alley entrance to the hotel where they too would be cut off in the event of trouble.

If they would try to hit him or take him, they would make their move before Keller reached the hotel, he judged. If he made it past that point, he could contact Angulo for help. There was no other alternative. He would have to risk it.

When Keller neared the hotel entrance on the pocket square, he noticed a shadow coming toward him from the mouth of one of the two other alleys feeding off the square in addition to the one through which he now walked. Turning, he saw that the surrounding alley mouths had been bracketed by men in windbreakers, and that all escape routes were apparently sealed off.

"Stay cool, Jack," one of the men said, speaking like an American. "We just want to talk, that's all."

"Then talk." Keller snapped. "But let's just cut to the chase. You know who I am and I know who you are."

"Who am I, Jack?"

"Casper the friendly ghost," Jack snapped. "Say what you have to say and then disappear."

"I'll spell it out in five words, Jack. Go back to New York. If you don't, it could prove hazardous to your health."

"Okay. You delivered your message. Now take a walk," Jack shot back.

His hand gripped the butt of the Colt pistol in his jacket pocket and he let the man who had addressed him see that he had it.

In that same instant he heard the sound of rustling cloth behind him. He had been wrong, Jack realized. They had deployed an asset in the alley.

"Tell your friend in back of me I'll blow a hole in you if he takes another step."

Keller saw the speaker shake his head, but otherwise neither of the spooks made an effort to leave the scene and end the standoff. It was clear to Keller they were considering a snatch, despite their claims to only be issuing a not-so-friendly warning.

They had not yet had their chance to talk with him, and with their kind, "talking" meant a one-way conversation while hogtied and gagged, and with bruises in places that didn't normally show as the minutes of the discussion.

Keller also knew that the situation would soon go critical. The speaker had positioned his people to make an easy retreat difficult. It would mean that he would probably challenge Keller, who would have to shoot him as he'd warned or lose credibility and be taken.

Keller saw the look in the speaker's eyes go hard and flat in a way that clearly indicated he had made his decision and was about to violently cross the line from assessment to action.

Keller steeled himself to shoot Casper in the belly when he heard a familiar voice behind him.

"I've got a gun in his back, Jack. Let me bring him out."

The voice belonged to Tanya.

Jack felt a dizzying mixture of elation, anger, disbelief, gratitude and relief that she had come to Venice as he stepped into the square. He kept his gun trained on the speaker, who took two steps backward at the same time.

Jack stepped to one side and remained flat against a wall as he covered the alleys to the left and right of the square. Another regulation hard man in a windbreaker came out, his hands raised high above his head. Behind him was Tanya, with the muzzle of a Beretta jammed against the small of his back.

Jack disarmed him and pocketed the small .380 Walther that he was carrying as well as the balanced throwing knife kept in an ankle sheath. Tanya frog-marched him toward Casper and backed off to stand on the other side of the alley mouth to bolster Keller's position.

"Like I told you before," Keller said. "We talked. I heard. Now get lost."

"It won't end like this," said Casper, no longer in control and barely restraining his rage. "Count on it."

Keller smiled grimly.

"You scare me," he rasped.

Casper and the man from the alley both backed off. So did others who Keller only now saw clearly. They moved from positions in shadowed hiding places along the widest of the three feeder alleys, quickly disappearing as they crossed the humpbacked foot bridge into another warren of narrow, twisting streets across the canal.

"Shouldn't we try to leave the district?" Tanya asked. "We don't have a boat and the immediate neighborhood will not be safe."

Keller shook his head.

"We're better off staying in the hotel until daylight when the streets get busy," he thought aloud. "Then we can make up our minds about what to do.

"By the way. What were you doing here? And don't tell me 'waiting for a street car.'"

"I arrived here about an hour ago. The concierge told me you had gone out but were expected back shortly. I waited for you in the lobby but got tired of sitting around. I came out and sat on one of the stone benches in the hotel courtyard looking out at the canal.

"Venetian stone plays tricks with sound. I heard men speaking in low voices from the foot bridge that crosses the canal. They were talking about you. I drew my weapon and hid in the darkness of the alley, waiting for them to make their move."

"I hate to say it, kiddo," Jack replied, "but it's a damn good thing you did."

They walked into the darkened alley leading to the Carpaccio's entrance, negotiated the right-angle bend between the two buildings that flanked it and felt somewhat better after shutting the heavy iron bars that fronted the hotel courtyard behind them. They warily entered the hotel, but the deskman's smile at the beautiful woman who accompanied the single male to his room did not seem to indicate anything amiss.

Locking the door and drawing the window drapes, Keller looked at Tanya.

"Your hand. It's shaking, Jack."

It was.

"So is the rest of me," he rasped. "The prospect of shooting a guy in the guts at pointblank range always gives me the shakes."

Neither said anything more. No words needed to be uttered. In the giddy aftermath of long, tense moments, the understanding that passed between them like an electric shock spoke with an eloquence that no language on earth could equal.

Jack took three steps across the room and swept Tanya into his arms, crushing her to him, feeling her breasts against his chest. They kissed softly, timidly at first, then more quickly, again and again in a heated rush, their mouths fused together, their tongues searching and connecting.

A church bell tolled from beyond the maze of dark, deserted alleys. A foghorn pierced the silence and voices on the night breeze drifted across the empty canals.

"Easy, Jack," Tanya gasped as Jack kissed her throat. "I want it easy."

"Then I'll be easy," he said softly in her ear as his hands found the zipper of her dress. "I'll be whatever you want me to be."

His mouth kissed her breasts and moved down her alabaster body, and soon they were naked together on the starched white sheets of the newly made bed.

Somewhere in the middle of it all, Jack looked up and saw their bodies entwined in the reflection on the convex surface of the white plastic lamp on the bureau while she clutched at his hair and he held her face close against his with his hands beneath the pillow.

And then the moment came, and Jack lost all sense of place and time as Tanya gasped beneath him and a bell tolled twice from some distant, empty, fog-shrouded square, to linger and then die away again as though it had never been.

Twenty-eight

*L*ike a latter-day incarnation of a Renaissance nobleman, Anjulo had offered his protection to his two guests. Jack thought that his friend seemed to relish playing the role of *podesta*, as if it allowed him to fulfill his destiny as the scion of his blue-blooded forebears.

"You, Keller, are a fool," he had chided when he had learned about what had happened after he had left Jack at Ignazio's the previous night. "You could very well have been killed."

"I know that, Anjulo," Jack had acknowledged.

"You should have accepted my offer of protection from the very beginning," he had gone on as if he had not heard Jack speak. He repeatedly slammed his massive fist down on the desk for emphasis, looking to his cronies for confirmation. "Immediately! *E fuor di dubbio!*"

"I completely agree," Jack had told him.

"But do not be concerned," Anjulo went on in gentler tones, "I, Gian Luigi Angulo, swear on my mother's sainted head that the fucking spooks -- may their pricks shrivel up like rotten peppers -- will not touch you here."

CHAIN REACTION

"Thank you, Anjulo," said Jack.

"My men will always be close at hand, and will be as vigilant as the partridge which sleeps with one eye perpetually open. If the spooks come around, the lupara will speak and their balls will go flying into the canal to be devoured by hungry fishes. In a short time, I will have gathered the information you need and will further assist you in any way I can."

"*Si, padrone, mille, mille grazie,*" Jack said. "Can we go now, padrone?"

"Not before I say one more thing," Anjulo went on, getting up and walking over to Jack and Tanya. "You told me before about your beautiful woman. But I had no idea that she would turn out to be as *molto bellissima* as Tanya. I would rather die -- die a thousand deaths -- than leave such a woman for even a moment's time."

■

"He's a sentimentalist beneath that cynical exterior," Tanya had remarked after they had taken leave of Anjulo. "I like him."

"So do I," Keller said. "Anjulo is one of the most honorable persons I have ever known. I would trust him with my life ... and have on more than one occasion. The fact that he skirts the law means nothing. The CIA runs more guns in a week than he does in a year. Compared to them he's a saint."

■

"Approve of the accommodations?" Jack asked, holding the two medium-sized carryalls containing his and Tanya's personal belongings.

"They're splendid," Tanya said approvingly.

The grand hall had a floor of polished terra cotta whose mosaic of inlaid colored tiles depicted a great map of Venice and the Levant during the city's sixteenth century glory days, complete with high-masted sailing barques and a huge face with puffed cheeks blowing wind into their bellying sails.

The floor gleamed beneath the ornate chandeliers which hung from a lunetted ceiling decorated with scenes from Greek mythology, commemorating Olympian triumphs of love and desire, picturing Leda and the Swan, Jupiter and Antiope, the Rape of Ganymede and the Virgin and St. George.

"That busty woman looks like she really enjoys what the big white swan's doing in that fresco up there," Jack opined as he scanned the ceiling decorations, smiling sardonically.

"First of all, Keller, that's not a fresco," Tanya told him. "Those are oil paintings up there, and if I'm not mistaken they're Tintorettos."

"Come again?" Jack said.

"Tintoretto was a Venetian artist of the Pagan Renaissance. I recall that he did a series just like this after one done by Correggio for the Medicis in Florence. These could be copies by a gifted pupil, but somehow I don't think so."

"Tintoretto, Schmintoretto," Keller said. "But I'll give your compliments to the *padrone*," Keller replied puckishly.

"You, Jack Keller, are a Philistine," she said and kissed him lightly on the lips.

"What was that for?" he asked.

"For being a Philistine," she said.

They were to have the entire upper story of Anjulo's palazzo to themselves during their stay. Anjulo had beefed up the security with more men who were stationed not only within the high iron fence but in the street as well.

Both street and water approaches to the palazzo were closely monitored by closed circuit television around the clock.

At the same time, Anjulo's extensive network of informants, thieves, prostitutes and mercenaries operating in and around Venice were putting out discreet feelers. Jack and Tanya were as safe as could reasonably be expected anywhere on earth.

At the end of the grand hall was a balcony fronted by curtained French doors. Jack threw them open and stepped out onto the balcony, beholding a panoramic view of the Grand Canal as a wind smelling strongly of Adriatic brine blew cold and hard against his face.

Boats plied the waters, horns tooting, windows and hulls glinting in the light, and shrieking sea birds wheeled through the crystalline blue skies. A church bell chimed the hour from somewhere in the distance, its clanging tones echoing loudly then slowly fading away.

Jack felt a hand on his shoulder and turned to look into Tanya's face. The wind toyed playfully with her long black hair and blew strands of it across her mouth and her eyes. With all of Venice behind her and the sunlight making her skin glow, Jack was again struck by her winsome, classic beauty.

He realized then that he was deeply in love with Tanya. It went beyond reason, beyond his ability to explain, beyond the fact that he was weary in mind and spirit and might not be thinking straight or that she was beautiful and that he had been alone for too long. But it was true, nevertheless.

They slid into each others arms and their mouths locked together. Intoxicated by her perfume, and the press of her slender body against his own, Jack kissed her throat and her eyes and clasped her tightly against him, oblivious to anything else in the world except for the warmth of her and the smell of her and the taste of her and the knowledge, unspoken yet certain, that she loved him as fully and as totally as he loved her.

But there were other, darker thoughts that Jack fought with all the strength of his will to push from his mind, thoughts that he would not permit to take form; not yet, not now, at least not for a little while longer.

DAVID ALEXANDER

■

The frosted glass door bearing the word H-A-R-R-Y closed behind Jack and Tanya as they emerged into the drizzle of a foggy Venetian night. The food at Harry's Bar was not as legendary as the ambiance of the famous establishment, but then again, food was not that of which patrons came to Harry's to partake.

They came to Harry's to view or be part of the menagerie of rich and disreputable high-rollers who made Harry's a regular meeting place and were its main clientele. Jack got the distinct impression that he was the most hated man in the place that night, on the arm of a woman who was the envy of all others.

They had eaten sparingly but drank liberally, putting away two vintage bottles of tart Frecciarossa wine. The visit to Harry's was courtesy of Anjulo, whom Jack by now referred to almost constantly as "the padrone," as were the two bodyguards assigned to protect them.

Jack slipped his arm around Tanya's slim waist as they turned the corner onto the Riva degli Schiavoni, the quayside that fronted the Grand Canal, and continued walking with the bodyguards in train.

They passed St. Mark's Square with the twin pillars that had served as the traditional site of important executions for hundreds of years, and the Venice Aquarium with its comically hand-lettered sign. Two waterbus-vaporettos slid by going in opposite directions, casting golden beams on the surface of the sinuous black canal water. Their horns bleated in greeting as they crossed in the night.

They stopped at the Bridge of Sighs and Tanya pointed out the ornate filigree designs along the middle of the bridge that masked a more sinister purpose. On their way to a beheading between the St. Mark's pillars the condemned could view the beauty of Venice for one last time and die with a pang of loss in their hearts greater than that of leaving life itself behind.

They turned and walked through St. Mark's Square. A Vivaldi concerto was being performed beneath fluttering banners and they stopped to listen for awhile before moving on into the claustrophobic warren of back streets lying beyond it. Away from the broad, lighted square, the streets were narrow and dark, and the chic shops of the Mercateria, the prime Venetian shopping district, were shuttered against thieves and closed for the night.

Behind them walked Anjulo's bravi, their hands never far from the weapons concealed beneath their long coats. The guns they carried in special elastic rigs were not lupara in the strictest sense, but compact Franchi SPAS-16 bullpups, their deadly modern counterparts.

The tactical shotguns were capable of dispensing the equivalent of one hundred .38 caliber bullets with the speed of a machinegun to devastating effect, and the bodyguards' vigilant eyes continued to sweep the dark alleys for the danger that might at any moment erupt with lethal consequences for those whom they had sworn to protect.

■

"I hope I am not interrupting," Anjulo said as he entered through high oak doors into the grand salon past the two armed guards that flanked the entrance.

"Nothing at all, just some incredibly good sex," Keller said.

"Stop it, Jack."

"He is always making jokes," Anjulo remarked, pinching Jack's cheeks between thumb and forefinger. "And you, cara, are too good for him. But now it is time for serious talk," he continued gravely. "I have some solid information for you both."

As one of Anjulo's men brought coffee and tea, they sat in the salon on comfortable chairs encircling a low table on which Anjulo had spread a variety of documents including tactical maps he had drawn himself. There was good news and there was bad.

The terrorist Keller was searching for had been pinpointed conclusively by Anjulo's global network of contracts at a secret training facility in northern Iran. The precise nature of the training exercises was not completely known and was the object of tight secrecy. But it was assumed to have something to do with a major offensive in the offing which would be led by Vanesco.

In Iran, the blond killer would be beyond Jack's reach, legally or extra-legally. But Anjulo's sources had also informed him of a development that nevertheless offered some hope.

Vanesco would be leaving for Brussels in twenty-four hours. The reason for his trip was to secure a consignment of specially-designed weapons from the Belgian arms manufacturer Fabrique Nationale and arrange for their rapid shipment to Iran where they could be examined, modified as necessary and distributed to elements of his strike unit.

"I have also spoken with connections in the Union Corse which has dealings in Brussels," Anjulo said. "For a financial consideration they would be willing to assist you in killing or abducting your man. I would suggest you take them up on the offer. I can vouch for their effectiveness personally."

Jack studied one of the tactical maps that Anjulo had drawn as a possible snatch scenario involving a moving ambush. Jack thought that Anjulo's plan had possibilities.

"I don't know how to thank you, padrone," he told his host.

"Just stay alive, Keller," Anjulo replied gravely, his normally cheerful eyes grown suddenly cold and dark. "That will be thanks enough."

∎

Anjulo stood watching the jet plane turn its white belly to the newly risen sun as it lifted off from the runway at Marco Polo International Airport. Anjulo had embraced both Jack and Tanya and all three had experienced deep surges of emotion during the leave-taking.

"Here is a direct secure phone number," Anjulo had said, giving them the numerical sequence. "Remember it. Use it to contact me at any time should you require my help."

After they had gone Anjulo had returned to his speedboat and sat on its deck smoking a cigaret, lost in somber reflection. Marco Polo Airport is built on an island in the Venetian lagoon and Anjulo watched sooty gray gulls wheeling overhead as he dragged the pungent smoke deep into his lungs.

His every instinct had been to prevent his friend and a woman for whom he had come to feel a close, almost fatherly affection, from embarking on what might very well become a suicidal mission. But he had known that there was no way to prevent them from going.

Both were seasoned professionals, and though Jack had never made it clear, he suspected that the woman was a trained operative as well.

Anjulo stared at the plane until it had become a mere speck in the clear azure skies and flung his cigaret into the Adriatic where it struck with a hiss and bobbed lazily in the current.

He would simply have to hope for the best. There was nothing else to do.

"*Hoi! Andiamocene!*" he shouted to his men who lounged along the dock smoking and talking. Climbing into the boat, he started the powerful engines and pointed her sleek prow toward Venice.

CHAIN REACTION

Twenty-nine

*T*he tall blond man in the black leather trench coat stepped off the crowded municipal tram and walked along the ancient cobbled street in the Marolles quarter of Brussels.

On either side of the spacious square were arrayed guildhouses with steeply pitched roofs and ornately decorated facades constructed in a unique building style that dated back to medieval times. The guildhouses still flew the colorful, fluttering pennants of the various unions of artisans that had erected them six hundred years ago.

The spray of water from a fountain in the middle of the square caught the rays of the midmorning sun, breaking them up into a thousand rainbow-colored shards, and sent dark rivulets streaming along the stone-flagged pavement.

Vanesco was blind to the sights and sounds around him, except as far as whether or not they posed him any threat was concerned. He had not made the tedious and dangerous journey from the training camp in Iran to Belgium's capital city to enjoy a tourist junket.

In fact, had there been a way to avoid making the trip, Vanesco would have taken it. He was intensely involved in the training procedure and the final planning for the mission. Furthermore, his capture, incapacitation or death at this point would severely jeopardize the entire scenario.

The many details attending to the operation consumed his every waking thought and reverberated through his dreams when he slept at night. So wrapped up in the fever of the mission was he that for weeks he had not craved a woman, though there was no shortage of available females among the terrorist cadres from a dozen national insurrectionist groups at the Tal Mindar camp.

No, had he seen any way around it one of his underlings would have come here in his place. But as things stood he had had no choice but to go directly to Brussels and attend to the transaction in person, as operationally unsound as this action might have been. The weapons being used by the trainees were not up to the parameters that Vanesco had built into the overall strike plan. That was the be-all and end-all. The weapons had to be right.

He had intended for his troops to carry FN Minimi light machine guns. The Minimi was capable of unleashing steel tumblers from its barrel at a variable cycling rate of 750 to 1250 rounds per minute. The lightness of the weapon contributed to its lethality. So light that it could be fired one-handed, the Minimi was as controllable as a conventional assault weapon even in full-automatic firing mode.

In this particular case, the Minimis on order had been specially outfitted by the manufacturer to accept Sionic-type silencers that had been computer-tuned to match the native acoustics of the weapon.

Ballistic firings of the Minimi had been monitored by an application that graphed the noise made by the discharge of bullets in an acoustic test chamber. The silencers had been custom-machined to precise tolerances that insured optimal performance.

The modification would permit the powerful weapons to be deployed speedily and silently during the tense critical seconds as the strike commenced.

DAVID ALEXANDER

The manufacturer had promised delivery of the weapons, but at the last moment had hedged, pleading production difficulties. Vanesco had the alternative of contacting the Singaporean manufacturer which produced the Ultimax, a weapon of nearly equivalent firepower and performance, but he had already given Fabrique Nationale a sizable cash deposit. Besides that, the Ultimax was not the gun he had carefully selected. The Minimi was. His purpose in Brussels was to personally take delivery of the shipment and arrange for it to be in the hands of his men as soon as possible.

As he prepared to cross an intersection between the square and an adjacent street, Vanesco felt a sudden pressure against his ankle and pivoted in place. His hand gripped the butt of a compactly-sized Uzi machinepistol, carried with a round chambered and bolt action cocked that was reachable from the deep pocket of his coat.

Looking down, he saw the colorful rubber soccer ball that had struck him lying beside his foot. A small boy was rushing toward him, followed by his mother.

Vanesco relaxed and stooped to pick up the ball.

The boy raised his hands and held them open, eager for the ball to be thrown to him. Vanesco tossed it lightly into the child's grasp while the mother watched him, a steadily darkening look crossing her plain hausfrau's face. As Vanesco levelly returned her gaze she took hold of the boy's hand and dragged him away without ever looking back.

■

"Here comes the bastard now."

Jack was sitting in an unobtrusively parked vehicle a half block down and across the street from a building in the Brussels warehouse district that housed the offices of a Belgian shipping company.

He, Tanya and one of the five Corsican mercenaries working under contract were in the first of the two vehicles used to run mobile surveillance on Vanesco. The rest of the team was in the minivan farther down the street, whose purpose was to burn any countersurveillance that the terrorist might have set up as a precautionary measure.

Jack and Tanya had arrived in Brussels the previous day to discover that the Corsicans had sent a man to the airport to pick them up.

Once convened in the basement of a souvenir shop in the Saint-Gilles quarter from which they operated, they had informed Jack that they had already put Vanesco under partial surveillance. He had arrived the night before and had gone directly to the Fabrique Nationale business offices first thing the following morning.

Jack had called the shots from that point on, and they had shadowed the blond killer's every move through Brussels, sometimes alone, most often in the company of a beefy driver who they figured doubled as his bodyguard.

It was now sometime before twelve o'clock in the afternoon, and Jack was watching Vanesco emerge -- his collar turned up against the biting north wind -- from a low-rise concrete structure that housed the offices and warehouse space of a shipping company.

CHAIN REACTION

"Marcel, your crew takes the lead," Jack said into the compact Motorola transceiver unit he had brought to his ear. He kept his eyes trained on Vanesco.

"*Mais oui,* Jack," he heard the Corsican reply a moment later.

Keller now felt -- as he had done since first laying eyes on the blond man in Brussels since his first violent brush with him in New York -- the urge to step out of the car and shoot him down in cold blood.

Jack's darker side urged him to put him down like a dog, in exactly the same manner that he had killed Augie and massacred a host of innocent bystanders for nothing but money and the twisted pleasure that the taking of lives brought him.

It took every ounce of self-control that Keller possessed to keep matters in their proper perspective. Apart from the possible legal repercussions of committing such an act, there was a moral dimension to it as well.

Vanesco had killed indiscriminately, killed like a mad beast. Keller wanted to see him die. But he was a cop, and everything he stood for told him that

Vanesco had to face his accusers and be tried for his crimes prior to receiving his well-deserved sentence of death.

The group was armed, and was prepared to kill their quarry, but only as a matter of last resort. Unless the escapade hit a serious snag, a snatch-and-grab operation was the way it would go down. The Corsicans had agreed with Anjulo's proposal of staging a moving ambush to take down the target, and it was one that Keller accepted.

The plan was to run Vanesco's car off the road on some suitable stretch of Brussels back street, carjack the vehicle, tranquilize him by using a syrette containing APAP/50-50, a fast-acting barbiturate compound, and bundle him off into the back of the van. After that he could be delivered to the US Embassy in Brussels for extradition to the US to stand trial for the multiple homicides in New York and whatever other charges might ultimately be brought against him.

There was legal precedent for such an act. Panamanian dictator Manuel Noriega had been abducted to stand trial in the US in 1989. The Achille Lauro hijackers who had murdered American tourist Leon

Klinghoffer had been forced to land in Sicily by American jet fighters after making an escape in a commandeered plane, and stand trial despite previous guarantees of safe passage to a friendly Arab state. The same would have applied to Saddam Hussein, had he been captured outside Iraq. It should have applied to bin Laden, too.

Keller gunned the engine and put the vehicle into drive as he watched Marcel's crew follow the Mercedes driven by the bodyguard, trailing the car at a discreet distance.

As he drove, Jack already had made a decision on how and when to take Vanesco. The missing puzzle piece was where to work the snatch, which would be finalized by a discussion with the Corsicans later that day.

Thirty

*E*ven for late autumn it was unusually dark the following morning. The streets bore a light glazing of rain that had fallen during the night and it continued to sift down throughout the morning in a cold, stinging mist that rivaled the "angel spit" of Keller's boyhood Brooklyn.

They had decided to stage the snatch on a stretch of lightly traveled back street in the Schaerbeek warehouse district not far from the shipping office shortly after Vanesco had left.

The ambush zone was selected because the street, which extended from the main avenue, formed an easily sealed off jug handle to the avenue. The rounded corner of the jug handle abutted the Frazenius Canal, while vacant lots and condemned buildings were to be found on the legs of the large inverted "U." The ambush would have few, if any, witnesses if it happened quickly enough.

It had been determined that Vanesco would have to return to the shipping office in order to make a final spot inspection of the arms cargo before permitting the crates to begin their circuitous clandestine journey to Iran. The weapons had arrived from the Fabrique Nationale plant late the previous afternoon via an independent trucking company.

If Vanesco held true to form, he would go there early in the morning and leave well before the noon hour. As for the shipment itself, the Corsican mob could deal with it at their leisure once Vanesco was out of the picture.

Because of the narrow time frame involved, the weapons would be worthless unless Vanesco succeeded in shipping them out within twenty-four hours at the latest. Keller suspected that the Corsicans were eying the weapons as an added prize that could prove worth a small fortune on the black market. He also suspected that Anjulo would almost certainly be a conduit for the sales. But he didn't much care what happened to the guns as long as they were denied Vanesco.

To help channel their quarry into the snatch zone, two of Marcel's men wearing the uniforms of municipal employees -- *fonctionnaires* -- would set up detour signs that would force the driver of the Mercedes to forgo the main avenue, and turn onto the jug handle road where the planned ambush site was located.

The car, like the other vehicles to be used in the ambush, had been supplied by the Corsicans who had the best mechanics in Europe working for them. From the way the car handled, Keller knew that it had been maintained by experts.

Jack glanced at Tanya, her eyes half-hidden behind tinted sunglasses, as he sat behind the steering wheel of the white Opel Speedster. Concealed on the floor beneath Tanya's seat was a compact Uzi submachinegun.

Though neither of them had articulated it in words, there existed a silent compact between them.

Until Brussels was over, until their quarry had been dealt with, one way or another, what passed between them would be strictly business.

A part of Jack ached to reach out to touch her hair and stroke her face and he wondered if Tanya felt as composed on the inside as she appeared on the outside. He had suppressed his own emotions as best as he could. But he knew that just beneath the surface they were there, like a school of ravenous sharks milling beneath the placid waters of a cool green sea.

Jack's thoughts were suddenly interrupted as he saw the blond man with the scar face reemerge from the shipping company building and head for the Mercedes parked nearby, his hands tucked deep into the pockets of his black leather coat.

"Get ready," Jack said into the radio, addressing the Corsicans dressed as *fonctionnaires* who stood poised to erect the detour signs and the other men riding with Marcel in the minivan unobtrusively parked several car lengths down on the other side of the narrow street. "The show's about to start."

He and Tanya both pulled on black Balaclava hoods and fingerless tactical gloves, and they checked their weapons one final time.

■

The Mercedes took the detour as they had anticipated it would. Jack could see the driver gesticulating in annoyance as he swung the wheel and downshifted to turn the black Mercedes Kompressor in the direction of the reflective arrow signs while one of the workers in dun-colored municipal overalls directed traffic toward the detour.

"He's on his way," the Corsican beside the truck said into his commo unit as soon as the Mercedes had cleared the area.

His partner was already throwing the detour signs into the rear of the truck that had been hijacked from a city garage the previous night, replacing them with signs stating that the street was closed. The minivan driven by Marcel turned the corner and the two fonctionnaires jumped inside, pulling Balaclavas over their heads and porting their loaded and cocked submachineguns.

As soon as the Mercedes was well into the ambush zone, up one fork and nearing the curved portion of the jug handle, Jack and the Corsicans swung into action just as they had rehearsed the operation time and again.

Leaning on his Speedster's horn, Jack mashed down on the accelerator and shot past the Mercedes until the Opel was right in front of it. Less than a foot separated the Speedster's rear bumper from the Kompressor's front end.

Jack suddenly depressed the brakes and slowed the Opel to a crawl as he downshifted the synchromesh gearshift into first.

The driver behind him blared his horn and shook his fist in annoyance, cursing a blue streak at the insolent Belgian in the white sports sedan. But despite his irritation he had no choice but to slow the Mercedes and match the velocity of the equally powerful Opel; Jack's breaking action forced the Mercedes behind them to drastically cut its speed.

When the trailing car had slowed sufficiently, Jack suddenly leadfooted the gas pedal and powershifted to fifth gear. Shooting ahead again with a squeal of tire rubber, he yanked on the parking brake to put the Speedster into a screeching bootlegger's turn, placing the Opel's driver's side flank perpendicular to the Mercedes and cutting off the road.

As the Opel screeched to an unexpected and noisy halt, the Fiat minivan behind the Mercedes came to a juddering short stop almost bumper-to-bumper with the Kompressor. Its rear doors immediately flew open and the hooded Corsicans emerged, black, ski-mask-like Balaclavas covering their faces and automatic weapons held menacingly in their gloved fists.

Jack had his silenced semiautomatic pistol up against the throat of the driver of the Mercedes, the stubby end of the Hush Puppy suppressor stamping a cold circle into the soft flesh just beneath the point of his chin.

Everything had gone like clockwork and the operation had unfolded too quickly for either the driver/bodyguard or Vanesco to think. This factor was critical in an operation. Give the opposition time enough to regain their wits and they can and will retaliate, often effectively.

"Turn off the ignition," he ordered, flicking his eyes across the street to take note of some construction workers engaged in a gut-rehab of a two-century-old building who had stopped to watch the commotion. When the stunned driver didn't immediately obey him, Jack shoved the gun harder into his right temple until the man did as instructed.

Vanesco said nothing but stepped out as he had been commanded to do. There was no shock in his darkly glittering eyes, only cold, reptilian menace. In a tactically poor position, he had adopted a posture of watchful waiting until an opening to act presented itself.

"It's a small world, isn't it?" Jack told his captive in a sandpaper rasp.

As he had expected, Vanesco did not reply.

Knowing how dangerous Vanesco was, Jack immediately put him up against the hood of the car and frisked him quickly and expertly, taking away the Mini-Uzi that he carried in an elastic rig beneath his long, black leather coat and handing the deadly little submachine to one of the Corsicans.

Tanya and two of the other Corsicans stood lookout with their weapons unsafed and ready. The remaining pair of Corsicans waited in the van, Marcel sitting behind the wheel, the other man behind the open rear doors ready to accept custody of their quarry and administer the syrette.

Jack pulled the disarmed blond man up by the back of his collar and handed

him off to one of he Corsicans who
shoved him at gunpoint toward the van,
meaning to drug him with the syrette the
moment he was inside while Jack stood
lookout.

Suddenly Jack heard shouts from the
direction of the construction site. To his
horror, he saw that a large steel hopper
brimming with construction debris was
careening down the sloping street from
the building under renovation.

Before he could react, the three-ton
steel hopper smashed into the side of the
minivan, staving in the midsection of the
vehicle with a sickening thud before
rebounding into the street.

Whether or not the collision was an
intentionally reckless act or a result of
carelessness on the part of the workmen,
the momentary distraction gave Vanesco
the opportunity he needed to make a
break.

■

Repeating the actions that had so
impressed al-Sharqi in the dictator's
Bedouin tent weeks before, Vanesco
pivoted quickly and grabbed the receiver
of the bullpup weapon trained on him by
the   Corsican,   simultaneously

sidestepping to avoid accidental or deliberate muzzle discharge in his direction.

Vanesco had wrenched the weapon away in a second and now trained it on its former wielder. A two-second burst cut the Corsican down, tearing away half his face and hurling him bloodied against the car.

Jack became caught up in an apocalyptic moment of sickening déjà vu as he saw Tanya raise her weapon and point the submachinegun at Vanesco, who had swung the bullpup's barrel around again.

The ghostly image of Augie Watson running from the cafe, his coat tails flapping, his service pistol held high, through the Grand Central Terminal main concourse weeks before flashed through his brain. Time moved in slow motion and events kaleidoscoped into a spinning vortex of violent shapes and harrowing colors.

Jack heard his voice shout out "Tanya! Don't do it!" as he vaulted the hood of the Mercedes and raced toward her, pointing his SMG in the process in the direction of the tall blond man in the black leather jacket. But he knew that it was already too late.

He heard the blowback-driven bolt clatter of the bullpup in Vanesco's hands as a burst of automatic fire cleaved the air, saw Tanya fling out her arms as she teetered sideways with her weapon flying from her grasp and clattering to the cobblestones.

Jack had reached her almost as she fell and spun to face Vanesco. With a snarl of rage on his lips, he cut loose with a burst of automatic fire and felt something strike him low in the side with great impact as Vanesco broke away and darted from the scene of the debacle.

Jack wanted to follow him but he found that his legs would not obey the commands of his brain. He managed to raise himself painfully to one knee, and that knee was soaked with blood from a pool on the blacktop pavement. He reached down to pull the Balaclava from Tanya's face.

Her unseeing eyes were open and covered with a milky glaze, and he closed them, and kissed her bloodied face and hair, mingling his tears with the crimson fluid that poured from her veins.

"She's dead, *mon chef*," Marcel said as Jack felt himself picked up in the Corsican's strong hands. "We must go or there will be trouble with the gendarmes."

Jack could already hear the sound of two-note police sirens growing closer by the second.

He vaguely felt himself maneuvered into the minivan and laid on the deck as the badly dented van became mobile and hastily left the scene. But all he could see was Tanya's face as she lay in death, and his soul began to close up like the shriveling petals of a blackened rose.

■

The field used for charter flights was located away from the main terminal area of Brussels International Airport and the pilot of the twin-engined Cessna 233-F waited for the light passenger aircraft to warm up on the tarmac.

He did not like the idea of carrying the single passenger who had chartered the plane, even though the man had been able to pay him in American currency and did not balk at the inflated charges the pilot had insisted on to undertake the trip, ostensibly to bribe airport Customs and security to look the other way at an otherwise suspect charter.

The American was badly, perhaps mortally wounded, and the pilot was afraid that the man might expire in midflight, leaving him with a corpse whose presence would be impossible to explain without casting his business practices under a most unfavorable type of scrutiny.

He had furthermore heard rumors about what the injured party had been involved in and these rumors frightened him as well. But the man's rough-looking friend had a gun trained on him, and in the end he had seen no other recourse but to chart a flight plan for Marco Polo airport in Venice.

The Cessna received clearance to take off from the control tower and taxied down the runway. It rose as it gathered speed and soon reached its cruising altitude of twenty thousand feet.

The pilot turned on the autopilot and permitted himself to relax. He swung around in his seat and glanced into the passenger compartment where the man who had hired him sat hunched with a gun in his hands pointed toward the cockpit and informed his client that everything was going according to schedule so far and promised himself that he would not turn around again for the remainder of the trip and never accept a charter of similar kind, no matter how much he was offered.

Thirty-one

*A*njulo waited outside while the doctor completed his examination of the man lying in the bedroom in a semiconscious state. The smuggler and his retinue of armed bravi had been waiting at Marco Polo and had rushed Keller to his palazzo via fast boat as soon as he was off the plane.

The doctor had already been summoned and was on board the speedboat, inspecting the wound as the boat raced the clock toward Venice.

His initial impression had not been favorable.

"He has lost a great deal of blood and there is a strong chance of significant organ damage due to peritonitis. I'm afraid the consequences might be fatal for this man."

Anjulo had looked the doctor straight in the eye and spoke with carefully measured words so that there would be no doubt about his intentions.

"This man and I are like this," he said, holding out his right hand and entwining the middle and index fingers. "If he dies, I promise that you too will die."

CHAIN REACTION

It was apparent that the doctor had not taken Anjulo's threat lightly from his manner, which had changed from one of clinical detachment to fastidious interest in his patient's well-being. He was afraid to meet Anjulo's level, unblinking gaze as he carefully cleaned the wound and applied an antiseptic dressing of fresh bandages.

Once at the palazzo he had rushed Keller up to the bedroom and telephoned for x-ray, ultrasound and other diagnostic equipment as well as an experienced nurse to be immediately brought in.

The x-rays were enough to tell him that the injuries that Keller had suffered were extensive. The bullets that had entered his chest cavity had glanced off one of the large ribs, shattering it in the process.

Fragments had penetrated the liver and spleen, but had missed the heart entirely. The doctor was relieved to find evidence that if Keller did not die within a short time from shock trauma or loss of blood, he had a fair chance of making a full recovery.

He operated immediately and removed all but two of the slug fragments, which were lodged too close to the heart for him to attempt to deal with right away without far more specialized equipment than he presently had available to him.

"What are his chances?" asked Anjulo. His stubbled face was drawn and haggard and dark circles underlined the hollow sockets of his sunken gray eyes.

"Barring an unexpected turn for the worse, I would estimate better than sixty-forty at the present time," the doctor answered encouragingly. "But he must be kept under constant observation. Should he slip into a coma it could well prove fatal."

"You will remain as my guest until he is out of danger," Anjulo had said, too tired to couch the command in less direct language.

"Yes, of course," the doctor had agreed nervously, with no choice but to accept the dictates of his host.

Seeing that the doctor was exhausted too, Anjulo had dismissed him and sent him, accompanied by two of his men, to a room prepared in the palazzo. He then went into the bedroom and sat beside Keller's bed looking at his friend as he slipped in and out of delirium.

CHAIN REACTION

■

Anjulo dozed from time to time throughout the night's long, solitary vigil. Once he was awakened by the sound of Keller's tortured moans as he cried out fitfully and tossed his head to and fro.

"Tanya ... Augie ... no ... wait till I ... no, no, no ..." His cries had ceased as his voice dropped down to a bass note of threat. "Bastard, bastard ... I'll ... Yeah, yeah, don't beg, don't .... "

Anjulo's eyes had reddened and grown moist in their wrinkled sockets. He knew that somewhere deep inside Jack's tortured soul his friend was caught in the demonic grasp of a cyclical nightmare, reliving the events that had obsessed him and turning those events to a different conclusion than had been the case in reality.

Earlier that day he had gone to the Church of the Frari and lit a candle for the dead and the living in the chapel. Though Anjulo was the farthest thing from a religious man possible, he had prayed to Jesus and Mary, as well as St. Bartholomew, patron of all who are seriously ill, to let his friend live.

DAVID ALEXANDER

Now, as he sat his lonely vigil late into the night, Angulo wondered how Jack would be able to deal with Tanya's death when he recovered, and a pang of guilt took hold of him as he considered that he might have done the wrong thing by asking the Virgin to spare Jack's life.

He had seen Keller's personality undergo a profound change because of the love the woman had given him and he could not be sure that having lost her in the manner he had done, Keller would still be able to function. The death of his own dear Maria had been violent and sudden; the victim of a vendetta long ago between himself and a rival gang-leader, and the terrible memories of it still haunted him in his dreams.

But that had been a different case, and Anjulo was the product of a far different tradition than that of Americans, one only his countrymen could fully understand.

He was a Venetian from whose perspective death and life were closely intertwined, if not parts of the same whole, like the Janus-faced masks worn at Carnivale by those who sang lusty songs as the black water-hearses of funeral processions passed slowly along the somber canals on their way to the ossuary at San Pietro Island.

Might it not be better if Jack died? Maybe yes and maybe no, he thought. But whatever the final outcome, the matter was now in the hands of God, not Anjulo.

With these thoughts in his mind he drifted off again for the last time that night while a cold wind howled across the lagoon and rattled the tall windows of the palazzo in their old wooden panes.

■

"The doctor warned you not to smoke."

"The doctor can go jump in the nearest canal," Keller rasped. "Roll a cigaret for me and light it, padrone."

"You should not speak that way about the doctor, Jack," Anjulo said as he reluctantly acquiesced to the wishes of his guest. "After all, he did save your worthless life."

"That's another reason he can go jump in the canal," said Keller as he drew a stream of smoke into his lungs.

"Well, you should soon be well enough to take care of that matter for yourself," Anjulo suggested. "The doctor says he is amazed at your progress."

Keller had rallied quickly and had snapped out of his delirium. By morning of the second day after his return to Venice his fever had broken and he was well enough to take liquid food.

The doctor had dressed his wounds, commented that he was beginning to heal and pronounced Keller out of danger. Anjulo paid him handsomely and the doctor left under the watchful eyes of Angulo's gunmen.

Anjulo's immediate fears that Keller would have lost his mental grip upon his recovery proved to be unfounded. But little by little the smuggler began to fear that another change that was potentially even worse had occurred just the same.

The change was reflected in Keller's eyes, Angulo thought. Before Brussels, Jack's eyes had been clear and open, eyes that looked at a man with penetrating insight, yet with unmistakable compassion. Now they blazed with a cold, dangerous light, shining like the glittering eyes of a venomous serpent.

Jack had said nothing about Tanya and Anjulo had not ventured to mention her name, thinking that it would be best to allow Jack to set the time to discuss her when he was ready.

But Keller continued to make no comment concerning the woman, or much at all about anything else, for that matter. His only request had been to be given a telephone and left alone. He had an important call to make.

Proceeding from memory, Keller had punched the access number that Tanya had given him into the keypad of the glowing plastic slab. A Moscow-accented voice had come on the line, a voice that immediately gave the impression of the speaker's authority and military bearing.

"The kestrel flies above the storm," Keller had said, using the recognition code sequence given him by Tanya just before they had left for Brussels.

Her instructions had been to place a call to the number in the event of her death, recite the code, which she had given him in English, and wait for the countersign.

There was a momentary pause and the voice answered in perfect English, "The lioness guards her kill."

Keller said nothing and waited.

"My regrets. She will be missed," the voice continued without revealing emotion. "How may I assist you?"

Keller briefly and elliptically relayed details concerning the failed snatch attempt in Brussels and his knowledge, via Tanya's briefing onboard the Orient-Express, concerning the terrorist strike planned by Vanesco that was to go down somewhere in the former Soviet client states on the fringes of Eastern Europe.

Stopping Vanesco was no longer a mission, nor was it an obsession. By now it had become the closest thing to religion that Jack Keller had ever known. He would pursue Vanesco to the ends of the earth if he had to, with or without the Russian's help.

"I'll need some reliable people who know the area. Weapons and ammunition too," he'd continued into the mouthpiece.

"They will be provided you. Can you get to ...?"

He gave Keller the coordinates of a drop site on the Yugoslavian coastline, just across the Adriatic in Trieste, and a rendezvous time by which to make the meeting.

"I'll be there," Keller said and disconnected.

He had one more favor to ask of Anjulo. "Contact your smuggler friends, padrone, and see if they can drop me at a spot somewhere on the Dalmatian coast," he had asked.

Anjulo regarded Keller with concern, but finally nodded. "It is done," he said.

■

Keller was sore but improving. His wound itched maddeningly, but the doctor told him that this was a sign that the injury was healing.

Although there was still a constant pain from the mending rib and the two pinprick-sized bullet fragments still lodged inside his chest cavity, it had receded to the fringes of his consciousness. He no longer needed the codeine-based painkillers that he had been taking for days.

Jack was sitting in the walled garden of the palazzo watching a barn swallow pluck a small spider from the trunk of an acacia tree when Anjulo came by to bring him the news that he had made contact with the Yugoslavian smugglers.

A mothership would be waiting for him just off the island with the monastery ruins the following morning, immediately before sunrise at five o'clock.

Keller thanked his friend and asked to be left by himself. He had a great deal to think about and to plan ahead for, and even more that he desperately needed to forget.

Thirty-two

*T*he shotgun-toting guard posted on the palazzo rooftop did not notice the black-clad figure who had silently crept up behind him until the thin wire garrote was tightly wrapped around the base of his throat. By then he was a heartbeat away from death as a gloved hand was clamped firmly across his mouth to stifle his agonized screams.

The ninja-style attacker dropped the limp body to the rooftop, and gave two clicks on the miniature commo unit held strapped against his chest by load-bearing nylon webbing. It was the signal to the rest of the team that he had dispatched his target and that the operation could now proceed as planned.

■

Keller sat on a comfortable chair in Anjulo's study facing the document-strewn antique oak desk. The two men were making last minute plans regarding Keller's next series of moves. A black bottle of Courvoisier Napoleon brandy from Anjulo's well-stocked cellar sat half-finished amid the clutter on top of the desk.

DAVID ALEXANDER

Littering the table were maps and pages of printouts that had been churned out by the color laser printer at which they studied charts of the area of insertion.

"That's quite a setup you have there," Jack had remarked, admiring the machine's futuristically sculpted plastic case and its large, panoramic high-resolution screen. "Where did an old drunk like you learn how to work one of these contraptions?"

"The computer and some other new *gaggia* were bought on the advice, actually the insistence, of my daughter Teresa, who called my traditional accounting methods 'out of date,'" explained Angulo with a smile. "I confess to you as a friend that I have gotten hooked on using it, although I still make a point of complaining bitterly whenever Teresa comes to visit."

He now kept detailed military-grade, and officially classified, global maps on disk. They had cost him a goodly sum, he added, but they had proven invaluable in the past, just as they were at the moment.

The walls of the study were lined with some of the weapons that Anjulo

349

collected. Apart from the well-preserved specimens of swords, battle-axes, poleaxes, lances and the like, some of which had come from Hitler's personal collection looted from Vienna in World War II, there were also an assortment of handguns and small arms dating back to the colonial days of the nineteenth century.

The semiautomatic pistols that served double duty as paperweights on the desk, however, were not part of Anjulo's collection. They were locked and loaded, ready to be fired on a moment's notice should trouble come knocking.

Keller was dragging on a cigaret. Though beneath his shirt his chest was still bandaged, the pain had abated to the point where he could now ignore it except when he moved in unaccustomed ways or breathed too deeply.

The only thing that kept him going now was attending to the many details of the upcoming mission and the satisfaction promised in taking vengeance on his nemesis that would follow in the wake of its successful completion.

DAVID ALEXANDER

After the mission, after he had done the bastard, done him good and proper, there would be time for mourning and soul-searching and self-recriminations and might-have-beens of every kind.

Until that time came, though, the mission was paramount. To Jack it was the only thing that stood in the way of encroaching madness and depression that loomed like malevolent banshees on the badly frayed edges of his fragile psyche.

Hate was the fuel on which he ran. It was his nectar and his manna. Hate kept him alive, provided Jack with a reason to go on, and Keller had given up the notion of bringing Vanesco back to stand trial. In the first place it would not be a feasible option under the conditions that would prevail in the global region to which he would soon be departing.

In the second place, and maybe more importantly, Jack's priorities had undergone a red shift into the warp zone of terminal resolutions. He was out for nothing less than blood chit now, and blood chit meant going the full distance.

Jack had taken one of the maps that had just come sliding out of the color laser printer and was inspecting it when he heard a sudden thud from somewhere in the building, perhaps from an adjoining room on the same floor.

"What was that?" he asked, his ears pricked up and his senses on the alert.

"Nothing, most probably a rat," Anjulo said with a dismissive gesture without bothering to look up. "The entire city is infested with them."

Jack was unconvinced.

"I think I'll have a look around anyway," he said.

He picked up the automatic pistol and walked toward the door.

The window shattered.

Stuttering starpoints of yellow-blue flame erupted from the automatic weapons held by the blacksuited killers who rappelled through the window amid a shower of broken glass.

Anjulo was struck instantly by a fusillade of hollownosed nine-millimeter bullets that passed through his body and shattered the wide rectangular screen of the computer, sending flame and smoke exploding across the desk.

Jack pivoted and tracked the weapon toward the first man into the room.

DAVID ALEXANDER

With the hammer already primed, a slight finger pressure was all it took to fire the nine-millimeter round sitting in the chamber.

The bullet augured through the heart of the faceless killer who could not sight his weapon accurately through the acrid billows of smoke pouring out of the broken machinery.

Jack kept pumping the trigger.

Bullets tore away part of the wounded man's upper chest which disintegrated in a shower of blood as he cartwheeled sideways and thudded to the floor.

Keller crouched behind a heavy table as a wildfire burst from the second man's submachine raked the room, chewing up the woodwork behind him and leaving a jagged line of bullet holes in the plaster wall.

Drawing a bead on the second man, Keller fired from a half-crouch, and continued to jerk the trigger as blowback pumped the slide and ejected the spent cartridges from the breech in a steady stream of brass.

The fire was accurate and deadly and the second man took at least two direct hits to the midsection.

CHAIN REACTION

The high-velocity ammunition had a high ballistic energy transfer rate. The expanding slugs caused massive organ trauma.

The injured man put his hands to the blood-spurting gash in his abdomen and took two staggering steps forward. By the third step his knees buckled and he fell against the desk, striking his head on a sharp corner. And then he slid to the carpet leaving a blood-smeared track.

Keller raced to the window and stripped the dead mercs of their Heckler & Koch MP5 submachines and their load-bearing webbing of as many spare ammo clips as he was able to carry.

Keying the captured transceiver set taken off one of the corpses he listened in on operational chatter that told him unmistakably that a carefully planned, multilevel strike mission was well underway. From the appearance of things the entire palazzo was under sea- and land-based attack, and most of Anjulo's people had already been taken down.

Keller hastily shuffled papers off the desk and took a final look at Anjulo, grateful that by now he was too numbed by events to feel the intense anguish at having lost so many good friends in so short a time.

With fresh nine-millimeter ammo clips loaded into the captured submachines, Keller sprinted through the door and jogged through the corridor, hearing the sounds of automatic fire echoing through the building as he made for the stairs.

■

The black-garbed figure lifted the small black ball but was cut down by twin bursts from the "Hocklers" in Keller's fists.

As the grenade exploded, tearing a hunk of masonry out of the building wall, Keller raced toward the speedboat moored at the dock. The commotion of many pairs of feet and shouting voices warned him that he would not be alone much longer. He turned the engine over with a press of the start button and backed the boat into the canal.

An explosion from another tossed grenade sent a spray of pulverized stone and masonry showering him as he roared away from the beleaguered palazzo.

Keller pointed both submachines in the direction of the lighted dock and fired the weapons simultaneously, sweeping his hands back and forth to saturate the landing stage with massed automatic fire.

Those attackers at the front of the group were struck and killed by the deadly salvo while the others at the flanks were forced to split up and run for cover. Sporadic but unfocused weapons fire was directed his way as he pulled out the throttle and shot the speedboat into the darkened lagoon.

Keller heard the clamor of an engine revving behind him and saw another powerboat suddenly swing into the lagoon from a side canal and give chase. He turned and swept a long burst of parabellum bullets across the stern of the speedboat, leaning on the H&K's trigger until the weapon's high-capacity clip ran dry.

Suddenly a thunderous explosion lit up the walls of the buildings behind him with a dazzling flash of blinding white light. Some of the rounds had struck one of the fuel tanks of the pursuit craft and ignited the flammable mixture contained inside. Dismembered arms, legs and other body parts plopped to the oily black lagoon waters amid a Mephistophelean shower of burning debris that hissed and cackled as it struck the surface.

Keller rubbernecked and saw that the palazzo too was burning, but there did not seem to be any sign of renewed pursuit efforts.

Across the water and far to his left, across from Giudecca Island, he saw flashing colored lights and heard a chorus of wailing sirens. The barracks of the Venetian police and the Italian Customs Service were both located on the Giudecca and Keller knew that within a matter of minutes the entire area would be tightly sealed off.

Running without lights, he cut power and navigated the channel buoys solely by the miserly light of the large yellow moon.

As the adrenaline high that he had been riding on began to drain away, Jack felt a sudden wave of depression and despair come crashing over him. Keller fought off the emotional inundation, knowing that to succumb to these feelings would be to surrender to the forces that would mentally wear him down and prevent him from realizing his objective.

CHAIN REACTION

Almost an hour later, he had reached the monastery island. A check of his wrist chronometer told him that he was still running ahead of schedule.

Keller moored the powerboat, concealing it as best as was possible in a makeshift hide site between piles of rocks and rubble sticking out into the lagoon and he covered the boat with dry brush and branch cuttings.

Then Keller trudged across the island to the ruins of the abandoned Carthusian monastery and settled down to wait. On the other side of the lagoon he could still see the faint light that marked the blazing palazzo and the many colored, strobing flashes given off by the gumball lights on the boats of the civil and municipal authorities that had arrived to investigate.

Keller soon became aware that a low-slung black shape was nearing the island, making barely a sound as it approached.

Watching from concealment he recognized the modified Boston Whaler as the same vessel he had seen days before when accompanying Anjulo on his smuggling run to the island.

DAVID ALEXANDER

Crouching amid the windswept monastery ruins, Keller flashed his light in the predesignated code sequence.

It was returned.

Men disembarked and approached him silently in the darkness.

The automatic weapon clutched white-knuckled in one hand, the torch gripped in the other, Keller sighted the gun along the flickering beam

CHAIN REACTION

Thirty-three

*T*he Russian Condor-class military transport aircraft lumbered down the clandestine airstrip and lifted off into the black, moonless night that shrouded the arid landscape of northern Iran.

A highly specialized piece of heavy military hardware was nestled inside the cavernous belly of the monstrous metal bird. Upon reaching the plane's destination it was to be disgorged like the sinister egg of a fury out of myth.

Trailing the Condor by fifty meters but matching its speed exactly and maintaining constant encrypted radio communication with the pilot of the aircraft, were two helicopters.

The one on the right was a modified Russian-made Mil Mi-24 Hind-D gunship, the feared "Devil's Chariot" of the Afghan war and other conflicts.

It, like the Condor, had been secretly flown from Uqba-bin-Nafi air base in northeastern Libya to a secret base deep inside Iran where its Libyan colors had been painted over with a camouflage pattern bearing no national markings to distinguish its country of origin.

DAVID ALEXANDER

The Hind was a heavy rotorcraft with almost three thousand pounds of its twenty five thousand pound weight solely devoted to weaponry.

A 12.7 millimeter chain gun and thirty millimeter twin-barreled cannons and crew-operated 7.62 millimeter Gatlings could pour sustained withering firepower on a target with precision accuracy. Swatter, Sagger and Spiral missiles could be vectored down on harder targets such as tanks or bunkers.

The third aircraft flying the mission sortie was a longer and lighter helicraft.

Like its sister chopper, this helo was also of Russian-origin, and had originated in the extensive military arsenal of Nafeeq al-Sharqi, whose recent low profile masked an extensive, ongoing military acquisition program that continued unabated despite the outward inactivity of the regime in support of global insurrectionist movements.

This helo, a Mil Mi-6 Hook, was a troop carrier aircraft comparable to the American Blackhawk and possessed similar capabilities. It could remain airborne at a low and very stable hover while the troops on board STABO (stabilized tactical airborne operations) dropped down to their targets by fast-roping from the chopper's open side hatches.

Sitting at the head of the crew compartment strapped into a canvas cargo sling, applying a woodland pattern of green, black and brown streaks of heavy greasepaint to his lean, almost cadaverous features, Gregory Vanesco looked at his men and flashed a grim smile across the cabin.

He had trained them well and they were mission-ready. Despite a number of recent setbacks, including the narrowly escaped ambush in Brussels where Vanesco had recognized the cop from New York who was obviously running a personal vendetta against him, the mission itself was still on sound footing.

Vanesco had no doubt whatever that the operation would be successful and that he and his fighters would soon be basking in the glory and reaping the gold that would follow in the wake of having carried out a terrorist action that would remain unmatched in the blood-drenched annals of human warfare.

DAVID ALEXANDER

Thirty-four

*E*ighteen nautical miles off the coast of Dubrovnik, Yugoslavia, the Jutka Star labored through twelve-foot seas against a two-knot northwesterly wind. The time was 200 hours GMT and the night was clear but moonless. The thirty-year-old freighter proceeded on a southeasterly heading with running lights doused at an approximate speed of fourteen knots.

The mothership had been lying at anchor in the Gulf of Trieste some ten miles from the line of treacherous fossil reefs that marked the extreme edge of the Venetian lagoon.

When Chotek's crew had rendezvoused with Keller at the monastery island, they had insisted on taking Anjulo's speedboat along. One of Keller's motives in hiding the boat was to prevent its being taken as booty. But in the end he had been forced to let the smugglers lash it to a hawser line from the stern of their Boston Whaler as part payment for services rendered and tow it out to sea.

CHAIN REACTION

Chotek had been on deck to greet Keller when the launch returned to the mothership.

Despite or because of the fact that he had just strong-armed himself a half-million dollar speedboat that had not been part of the original agreement, Chotek greeted Keller like a long-lost friend and boon companion. He threw his brawny arms around Keller in a comradely bear hug and clapped him soundly on the back.

"My radioman has been monitoring the emergency bands," he told Jack. "I know that there's been a problem with Anjulo. Tell me the rest."

"I don't know much myself," Keller informed him honestly. "There was a commando-style raid, a very well-coordinated operation. Two masked killers porting automatic weapons gunned Anjulo down right before my eyes. Other personnel were all over the building, and they were not taking prisoners."

"Who do you think was behind it?" asked Chotek. "One of Anjulo's competitors? The Sicilian Mafia maybe?"

Keller shook his head.

"The shooters were spook paramilitaries. Contract mercs but working for a well-connected intelligence apparatus," Keller told him. "I'd received a warning recently. Neither myself nor Anjulo had taken it seriously enough, I'm afraid."

"The strike was connected to your present plans, then?" Chotek surmised.

"That's the short answer, yes," Keller acknowledged.

Chotek nodded and asked Keller no further questions. "I'm genuinely sorry about Anjulo's death," he said. "He was one of the few who never tried to double-cross me."

He paused a moment then exhaled heavily. "Come with me to the bridge," he continued. "I want you show you something."

As Keller accompanied Chotek toward the helm, he took note of the physical layout of the freighter. Though bearing an outward resemblance to other cargo vessels, a closer look revealed a number of modifications that were anything but standard.

Radomes large enough to support sophisticated long-range radar telemetry, satcom dishes and antennas for microwave reception and transmission, and other advanced fittings were in evidence near the smokestack assembly.

Here and there, canvas tarp lashed down against the weather concealed the bulky outlines of what Keller surmised would be heavy deck guns. The freighter was a great deal more than met the eye. Keller surmised that he had only scratched the surface regarding the modifications made to it.

∎

He was not wrong, he soon discovered. Chotek's purpose in bringing him forward was to show off some of the sophisticated electronic and navigational gear installed on the bridge.

In total darkness except for the sterile light cast by an array of color flat-panel screens on pivot-mounts, flashing digital readouts and marked, illuminated push buttons on several large control consoles, the bridge resembled a space-age war room more than it did the helm of a tramp steamer plying the waters of the Adriatic, the Mediterranean and the Aegean.

DAVID ALEXANDER

Proud of his extravagant toys, the Yugoslavian smuggler showed them off to his guest.

"You are in good hands with us, Keller," Chotek declared. "We have the most sophisticated GPS, SATNAV, marine wi-fi and digital weather and tactical radars available. The original boilers were pulled out of this tub by the German specialty firm TKMD and military-grade retrofits installed in their place. We can do thirty-five knots if we have to."

Chotek pointed to a large, flat-panel multimode display screen. Graphical icons overlaid on a digitized topographical map had replaced the sweeping green line and fuzzy blips of an earlier era. Using a trackball to control a screen cursor, the radar system operator could open and close viewing windows, zoom in on selected focus areas and instantaneously play back previous data with the apparent ease of running a catalog search at the local library.

"It's impressive," Keller offered, studying the screen and noticing that some of the icons were closing with the ship. "Looks like we've got some company."

"Yes, we've been tracking some vessels belonging to the Italian Coast Guard for some time since steaming into the Adriatic from the Gulf of Trieste," Chotek said. "But don't worry, they don't have any reason to look at us too closely."

Keller's attention was drawn to the representation of the long coastline of the Balkan Peninsula, whose numerous outer islands and cays created a thousand hiding places for smugglers like Chotek who, despite the civil wars, and their lingering aftermath, had continued to prosper and who did business with all sides.

Chotek spoke a few words to the RSO in a Serbo-Croatian dialect and the man used the trackball to change the onscreen display. The screen now showed a section of the Balkan Peninsula situated several miles southeast of their present position.

A broken line topped with an arrowhead represented the projected course of the freighter. A flashing red circle marked a site on one of the cays near the Albanian coastal town of Vlore.

"Our destination," Chotek said to Keller, pointing a stubby finger toward the screen. "If all goes well, we should be arriving before first light."

■

Keller stood on deck, warmed by the steaming hot cup of strong black coffee from the ship's galley he had just drunk and the plate of hot oxtail stew he had just eaten, as well as by the hooded anorak that he wore against the chill sea wind that blew in from the north across the spur of land above the heel of the Italian boot and swept across the freighter's deck with the sharpness of a slashing straight razor.

The false dawn was passing, and in the first spill of purple light that painted the black reflective seas with a shifting palette of multicolored hues, he could see the brooding Italian mainland on his left and the rugged Albanian coast on his right.

Not long before, the freighter had plowed its way from the broad expanse of the Adriatic Sea into the narrow Strait of Otranto. The two Europes were on either side, and so were Keller's past and future.

CHAIN REACTION

In a short while he would be taken by launch to the drop site on the beach where he was to be met by the chopper promised by General Antonov.

From there, assuming that the chopper showed as promised, events would progress swiftly and violently. Keller would be flown east across the Balkans to link up with a classified Spetsnaz unit assembled in secret by Antonov and the final confrontation would commence.

Keller did not think about the events that had propelled him forward, driven him to the deadly brink of savage confrontation with the object of his obsession. The time for meditation would come later, after the scenario played itself out, and only if he survived the coming hours and days.

He cast his thoughts forward, fixing his entire being on what he needed to accomplish, at any and all costs, and he found to his surprise that his soul was now completely at peace.

Thirty-five

*T*he huge Condor transport aircraft reached its final waypoint after rendezvousing with an orbiting tanker plane over the Gulf of Sidra for air-to-air refueling.

The Condor went into a loiter pattern, circling the mission zone while the trailing Hind and Hook choppers broke formation and swooped down through the darkness, guided to their objectives by terrain-mapping infrared radars.

Although the base had been placed on high alert and its defenses beefed up with a contingent of additional troops, the quality of defense was poor, security measures either in disrepair or lacking entirely, and the troops little more than time-servers who even on their best days teetered precariously on the edge of insubordination and outright desertion.

While the Condor held its loiter pattern in the predawn skies above the installation, the two helos followed their well-rehearsed actions.

The Hind came in first, its gun crew tracking their electrically operated 7.62 millimeter Gatlings to saturate ground targets with deadly, swirling cones of green tracer fire. Every forth bullet on the feed belt was a tracer round. Apart from permitting the gunners to accurately tape their targets, the green tracers created a psychologically debilitating vortexing effect when fired.

As the gunship opened up, the yellow muzzle flashes of AK-47 and similar light weaponry lit up the compound of the installation. A heavy Norinco G-AA-01 twenty-three millimeter twin barrel flak gun boomed in deep counterpoint to the ratcheting of the small arms. Strobing sheets of blue-white light pulsed eerily across the compound as the flak gun's muzzle discharged bursts of antiaircraft artillery fire that rose skyward in a deadly, glittering stream.

The gunship mercilessly continued to strafe the compound, killing a large number of shooters in a matter of seconds. But its first priority was to take out the communications center, a prefabricated dome at the far end of the compound marked by satellite dishes and other antennae which were affixed to a nearby steel mast some thirty feet high.

DAVID ALEXANDER

The pilot of the Hind gunship selected two Sagger general purpose air-to-ground munitions and sent them whooshing from their stub-wing-mounted dispensers with a press on the fire control button of his joystick.

As the communications center went up with a bright flash in a roiling toadstool of yellow-and-black flame that sent thunder booming through the predawn blackness, the gunship gained altitude and swung hard around to deal with the troops manning the Chinese G-AA-01 gun which was firing triple-A rounds at the agile and deadly rotorcraft.

While crew dogs stationed behind the Gatlings continued to pour fire into the base, saturating the compound with heavy caliber rounds, the pilot selected a third Sagger, achieved confirmation of target acquisition, and loosed the rocket on an inclined groundward vector.

The missile plowed into the sandbags surrounding the earthen revetments protecting the G-AA-01 gun emplacement and an impact fuze detonated the shaped conical charge in its nose.

The highly concentrated fragmentation blast ripped into the emplacements, instantly turning the big gun into twisted, molten wreckage and cooking off hundreds of rounds that were stored in ammunition caissons nearby.

Since the chance of a random hit from the exploding ammo dump posed a deadlier threat to the Hind than that of the original triple-A from the flak gun, the helo driver gained altitude and yawed the chopper out of the zone of immediate threat until the danger finally passed.

Seconds ticked off until the slick carrying Vanesco's elite shock troops received the all-clear signal.

Vanesco gave the thumb-up sign to his troops and they sprang into the pre-rehearsed actions that had been practiced to perfection in live fire drills over the course of many months.

The drop manager tossed the reverse-woven nylon climbing rope over the side and a dozen men were lowered down its forty-foot length to the ground, executing a rapid STABO insertion from a dead hover over the compound with flawless precision.

As Detachment-2 STABO-deployed from the chopper, the first commando unit was already sweeping across the compound, their Ultimax light machineguns and Armscor thirty-millimeter autogrenade rifles dealing swiftly with those members of the opposition who had chosen to fight rather than surrender. Acting in concert, other assault elements subdued the wiser few with plastic cable ties and placed them face-down in a guarded corner of the base.

Those who surrendered would be useful later. For the time being, they would stay alive.

■

A heavy steel door barred entry into the blockhouse leading to the underground portion of the installation. While his men covered him with their weapons, Vanesco applied a prism-charge to the door and set the digital time detonator on the door-blowing munition for a five second delay.

Deploying for cover, the strike unit silently ticked off the seconds. At the zero mark they felt the ground tremble and heard a thunderous report as the heavy steel plate door blew from its frame amid a dense cloud of pulverized rubble and cascading dirt.

CHAIN REACTION

Their eyes shielded by specially tinted goggles, the strike crew next tossed flashbang grenades into the smoke-filled interior. The grenades gave off a series of bright flashes and deafening percussive reports capable of incapacitating any troops in the area of their thirty-foot detonation radii.

As the flashbangs went off, the black-clad and face-masked strike unit swept into the confined space of the accessway, loosing automatic fire at any and all targets of opportunity with intuitive shooting skills developed by the intensive range training at the camp in Iran.

At a junction in the corridor network that branched off from the command and control center to a circle of fifty foot-deep pits protected by two-ton concrete blast covers, the team split up, with Vanesco leading the commando group that made tracks for the base command and control center.

The layout of the base was as familiar to every member of the team as were the backs of their own hands. They had drilled and drilled and drilled until they had become well-acquainted with every twist and turn of the installation's corridors.

After Vanesco shot and killed an armed guard who had not brought his hands up quickly enough, the rest of the defenders surrendered and were quickly stripped of their weapons, made to lie face down on the floor, and restrained with plastic cable ties. Vanesco smiled behind his molded, bullet-resistant Kevlar tactical mask as he approached the base command center.

He knew that he had now begun the endgame.

In a matter of moments, the commo unit mounted at chest level on load-bearing webbing crackled with the news that the other elements of the strike detail had in turn taken their objectives without significant casualties.

Vanesco was elated to learn that the base was now secure. Keying the compact black transceiver he hailed the pilot of the orbiting Condor and instructed him to LAPES-drop the special cargo that had been brought along in its capacious hold.

■

CHAIN REACTION

The soldier had been selected at random from among those captured in the raid. Vanesco had nothing against him personally. But he had need of a subject to teach an object lesson and it was the man's misfortune to have been the first individual that he had set his eyes upon.

The portable communications equipment had been broken down and initialized. The digital video camera that had been set up on a tripod and manned by one of his troops was now in operational mode, the red light beneath its irising lens steadily glowing.

Vanesco punched the key that would electronically search through the frequency range for the transmission channel that he had programmed into the sophisticated signal-hopping unit. He soon received a visual confirmation that the channel was open via the LCD message display located on the unit's front panel.

"You have by now learned that the former Soviet missile base located in the district of Gissarskiy Khyr in the Tadzhik Republic has been commandeered by freedom fighters," Vanesco began, facing the videocam.

"Confirm this transmission and I will proceed with further data of great concern to you."

After a long moment's pause a voice came on over the line, almost completely free of static due to the digital oversampling capabilities of the advanced electronic equipment.

"Who is this?" the voice demanded.

"Identify yourself please," Vanesco counterproposed.

He would establish from the onset of the game that its rules were his alone to make.

Now a harsh tone began coloring the voice.

"This is General Sergei Valentinin of the Russian Strategic Rocket Forces," he replied indignantly, using the equivalent term for the American Strategic Command. "Now who the hell are you?"

"Thank you," Vanesco replied with a smile. "You may call me 'Mustafah.' I am a member of the Battalion of the Prophet Mohammed, an Islamic liberation group opposed to the Imperialist aggression of the former Soviet warmongers who are engaged in a campaign of genocide against my oppressed people."

Vanesco paused for effect and went on.

"I assume you are recording this transmission, but in any event make certain that our demands, which are to follow, are understood, as I will not repeat them.

"We require that the former Soviet Muslim Republics, now part of the Commonwealth, be immediately annexed to the Islamic Republic of Iran and the sum equivalent to one billion US dollars paid to the government of Iran in reparations for heinous crimes committed against the oppressed Muslim minorities. If these demands are not met, we are prepared to launch a nuclear strike against Moscow and other selected targets directly from this base."

There was a pause during which the listeners on the Russian end of the communications link were making a necessarily hasty threat assessment and discussing the terms that had just been presented.

He could imagine the chaos that was already prevailing as telecommunications lines lit up like a network of irritated red veins emanating outward from Moscow in all directions.

Vanesco only permitted himself a faint smile as he waited in silence.

He had the *apparatchiks* in his fist and would squeeze until they broke down and gave him everything he wanted.

After awhile the general came back on the channel.

"You have nothing to bargain with. The missiles cannot be fired without the launch codes and the codes are secure. Beyond this, the launch systems are old and no longer functional. We will make an example of you and your band of so-called freedom fighters. To a man you will rue the day you were born."

"I don't think so," Vanesco said with calculated sangfroid. "You will better understand the situation if you examine satellite imaging from the vicinity of the base as your Bright Star-10 orbital surveillance platform comes overhead in precisely...." he paused to consult his watch ... "ten minutes more. When you have examined it to your satisfaction, call me back on a one hundred megacycles frequency channel."

"You may be certain we will examine our data, my friend," the general retorted, uncertainty now having returned to his voice.

"Good. And one final point to assure you that we are entirely serious," challenged Vanesco.

His eyes flicked to the two commandos holding the bound and gagged soldier by the arms, signaling them to bring him toward Vanesco. When the man stood in front of him, Vanesco removed the strip of duct tape covering his mouth with a sharp pull.

"To further demonstrate that we mean what we say, we will now execute one of the installation's defenders, a man captured during the attack and selected at random to receive this punishment. Stand by."

The guard's eyes had gone wild and he had already begun to plead for his life and shake his head frantically. His pleas soon became impotent bleats of terror as he saw the combat knife with an eight-inch serrated blade that Vanesco had unscabbarded from his military webbing and now held menacingly close to his beating throat.

DAVID ALEXANDER

The captive's screams intensified, becoming animalistic howls, as the tip of the blade bit into the soft flesh covering his windpipe and hot, dark blood began pouring out of the severed jugular vein.

Vanesco wiped the dripping blade on the victim's uniform and ordered his men to let him go. The soldier flopped to the floor where he went into convulsions as the blood continued to pour out of him in pulsating jets.

Though it was all over in a matter of seconds, the screams of the murdered captive seemed to echo across the control room long after he had fallen mortally silent.

"Savage!" shouted the Russian. "You will -- "

Vanesco cut him off.

"A videotape documentary of the execution of the Slavic oppressor has been recorded and will be made available to global media. You have precisely one hour from this point to come to your decision. Use it well."

Vanesco abruptly severed contact and ordered his men to take away the corpse and clean up the blood that had spilled onto the floor and had already begun fouling the air with the sickly sweet odor of death.

The Russians had not believed a word of his story, of course. But once they got a look at what the satellite photos showed, they would have no choice but to take the bait, hook, line and sinker.

Thirty-six

*T*he rubber Zodiac stopped short of the waterline. Keller climbed out and waded through the cold shallows toward the spot on the beach where the signal light had flashed the recognition code minutes before.

Humanoid shadows detached themselves from the darkened dunes near the foot of craggy bluffs that towered above the windswept crescent of white sand beach. As they neared his position, Keller noted that the two men wore the Warsaw Pact variant of NATO woodland camouflage BDUs and the red berets of Spetsnaz -- Russian special forces -- troops.

"There is a chopper waiting nearby," the man in front said to Keller as the second man's eyes swept the landing party and the beach zone for signs of threat.

Keller turned and shook hands with the two Yugoslavian seamen who had taken him in to shore. "Thanks," he said. "Tell Chotek to enjoy the speedboat."

The landing party went back into the Zodiac and heeled it about, splashing in the shallows. It was soon plowing through the surface chop toward the dark bulk of the mothership anchored close by the harbor mouth and spectral against the slowly lightening horizon.

"I am Grigory," the man who had spoken said. "This is Piotr," indicating his identically attired companion.

"Jack Keller."

The two Spetsnaz climbed the bluff and after reaching the top began to dog-lope toward a stand of olive trees about fifty yards from the edge of the cliffside.

Though it had been masked by the sound of the waves and the roar of the cold sea wind, now that Keller was away from the beach zone he heard the sound of helo rotorblades slowly revolving in a recognizable idling mode.

Keller climbed into the open hatchway of the rotorcraft he identified as an Mi-26 Halo transport helo. Hard behind him, the two other men jumped inside, with the man who had identified himself as Grigory speaking to the pilot in rapid Moscow Russian.

The pilot immediately pulled back on the cyclic pitch stick and pushed down on the collective pitch controls.

DAVID ALEXANDER

The revolutions of the spinning blades increased in speed with a similar rise in their throbbing clatter and the drone of powerful turbines filled the air. The craft waveringly lifted on its skids and then quickly rose straight up to its translational altitude of thirty feet. It banked and sped due east into the night.

"There has been a development," Grigory informed Keller as he gestured for him to strap himself down onto the sling seats just as he himself was doing. "The base has already been taken by a group of self-styled terrorists."

Seeing the look of shock on Keller's face, the Spetsnaz went on. "We are left with no choice. Preemptive interdiction is obviously out. If they succeed, all is lost. We must now take the force option."

■

The jet-assisted helicopter reached its designated landing site in just under an hour's flight time. Below, the ground crew had been informed of the imminent touchdown and had made preparations.

They had placed glowing chemical light sticks in a diamond pattern to mark off the landing zone. The helo driver had little trouble setting the chopper down for a perfect landing on the well-marked LZ.

Once out of the helo, Grigory made rapid introductions to the members of his unit, telling them in Russian that the American cop was to participate in the strike as a full-partner.

Keller suspected that this speech was made more for his benefit than for that of the commandos, as the strike unit was obviously in a state of full readiness to go into battle and had doubtless been thoroughly briefed on all known contingencies, including the role that he was to play.

In any event, the troops looked formidable and battle-ready, Keller observed.

They were outfitted for commando operations in camouflage BDUs worn bloused over paratroop jump boots, their faces and hands cammied up. Hold-alls on some of their packs secured SA-14 Gremlin anti-armor rockets comparable to American Stingers while the strap rings and other metal surfaces of their AKR-Krinkov short-barreled automatic rifles were appropriately taped in order to reduce both noise and reflective glare.

DAVID ALEXANDER

The troops had the look of capable professional soldiers, but Keller remembered back to the GIGN cadre in Paris who had also seemed impressive. They had looked good too, as they had crashed their way into an empty apartment concealing nothing but the corpse of one of Vanesco's innocent victims, and had otherwise bungled every move.

Appearances, in the end, could be and often were deceiving, and only the outcome of the mission would offer conclusive evidence to Keller of the capabilities of these Russian specwar people.

Although Grigory -- like the others in his group -- wore no identifying badges or insignia of rank, he was clearly the unit leader and quickly and efficiently issued instructions for the contingent to pile into the transport chopper prior to liftoff.

Heavily freighted with men and materiel to its maximum load capacity, the Halo chopper wobbled unsteadily as it slowly rose from the ground, but soon achieved translational lift.

CHAIN REACTION

Once out of what pilots called the "thick air" close to the ground, and with added torque from the twin jet turbines mounted to port and starboard, the helo rapidly gained velocity and progressed at its full air speed of forty knots toward the distant strike zone.

Thirty-seven

*I*n the underground control room of the captive base, Vanesco was startled by the unexpected clamor of automatic weapons fire that he heard dimly from the surface level of the installation.

"What's happening?" he asked over his transceiver.

"We're taking fire on the perimeter," said a voice Vanesco recognized as belonging to the Detachment-2 leader. "The entire base is under attack!"

"Keep the attackers out at all costs," Vanesco shouted. Before going off-line he added, "I want a full profile as soon as possible."

"Affirmative. Out."

Moments ticked by while he ran through the possible scenarios that might explain the sudden attack. The base had been under his control for only a brief span of time and there had not been a chance to mount an effective counterstrike by Russian Spetsnaz units.

While there was always the possibility that he was mistaken, Vanesco chose to believe for the moment that a ragtag group of soldiers from some nearby military base had been pressed into service in an ill-considered bid to hit the base by some fool of an *apparatchik* in Moscow. Vanesco's pulse rate slowed as he realized that this must be the correct explanation. There was no other realistic possibility.

He would, however, have to make them pay for their mistake in underestimating him. Vanesco keyed the long-range transmitter and soon had the Russian general back on the line again.

"Attacking the base was a serious mistake," he said in flawless Russian. "I am going to kill more hostages and execute any members of the raiding force not already dispatched by my troops as a warning against future indiscretions of the sort."

"Raid? I know nothing about any raid," the general replied.

"Don't lie to me!" Vanesco shouted. "Do you expect me to believe you don't know there are troops attacking as we speak?"

"I have told you that I know nothing," the general repeated, in a strident voice which betrayed not the slightest sign of duplicity.

A muscle on Vanesco's jawline pulsed as a wave of heat rose from the center of his belly.

"I will be in touch," he said curtly and severed the direct comlink to Moscow.

Vanesco now began to think that the explanation that he had offered himself earlier was no more than a shallow prevarication to mask an unwanted awareness of actual truth.

As the sound of automatic fire intensified, he had no choice but to accept the very real possibility that a well-coordinated counterstrike not directly sanctioned by the Kremlin and employing special forces units had indeed been launched against the base.

"Chrome-Two, say your position," he spoke into the handheld radio unit as he hefted his rifle. "I need a profile now."

"We're taking casualties," the voice of Detachment-2's leader reporting from the surface level came back immediately. "These are trained commandos hitting us. Company strength at least. Probably more. Airborne and ground assault."

"I copy, Chrome-Two. Keep me posted."

CHAIN REACTION

Vanesco immediately knew with terrible certainty that he had a major problem on his hands as he stowed the commo set. Although he had prepared a fallback option in the event of just such an eventuality, he had not been mentally prepared to use it.

Nevertheless, there was now no other choice.

Going into the fallback, Vanesco succinctly issued instructions to his troops stationed with him in the command center. They were to go topside and protect the Libyan-supplied Hind-D gunship, preparing it for immediate takeoff while he attended to other phases of the backup scenarios.

As the troops left the command center, Vanesco turned toward the black computerized fire control mechanism that was linked by cable to the mobile medium-range ballistic nuclear missile that had been LAPES-dropped by the Condor immediately after the base had been secured.

There was no recourse now except to launch the missile preemptively.

At the heart of the more complex operational scenario that Vanesco had developed there had all along been the clear intention of hitting Moscow with a tactical nuclear strike. The outcome of the negotiations would be deliberately steered toward failure.

Once that happened, a domino chain reaction would take place, resulting in a far-reaching redistribution of power throughout the region.

The fascist hardliners on the Russian right would have their nuclear Reichstag Fire and could re-annex the breakaway republics on the rump of the former Soviet empire. Iran, to the south, would take the Muslim territories on Russia's fringes, while a return to Cold War-level tensions would stimulate military expansion and nationalistic paranoia in the West, which if past history was any kind of guide, would result in predictably reckless military adventures by Washington.

All that would really change would be the timing of the strike, thought Vanesco. Now it would have to occur sooner rather than later.

Using a key attached to his belt to unlock the protective cover of the arming mechanism, Vanesco input the predesignated launch clearance codes at a keypad on the remote handheld unit. The liquid crystal digital readout panel confirmed that launch clearance had been granted and that the missile's targeting and navigational data was mapped into onboard memory. Vanesco depressed the lighted red button that would automatically raise the missile and initiate an immediate ballistic nuclear launch.

Vanesco's eyes flicked to the readout panel for confirmation of the launch order. But to his chagrin he instead saw the message informing him that the launch system had malfunctioned.

With a curse forming on his lips, Vanesco pressed the button again and again, but he still could not succeed in initiating the launch of the missile. There were two possible explanations. Either the missile ground component's server had taken a hit or sustained some form of EMI impairment, or the main data cable connected to the mobile launcher had been disconnected or damaged during the attack by the opposition assault forces.

He had acted too late! he thought, and gnashed his teeth in silent rage.

But there was still a way to get the missile airborne, he realized all of a sudden -- providing it was the cable that was at fault as he guessed it probably was. A backup feature would enable Vanesco to initiate manual launch directly from the mobile platform if necessary.

The launch control interface unit could be plugged directly into a STANAG Type 2 connector located on the chassis of the MAZ 543 tracked launch vehicle by means of a locking patch cable in order to permit activation from close proximity. Vanesco placed the launch controller into a rucksack and hefted his Ultimax light machinegun. Then he got moving at a fast jog along the corridors of the embattled missile base.

■

On the surface, he found that the installation was in a state of utter chaos. The attackers had made short work of his men and were very rapidly consolidating their gains against pockets of determined, though steadily dwindling resistance.

CHAIN REACTION

Vanesco had one fear, and this was that the mobile launcher had already fallen into the hands of the raiders. But on reaching it he was relieved to find that the MAZ was still being held by his own troops.

Amid the racket of intensifying automatic fire, he rushed toward the launch truck, just as he saw a fireball erupt from the Hook transport chopper parked across the compound as incandescent tracer rounds struck it amidships and set off the highly flammable fuel in its storage tanks.

It would be prudent to get the still intact Hind gunship airborne and strafe the compound, he thought. But that would certainly complicate his own plans to stage a fighting extraction from the base as soon as he had launched the intermediate-range nuke on Moscow.

With his troops covering him, Vanesco unshipped the launch controller and plugged the back-up interface cable into the dataport connector on the side of the MAZ mobile launcher.

The handheld unit's readout display now showed that the system was fully operational, confirming his original guess that it had been damage to the main data cable that had caused the initial malfunction.

Untethering the secondary cable to its blast-safe length of twenty meters, he used the small joystick on one side of the control panel to manually raise the missile into a vertical launch position. With the high-pitched whine of pneumatic lift actuators responding to his commands, the missile slowly began to rise from a horizontal attitude on the back of the launch vehicle and assume its fully erect launch posture.

In only a matter of seconds, the medium-range ballistic nuclear weapon would be ready to fire. Vanesco had then only to re-input the launch clearance codes and it would be done.

Thirty-eight

*T*he commando beside Keller suddenly gasped as the rear of his head exploded in a shower of blood and spinning chunks of shattered cranial bone.

The Spetsnaz tripped over his own legs and went down hard on his face and lay on the ground without moving. Keller fired on the run and tossed a fragmentation grenade at the source of the weapons fire that had taken down the Russian, simultaneously breaking to one side. Another surviving trooper tossed the grenade he'd pulled from load-bearing suspenders and did the same.

As the two fragmentation grenades exploded, Keller popped up and discharged a multiround burst from his Krinkov assault rifle into the cordon of troops protecting the heavy, six-wheeled, mobile launch vehicle on the back of which a missile was now standing in a fully vertical position.

Keller and the other Spetsnaz had seen the MAZ 543 mobile launch vehicle as they rounded a corner between two blockhouse structures and had immediately recognized the nuclear ballistic missile for what it was.

As they were met with fierce defensive fire, Keller glimpsed the blond man standing off to one side of the launch vehicle and manipulating a handheld electronic device linked via cable to the MAZ. An icy rage gripped his heart.

Vanesco was preparing to manually launch the bird!

The combination of the grenade strikes and time-on-target burstfire from the two automatic rifles had decimated the enemy troops. Keller now pitched a second grenade and ran headlong toward the MAZ truck, firing from a running crouch as he loped across the shattered waste ground.

There was a high risk of sustaining a lethal hit but there was no alternative. It was apparent that only moments remained before the missile was launched. Were that to happen everything else that had preceded tonight's counterstrike would have been in vain.

Keller heard a grunt and realized that the other Spetsnaz had taken a hit in the side as he crouched down to one knee and prepared to fire an SA-14 missile directly at the launch vehicle. The Russian commando fell to the ground in a heavy sprawl, grimacing in pain as the armed weapon went flying from his hands and skidded in the dirt. His hands clawed at the bloodied earth for a moment and then he went totally still.

Keller continued working the Krinkov, taking down the final two defenders with wide arcs of automatic fire, ejecting the spent clip and reloading on the run.

The rear of the heavy MAZ truck grew in his visual field as he came nearer to his destination.

His senses seemed surrounded by the dark cylindrical walls of a perceptual tunnel through which he could see only the blond man with his hand manipulating the joystick on the control panel and the other hand reaching for a weapon dangling at his side on the end of an elastic TEAM strap.

Vanesco's eyes locked with his and Keller burst-fired the Krinkov, hearing the sounds of bullets ricocheting off metal as slug fragments tore into the electronic mechanism clutched by the terrorist thrill-killer.

Keller squeezed the Krinkov's trigger again but the automatic rifle had either jammed or run dry.

With the rifle useless, Keller drew his combat knife and rushed at the blond man, reaching him as he fired a wild burst from the Ultimax into the air. The drum-fed automatic weapon went tumbling away from Vanesco's grasp. The two men fell to the frozen ground, each grappling with the other in a mortal struggle for supremacy.

Keller stabbed toward the blond man's throat with the combat knife, but Vanesco was both strong and determined to survive. Keller's death strike was deflected. In retaliation Vanesco managed to deliver a savage hand blow to Keller's face, stunning him and sending the knife clattering from senseless fingers.

Vanesco gasped for breath and rallied himself as he rose shakily to his feet. He risked a glance over his shoulder toward the waiting gunship. The Hind-D was still on the ground, intact and with its rotors dishing. But it would be dangerous to linger with the firefight to retake the base still at full operational tempo. The helo could be blown to bits at any second, cutting off his chances of escape with irreversible finality.

Nevertheless, he could not deny himself the pleasure of killing the cop whom he recognized from New York, the same one who had trailed him to Paris and Brussels and would have succeeded in capturing him there if not for a completely unexpected contretemps.

While Jack lay dazed on the ground, Vanesco calmly walked to where the dropped Ultimax had fallen and picked up the lightweight drum-fed machinegun.

Leveling its flash-suppressed barrel at Keller, he thumbed the fire-select button from burst mode to full automatic, meaning to empty however much ammo remained in its hundred-round capacity drum magazine into the cop's writhing torso.

A tremendous explosion made the ground shudder, almost knocking Vanesco off his feet.

The clamor of a fifty-five millimeter mortar detonation had suddenly erupted from directly behind him, and Vanesco turned in stark, wide-eyed horror to see that a huge smoking crater had been blown in the ground only a matter of yards from the idling Hind.

Dense, acrid-smelling cordite smoke and swirling dust rose from the mortar strike and sluiced across the compound in thick, billowing sheets, cutting off his view of the helpless man on the ground.

Vanesco could not afford to linger a second longer.

There would be other missions and other paymasters, and most importantly, other chances to pay Keller back with interest. The cop would live, but then, so would he.

Wheeling about, Vanesco ran toward the gunship, dodging stray rounds streaking across the blast-scorched earth as the last of his elite specwarriors fell to the superior invading force.

■

Keller rose clumsily to his feet and tried to orient himself despite his dizzily swimming senses. He heard the deafening clatter of the Hind's dishing rotorblades as the gunship lifted off and deduced what was happening in a sickening flash of comprehension.

Vanesco was making good his escape. Once again he would vanish and go to ground. Once again, Keller had allowed him to slip right through his fingers.

A sudden wave of dark depression crashed over Keller as he desperately cast about for a way to salvage the situation, though it seemed like yet another, and probably the final, shutout.

A mortar shell exploded nearby, lighting up the compound with a hellish white phosphorescent flicker and Keller's eyes suddenly fell on the long, tubular object lying near the corpse of one of the fallen Spetsnaz. Keller ran toward it with all the speed he could muster, as though he had just seen the face of redemption itself.

■

As the chopper climbed rapidly toward its translational altitude, Vanesco surveyed the situation below with the calm, appraising eye of a man who was no longer caught up in the heat of battle or in any real danger of losing his life.

It was apparent that the Spetsnaz were quickly consolidating control over the base. He had executed his escape not a moment too soon. Only seconds more, and he would have either been killed or captured or the chopper now spiriting him to freedom destroyed beyond hope of salvage.

Vanesco regretted not having had the satisfaction of killing the cop, but consoled himself with the realization that this only meant that the moment of reckoning had been put off awhile, not lost entirely.

Vanesco made a mental note to pay Keller a visit at some point in the future when he had occasion to next spend some time in New York City. He would make the police lieutenant's death an especially slow and painful one, he promised himself, one he would recall with relish for years to come.

A drifting veil of dense smoke temporarily obscured sight of the ground below the chopper. But when it cleared, Vanesco was able to see something below that quickly changed the smirk on his face to a deeply articulated frown.

Almost directly beneath the chopper's belly, the American cop was holding a man-portable heat seeker on his shoulder. The SA-14 was as advanced as the American Stinger missile that had taken a serious toll in the Soviets' Afghan war of precisely the type of gunship he was now flying.

Vanesco immediately jumped behind one of the helo's electrically operated Gatlings and positioned himself to fire the weapon. Flipping on its activation switch he heard the high-pitched whine as the motorized barrels began spinning at tremendous speed. He angled the gun down toward the target below.

Depressing the spade-grip triggers, Vanesco felt the heavy gun shudder in his hands as he unleashed a continuous burst of green tracer rounds that rained down in a deadly spinning vortex.

Jack stood stock-still as the laser-designated rangefinder of the weapon on his shoulder began flashing and a low, growling tone signaled that the MANPADS unit had electronically acquired its target. Jack pumped the trigger and heard backblast whoosh from the rear of the launch tube as the missile shot from the pipe, rising into the air in a lethally straight trajectory.

Vanesco saw the missile growing larger by the second as it traveled on its unerring path toward assured destruction.

DAVID ALEXANDER

In the fraction of a second before it exploded, he realized with horror that he was about to die a violent, hideous death.

Despite himself, Vanesco began an agonizing scream of fear that was cut short as the missile's shaped charge detonated. The round had struck amidships, homing in on the heat of the engine exhaust. It had gone right down the pipe and exploded well inside the engine cowling where it could do maximum damage to the rotorcraft and aircrew.

White-hot shrapnel sprayed those inside the chopper as the round blew up. Close on the heels of the lethal splinter burst came a moving wall of broiling flame that melted the flesh from their bodies and practically cooked the aircrew in their own blood.

Before Vanesco could finish screaming, the fireball that was ripping apart the hull of the Hind tore his burning limbs from his threshing torso, and then reduced what was left to a cinder in the inferno that totally consumed the Hind in midair.

On the ground below, Jack flashed a baleful smile.

CHAIN REACTION

"Doom on *you*, motherfucker," he said softly.

Pieces of the destroyed rotorcraft had now begun pattering down in a blazing rain. But though the fallout of burning-hot and razor-sharp hull fragments was dangerous, Jack continued standing and looking up at dark puffs of smoke that indicated the spot where the helo had been hovering when the round had exploded.

A dizzily swirling montage of kaleidoscopic imagery flashed through his brain, and for a while he seemed to see Tanya's face etched against the cloud-choked sky.

Jack let the spent missile launcher drop to the ground and suddenly felt unsteady on his feet. He was mentally and physically exhausted and beginning to hallucinate from fatigue and the often precipitous crash that is the direct opposite of the neurochemical high experienced in the heat of combat.

But it was over.

Vanesco was dead. And, for the moment at least, the demons inside Jack Keller could be put to rest.

DAVID ALEXANDER

EPILOG

Thirty-nine

*K*eller sat in a plush-backed chair in the commissioner's office beneath portraits of predecessors dating back to the days of Boss Tweed. Abernathy sat at his side and chewed an antacid tablet as Jack got a royal dressing down from the chief policymakers of the New York City police department and mayor's office.

He had only recently arrived at JFK International on an Aeroflot jetliner courtesy of the Russian government and had been shuttled to what was tantamount to an Inquisitional tribunal convened at City Hall.

"You have overstepped not only the bounds of propriety, but the protocols of international law," the mayor's legal counsel had been pompously declaiming. "You do not make the rules, Lieutenant Keller. Society does. Your place is to uphold them, not invent them as you go along."

Keller had noticed that the little weasel in the dark business suit had done all of the talking while the department brass looked on and said nothing like wise, mute Chinese monkeys.

"If you were not regarded as a hero by the newsmedia, Lieutenant Keller, you would now be off the force," he went on. "As it stands, you can be certain there will be an investigation not only by police internal affairs but by appropriate federal agencies as well."

Keller listened and kept his silence. He still heard the sound of gunfire echoing in his ears. It seemed to drown out the words being spoken to him, reducing them to the insignificant chirpings of a bothersome insect.

The way Abernathy had explained it on the ride over from the airport, certain factions, headed by the mayor's chief rival in the next election, had been trying to make political capital out of Jimenez' decision to send Jack abroad. Having been deemed expendable, Jack was now to be thrown to the wolves.

"Do you have anything to say before we close this preliminary hearing, detective?" the weasel asked.

"Yes," Keller intoned as he rose to his feet and reached for the worn leather holder containing his gold detective shield that was clipped to the breast pocket of his sport coat. Walking up to the commissioner's desk he folded back the leather cover and placed the shield directly on top of its lacquered and well-polished surface.

"You can shove this up your fat fucking -- "

" -- Jack, don't be stupid!" Abernathy jumped to his feet and shouted, unable to tolerate what was happening a moment longer. As Keller walked out, he faced the commissioner, the weasel and the rest of the City Hall bigwigs assembled in the august chamber.

"Jack Keller has got more guts and integrity in his little finger than all of you time-serving assholes put together. If you hang him out to dry, if you try to make him into a scapegoat, I'll take the fall with him, and I can promise you that I'll flush a lot of people in this room right down the toilet with me."

CHAIN REACTION

■

Keller had reached the end of the hall when he heard the sound of heavy running footfalls and stertorous breathing behind him. Abernathy called his name but Keller did not slacken his pace.

"Wait up, Jack," he huffed as he reached him, out of breath from the run down the hall.

Abernathy dived into his jacket pocket and took something out. Keller saw that he was holding the gold lieutenant's shield that he had just flung atop the commissioner's desk.

"Take it, Keller."

"I already made it clear I didn't want it," Jack replied.

Abernathy's flabby, pallid cheeks colored and his gruff voice dipped an octave in pitch. He grabbed Keller by the arm and dug in his fingers with desperate force.

"Listen to me, you headstrong fuck," he growled. "I just put my career on the line for you back there. So help me, I never did that for anybody before in all my years on the force. If you don't take this badge right now, you'll be spitting in the face of the only friend you have right now in the department, and for an S.O.B. like you, maybe in the whole goddamn world."

Keller hesitated but said nothing. Finally he reached out and took the badge which he re-affixed to his breast pocket.

"You're a good cop, Keller," Abernathy told him as he placed a beefy hand on his shoulder, "an unregenerate, sociopathic asshole, but a good cop."

"Thanks, Frank," Jack replied, and his mouth formed a sort of smile. "The feeling is mutual."

Both men walked along the corridor and soon reached the municipal building's main hall. Pushing through the heavy brass doors, they came out onto the sunlit, bustling street and merged with the hurrying bloodstream of the mammoth city.

CHAIN REACTION

You might also like to read an excerpt from David Alexander's bestselling Mafia thriller, Brooklynese.

From the mean streets of New York City's prime Mafia boro, comes a chase after savvy and streetwise bank robbers and jewel thieves that crosses international boundaries and time zones with the speed of a jet plane. Alexander weaves everything together with the skill of a true master of the action thriller category in an unforgettable extravaganza of capers, mayhem, hot gems, hot dames, and accomplished criminals who will stop at nothing to gain possession of a treasure whose value is almost beyond calculation. When a billion dollar diamond deal cut by one of New York's heaviest crime families goes sour, and the consignment of rare gems is lost overseas, a crew of wise guys straight out of Brooklyn is ordered to get it back -- any way they can. This is an international caper novel to end all caper novels, a nonstop page-turner jam-packed with action from start to finish and one of Alexander's boldest books ever.

■

Editorial Reviews

"Brooklynese is an accomplishment by an author whose narrative skills are clearly at their peak and can sustain an ambitious plot, like the daring young man on the trapeze who flies through the air with the greatest of ease." -- Desert Sun

"If every crook could pull off a caper with the ease and skill Alexander ably demonstrates in Brooklynese, we'd all be broke." -- Globe Literary Supplement

"From the mean streets of New York City's toughest borough, comes a chase after savvy and streetwise bank robbers and jewel thieves crossing international boundaries and time zones with the speed of a rocket plane. Alexander weaves everything together with the skill of a true master of the action thriller category in an unforgettable extravaganza of capers, mayhem, hot gems, hot dames, and accomplished criminals who will stop at nothing to gain possession of a treasure whose value is beyond calculation. As crime thrillers go, Brooklynese is the boss of bosses." -- Brookline Beacon

■

Brooklynese by David Alexander.
An excerpt.

■

A briny grey fog swirled across the collection of low-rise cinderblock warehouse buildings that made up the South Brooklyn Industrial Park. Out on the dark waters of the Buttermilk Channel, a tugboat honked a loud Bee-ohh!

Whitey MacDonald took a last drag on the foul-tasting plain-end Lucky and flicked it like a piece of snot across the rain-glazed tarmac where it hit and quickly sizzled out.

The Irishman climbed into the high cab of the truck parked outside the warehouse. The computer printout cargo manifest he'd just glanced through stated the truck carried a sealed and bonded load of consumer electronics items. Televisions, stereos, fax machines, home computers, CD players. The grinding of the truck's engine echoed through the rainswept night in the deserted lot of the industrial park as Whitey put the truck in gear and lumbered toward the lighted guard station directly ahead.

■

By midnight the rain had tapered off to a slow, easy drizzle, but a heavy pea soup fog had rolled in off the Hudson and blanketed the streets with a cottony mist, whose rotten-egg stink of sulfurous gases, courtesy of the Bayonne, New Jersey sewage-treatment plant directly across the river, made it smell like a pay toilet in purgatory.

The side street in Sunset Park sloped down toward the gunmetal superstructure of the Gowanus Expressway extension overpass. The canal of the same name, known variously to local residents as "The Vile Nile," and "The Odor River" due to its own unforgettable fragrance, lay just beyond. The neighborhood took its name from Sunset Park, from which spectacular sunsets over the Hudson could be visible, but it might just as aptly refer to the fact that the sun had long since set over this urban wasteland from which Walt Whitman had once seen visions of "magnetic lands."

Squat red-brick industrial buildings, chiefly warehouses, flanked the deserted street on both sides. Spaced between them at odd intervals were vacant, weed-choked lots full of garbage that had somehow made it over the high chain-link fences, churches bearing huge neon-crosses and Spanish names, and two-story saltboxes with shingle siding rented by absentee landlords to a succession of Latino immigrants who rarely stayed longer than a few months.

With headlights doused, Wheats parked the car in front of a closed-down chicken slaughterhouse. The stench of enough chicken blood to fill the Gulf of Mexico from the barnyard fowl butchered since the shop first opened up in 1908 permeated the building and added its stench to the infernal-smelling fog as they waited for the truck to make its appearance. If chickens ever ruled the world, they would make this their Auschwitz. A fine film of blood had permanently stained the sidewalks brown.

Joey and Frankie-Boy checked their pieces. The Glock semiautomatics were cleaned and oiled and there was a round chambered just in case they were needed, although shooting never had been necessary before. The black nylon stocking masks, the same tactical face masks used by police SWAT teams, remained for the moment out of sight. They would come on just before the score went down. And come off again for the getaway.

The cops from the Seven-Eight who patrolled this stretch of Brooklyn South were like a classic Zen koan -- both a problem and not a problem. The boys in blue in this precinct did not get any more corrupt this side of the Bronx or Abu Dhabi. If they were not on the take, then they didn't last long. In the Seven-Eight an honest cop quickly became a dead cop.

Frankie-Boy had assured them that his father, and Joey's godfather, Don Antonio Casabianca, had seen to it that the right people had been paid off to do the right thing. But you never could be totally certain about the cops. In many ways New York's Finest were, de facto, the major crime cartel in the city. In some respects they put the Mafia to shame. They were great blue sharks that often swam past without giving a shit, but who could turn on you in a second and rip you to shreds in a mindless feeding frenzy if you didn't watch your shit.

Suddenly the Motorola handset squawked in the back seat.

"Melon to Prosciutto. You hear me, Prosciutto?"

"Yeah, yeah. I hear ya. I hear ya," Frankie-Boy said into the commo unit he'd pulled from the pocket of his brown leather jacket. "What ya got?"

"The truck's on its way. It just turned off Fourth Avenue to come down your street."

"Where are you?"

"We're right behind it."

"You see any security around?"

The freight dispatcher had checked and made sure that there would be no backup security tailing the truck, but plans could be changed at the last minute and you could never be absolutely sure anyway.

"We're the only other car in the area. And we cruised the streets a couple of minutes ago to make sure."

"You sure it's the right truck?"

"Hey, I can read a fuckin' license plate!"

The dispatcher had given them the plate numbers and truck number of the rig, but Frankie-Boy knew better than to count too much on the intelligence of the people who worked for him, especially freelance stick-up artists like Nicky and Paulie, two yo-yos from Baldwin, Long Island, a town where they grew yo-yos like other places grew squash.

"You know what you gotta do?" Frankie-Boy asked finally.

"Yeah, we know it. Don't worry. We're on the case."

Frankie-Boy squelched the radio and tapped Eddie Wheats on the shoulder. "Get ready, the truck's gonna be here any minute."

■

The telltale grinding of gears boomed and echoed through the dense, swirling fog. The spreading cones of two headlight beams shone on the rain-slicked street. The heavy truck lumbered around the corner from beneath the BQE overpass. One of the dispatchers at the freight transport company who had tipped them to the cargo load of high-tech consumer electronics knew his shit and knew that if he was wrong, he'd take his lumps. He didn't turn out to be wrong tonight.

"Go," Frankie-Boy said.

Wheats threw on the brights and stepped on the gas. The car bolted from the curb, tires spinning and screeching on the slippery tarmac. The truck's cab was bathed in an unearthly white light that seemed to freeze the raindrops in place, making them look like penny nails spilling from heaven as God built a better world someplace else. Joey could see the driver's big, white, meat-slab shanty Irish face contort in shock as he reflexively stomped the brake pedal.

As the truck came to a hard, screeching halt, Wheats fishtailed the Pontiac sideways. Frankie-Boy was already out the door; wired on coke he was faster than a speeding bullet. Two long strides brought him to the running board of the truck where he jammed the nine-millimeter automatic into the side of the driver's head through the cracked-open window.

"Stop the truck," the ice-cold doer in the black face mask said to the scared-shitless doee.

Whitey MacDonald threw the rig in park and killed the ignition. Frankie-Boy waved to Joey who bounded out of the car, his face now also masked. Joey's role was critical. The trucks were heavily alarmed. To foil hijacking attempts, the freight companies were engaged in an ongoing effort to improve security using a variety of high-tech gizmos and gadgets that would make James Bond throw up his hands in despair. It was a Cold War in the streets, with a fortune in hot merchandise at stake.

Joey jumped on the rig's opposite running board. He took a Maglite from his pocket and shone its sixteen thousand candle power beam inside the truck's cab. Beneath the dashboard he glimpsed a corner of a small computer keyboard.

"Here's how it works, okay," he said to the frightened driver. "You tell me the truth, nothing happens. You bullshit me, we fuck you up. You got that?"

"Yeah, I got it," Whitey replied.

"'Kay," Joey went on. "I want you to punch in the passcode that opens the doors without tripping any alarms. Then you get out and you give it to me so I can check it out myself."

Whitey glanced at the masked gunman and had no second thoughts about cooperating. He reached under the dash and keyed in a seven-digit access code. The locks popped and the door buttons jumped like obedient elves. Frankie-Boy pulled open the door and yanked Whitey out of the cab, nodding at Nicky and Paulie in the second car behind the truck.

Joey quickly climbed into the driver's seat and slid down under the dash, playing the high-intensity Maglite beam across every concealed nook and cranny. He snapped off the torch and nodded to Frankie-Boy who held the muzzle of the gun pressed to the driver's head.

"What's the code?" asked Joey.

"Four-two-five-oh-oh-four-four."

CHAIN REACTION

Joey keyed the seven digits. The locks popped. He tried the ignition. The engine started right up. There were no audible sirens, no alarms. The driver had been too scared to lie. Joey flashed Frankie-Boy the thumb's-up then slid over into the passenger seat. Frankie-Boy handed MacDonald over to Nicky and Paulie, holstered his piece and slid behind the wheel.

The truck groaned as Frankie-Boy shifted gears and pulled down the deserted, fogswept street. Eddie damped the brights on the Pontiac and followed in the first rental. As Joey and Frankie-Boy pulled off their face masks, Whitey found himself staring at the freshly vacuumed carpet between the front and rear seats of the second car.

"You stay like that till we tell you it's okay," Nicky said as he leaned over the front seat and got out a Camel. "You fuckin' move and I'll make you fart your brains out your asshole."

■

Ten minutes later, the truck trundled up the darkened ramp of a warehouse a couple of blocks away, just off Fourth Avenue. A crew of unloaders was waiting to take off the hot cargo load.

Frankie-Boy brought the truck to a stop and the drone of the hydraulics shutting the two-inch thick, three-ton steel entrance door echoed through the interior that stank of gasoline, moldering tires and rusting sheet metal. Joey hopped out and lit a cigaret as he pulled a VHS cassette-sized Hewlett-Packard palmtop computer from his pocket.

The first part of the score was the easy part. Getting the access code. The second part was the hard part. Defeating the silent satellite-uplinked

424

alarm that would instantly flash the truck's location on a grid position map of the city to a private security firm based in the World Trade Center in Manhattan if the doors were incorrectly opened. The code that opened the doors was known only to the supervisor at the warehouse to which the goods were being shipped. The driver didn't have it.

Joey slid under the truck and found the controller box he was searching for. Using a ratchet driver with a torx bit, he unscrewed four Allen lugs and removed the galvanized steel plate that protected the box. You'd think they would alarm the controllers but they never did. In an unpredictable world the security companies' Achilles Heel was that they were always predictable.

A printed circuit board containing a group of microprocessor chips was inside the metal receptacle. Lying on his back beneath the undercarriage of the truck, with the HP palmtop sitting on his stomach, Joey attached a custom-made cable to the computer's serial port. On the other end of the cable, where a standard twenty-five pin connector would normally be found, Joey had crimped on six color-coded mini-alligator clips.

Joey carefully attached four of the mini-alligator clips to the exposed pins of the large IC on the board, which bore the ID number 4803W on its surface. The IC was a 4803-series microprocessor chip, one of two types manufactured by either Westinghouse or Hitachi -- in this case the W suffix identified it as Westinghouse silicon -- but in both cases virtually identical. These chips were EPROMs -- erasable programmable read-only memory chips -- whose pins three, nine and fourteen on one side and five, eight and eleven on the other, were linked to memory registers containing alarm instruction sets. Once Joey accessed these, he could reprogram the EPROM so that the alarm would be neutralized and the truck doors would open.

Numbers flashed on the palmtop's backlit screen as Joey tapped out commands on the small keyboard.

The software loaded into the HP's three megabyte RAM memory interrogated the IC chip and would quickly extract the instruction sets. The HP was lousy for showing baby pictures but the old contender was perfect for this type of job. Joey had paid a hacker he'd found on the Internet to disassemble and rewrite a commercial data acquisition program from its source code. Nobody knew each other, nothing was traceable. Joey sent cash to a mail drop and downloaded the hacked program from a bulletin board mailbox.

Originally intended to monitor the performance of industrial machinery, the revamped software was now deactivating the alarm and locking mechanism. In under three minutes the palmtop emitted a low electronic warble as the DEFEAT SUCCESSFUL message flashed onscreen. Joey detached the cable, slid the palmtop back into his inner jacket pocket and crawled out from beneath the truck.

Nodding at Frankie-Boy, Joey walked around to the back and pulled open the truck's rear doors which were now unlocked. Like a well-oiled machine, the unloading crew -- four guys splitting four of the five thousand dollar payoff between them -- got immediately to work.

Unloading the truck completely would take most of the next hour, after which the crew would drive it a couple of blocks and abandon it under the Gowanus Expressway overpass, or some other convenient spot, such as the swamps around Marine Park near Plum Beach. If ever questioned, the night foreman of the warehouse, who was in on the score and got the last grand of the five thou, would say that he had no idea that any wrongdoing took place on his watch, well aware that nobody could ever prove otherwise.

Joey and Frankie-Boy walked out through a steel door set in the red brick wall next to the big corrugated metal partition covering the access ramp through which they had initially driven the truck. Eddie Wheats was sitting behind the wheel of the rental, whose motor was turned off. Joey and Frankie-Boy climbed into the car, which Wheats soon rolled into the rainy night, still thinking about eagles over the Marine Park Bridge.

■

Frankie-Boy took Whitey's commercial driver's license. "Just walk back to the warehouse and report a hijacking," he told him, stuffing a hundred dollar bill into his wallet and handing it back. "Tomorrow you report the license missing to the DMV."

"I'm gonna need proof," MacDonald said, his eyes wide.

Frankie-Boy nodded. He balled his fist and hit the driver square in the face. Blood spurted from his busted nose.

"There's your proof," he told him. "And don't forget we know were you live. You fuck with us, we kill you and your family. Your wife is dead. Your kids are dead. Your dog is dead. And you're dead too."

CHAIN REACTION

"The cops are gonna ask me questions."

"Just make sure you give 'em the wrong answers," Frankie-Boy advised, then turned and walked away.

Whitey MacDonald stood shivering in the rain with blood pouring from his shattered nose and running down the front of his jacket and watched the two cars drive down the street, turn the corner, and vanish into the night.